The new Zebra Regency Romance logo that you see on the cover is a photograph of an actual regency "tuzzy-muzzy." The fashionable regency lady often wore a tuzzy-muzzy tied with a satin or velvet riband around her wrist to carry a fragrant nosegay. Usually made of gold or silver, tuzzy-muzzies varied in design from the elegantly simple to the exquisitely ornate. The Zebra Regency Romance tuzzy-muzzy is made of alabaster with a silver filigree edging.

EVEN A RAKE CAN LOSE HIS HEART . . .

Alex reached out to tuck an errant curl behind her ear, letting the silky strands flow between his fingers. Cecily's eyes briefly closed against the sensations his touch evoked.

"I think about you, you know," he said.

Her eyes opened. "Do you? Why?"

"Because you are a most unusual girl. A beautiful girl."

"I'm not beautiful," she protested softly.

"Of course you are. Rakes know these things." His eyes went, of their own volition, to her lips, soft and full and slightly parted. Somewhere in his mind an alarm bell began ringing, and though he had always obeyed this signal of danger before, this time he ignored it. He knew only that this girl was bringing him back to life, and he no longer wanted to fight it. She drew him to her in a way he could not fathom. For the moment, she was his.

"Cecily," he murmured, and brought his lips down on hers . . .

DISCOVER THE MAGIC OF REGENCY ROMANCES

ROMANTIC MASQUERADE (3221, $3.95)
by Lois Stewart

Sabrina Latimer had come to London incognito on a fortune hunt. Disguised as a Hungarian countess, the young widow had to secure the ten thousand pounds her brother needed to pay a gambling debt. His debtor was the notorious ladies' man, Lord Jareth Tremayne. Her scheme would work if she did not fall prey to the charms of the devilish aristocrat. For Jareth was an expert at gambling and always played to win everything—and *everyone*—he could.

RETURN TO CHEYNE SPA (3247, $2.95)
by Daisy Vivian

Very poor but ever-virtuous Elinor Hardy had to become a dealer in a London gambling house to be able to pay her rent. Her future looked dismal until Lady Augusta invited her to be her guest at the exclusive resort, Cheyne Spa. The one condition: Elinor must woo the unsuitable rogue who was in pursuit of the Duchess's pampered niece.

The unsuitable young man was enraptured with Elinor, but *she* had been struck by the devilishly handsome Tyger Dobyn. Elinor knew that Tyger was hardly the respectable, marrying kind, but unfortunately her heart did not agree!

A CRUEL DECEPTION (3246, $3.95)
by Cathryn Huntington Chadwick

Lady Margaret Willoughby had resisted marriage for years, knowing that no man could replace her departed childhood love. But the time had come to produce an heir to the vast Willoughby holdings. First she would get her business affairs in order with the help of the new steward, the disturbingly attractive and infuriatingly capable Mr. Frank Watson; *then* she would begin the search for a man she could tolerate. If only she could find a mate with a *fraction* of the scandalously handsome Mr. Watson's appeal. . . .

The Rake's Reward
Mary Kingsley

ZEBRA BOOKS
KENSINGTON PUBLISHING CORP.

To Mary Carter, for helping me get through it.

ZEBRA BOOKS

are published by

Kensington Publishing Corp.
475 Park Avenue South
New York, NY 10016

First printing: August, 1991
Printed in the United States of America

Chapter One

Lady Diana Randall flung open the door to the Gold Drawing Room and hurtled across the floor. "Cecily! Is it true?"

"What?" The slight figure standing by one of the tall windows dropped the brocaded drapery she had been holding and spun around. "Diana, you gave me a start," she scolded, but her eyes twinkled. "Whatever would Mama say if she saw you enter a room like that?"

"Never mind Mama! Is it true?"

Cecily glanced out the window again. In the square below, a man could be seen climbing into a high-perch phaeton, its wheels picked out in yellow. "Is what true?"

"Is that him, just leaving? Oh, my, he is handsome." Diana joined her sister at the window and gazed down at the man as he picked up the ribbons and drove away at a sedate pace.

"Yes, but not much of a driver," Cecily muttered. "It might ruin his hair if he drove too fast."

"How can you say that! That rig is bang up to the mark!"

Cecily's eyes sparkled again. "You've been talking to our brother, I see. Such language, Di!"

"Oh, scold if you want, Cecily, I think the marquess is divine. Is it true? The servants are buzzing with it. Did he propose?"

Cecily raised her hand to her mouth and then quickly lowered it again, before she could gnaw on what was left of her thumbnail. "Perhaps you should ask the servants, if you really wish to know."

"Oh, don't roast me so, Cece! I shall expire on the spot if you don't tell me!"

"Will you?" Cecily extended her left hand, now adorned with a gold ring set with a single ruby and a diamond on either side. "Yes, he proposed, and yes, I said yes. What do you think?"

"He did! Oh, Cece, I'm so happy for you!" Diana grabbed her sister in a crushing embrace and then pulled away, lifting Cecily's hand to look at the ring. "This is never the Edgewater ancestral ring!"

"No, I fear there is no ring. No jewelry at all. Edgewater bought this at Rundell and Bridge."

"No jewelry!" Diana stared at her in dismay. "And instead he gives you this paltry thing?"

Cecily snatched her hand back. "You know I dislike ostentation, Di. Besides, I have my pearls, and Mama has promised me diamonds when I marry."

"Married!" Diana's eyes grew wide. "You really are going to marry, aren't you? Oh, you must tell me all about it!" Diana caught Cecily's hands and led her across the gold and white Aubusson carpet to a blue velvet sofa. "You must be the happiest girl in the world."

Cecily's nose crinkled. "Well, yes. I suppose."

Diana stared at her. "You don't sound too certain."

"I am!" Cecily protested. "It's what I wanted. But—"

"But?"

Cecily's nose wrinkled again. "He hasn't a sense of humor. I never realized that before. You see, he went down on his knee to propose—"

"Cecily! How romantic."

"Yes. Well, after he proposed and I accepted, I said he'd best get up, else the knees of his pantaloons would wrinkle."

6

"Cecily!" Diana gasped. "You didn't! When you know he's so concerned about the fit of his clothing!"

"I did." Cecily's tone was rueful. "It would have been bearable if he'd only laughed, but he didn't, Diana. He simply stared at me. It was most uncomfortable, I can assure you."

"Well, I think he's a wonderful catch, and you shouldn't criticize him just because he doesn't laugh at your jests. I never do," she added proudly.

"I know. Silly of me, isn't it?" Cecily said meekly. "But, there it is. I enjoy laughing with a person. I think it's so important, don't you?"

"Oh, pooh! What does that matter? He's so handsome, Cece. I'm sure if he called on me, I'd swoon with it."

Cecily's mouth quirked. "I'm sure you would, Diana." In fact, most girls would. Which made Cecily wonder why the Marquess of Edgewater, her intended, didn't have quite that effect on her. Handsome, he certainly was, charming, and more intelligent than he appeared, given his dandified ways. His intellect was very important to Cecily. In her second season, she was no green girl to be seduced merely by a handsome face. No, she wished for more from the man she would marry, though she didn't deny that she had been flattered when Edgewater had begun paying her attention. He was, as Diana had said, a most eligible *parti,* titled, monied, popular. Cecily wrinkled her nose again. It all made her wonder why he had chosen her.

The door was opened at that moment by a bewigged footman wearing the Marlow green and gold livery, and the Duchess of Marlow glided in. "Oh, my dear child," she said, holding out her hands as both Cecily and Diana rose, "is it true?"

"Yes, Mama." Cecily raised her cheek for her mother's kiss. "I am betrothed."

"Oh, I am so pleased." The duchess sank gracefully into a chair, the layers of her morning gown fluttering around her. "I knew you could bring him up to scratch, my dear." A look of horror crossed her face. "Gracious, you surely didn't receive him looking like that, did you?"

"Like what?" Cecily glanced down and saw that her sash of pale green grosgrain was twisted. "Oh, dear." And here she had taken such pains to look her best. Her morning gown of white muslin was unexceptionable, with its chemisette filling in the low neckline drawn to a frill at her throat, and ruching at the wrists of the long sleeves. Even her hair was neat, bound up by a ribbon to match the sash. Why could she never look bandbox perfect, like Diana, no matter how hard she tried? "The marquess didn't appear to notice, Mama."

"I should hope not! I begin to despair of you, Cecily. Sometimes I wonder how you can be my daughter."

"Yes, Mama," Cecily said wryly. Diana was the one who most resembled their mother. Unlike Cecily, both were tall, slender, raven-haired beauties. Nor was she fair, like their father. Instead, she was somewhere in-between, with golden skin that looked positively sallow if she wore the wrong colors, and hazel eyes that were fortunately fringed with long, dark lashes. Her features weren't bad, she allowed, though her mouth was a trifle too wide, but best of all was her hair. Neither brown nor blond, but, again, in-between, it framed her face in short, feathery curls, a style that while no longer fashionable, suited her admirably. It didn't make her a beauty, though. Nothing could do that. "I do wish I knew why he chose me."

"Why, because you are the Duke of Marlow's daughter, of course," the duchess said.

Cecily winced. "I'd rather be chosen for myself than because of that!"

"But it is the way of the world." The duchess's face softened. "Come, sit by me," she said, gesturing toward the tapestried footstool. Cecily perched on it, flinching as her mother took her chin in her hand. "Now, don't fidget, child. It is a most suitable match."

"He doesn't love me, Mama."

"My dear child, what has that to say to anything?"

"Cecily!" Diana sounded horrified. "Don't you love him?"

"I like him very well." She looked imploringly up at her mother. "Love will come, won't it, Mama?"

The duchess waved a hand in dismissal. "Silly child, that is not how things are done in our world. And if love should come—" she shrugged—"it's all very well, Cecily, but it doesn't really matter, does it?"

"No, ma'am," Cecily said, her head bent.

"Tcha. I never thought you were a foolish romantic."

"I suppose I am."

"Why are you marrying him?" Diana asked.

"Because I like and respect him, more than any other man I've met." Cecily turned back to see her mother regarding her with unexpectedly sympathetic eyes. "I am persuaded we shall deal well together."

"Deal well! If that's not the most odiously practical thing I've ever heard—" Diana began.

"Well, I am practical, Di," Cecily said mildly. "I realize I shall have to marry someday. You know what Father said. Neither you nor our sisters can marry before I do."

"Oldest first. Yes, I know." Diana made a face. "It's so unfair."

"Why?" Cecily's eyes danced again. "Have you a *tendre* for someone I don't know about?"

"No, but perhaps I might have flirted with Edgewater myself."

"Children," the duchess said in a tone that though mild made them both attend to her. "Now, we must start making plans. Madam Celeste will make your gown, of course, and we must find when St. George's is available."

"The marquess might have some ideas, Mama,"

Cecily said.

"As if he would! He's only a man," the duchess exclaimed. Cecily and Diana exchanged amused glances. "If we left it up to men, your father would have you married in the country at Marlow, like some hole and corner affair, and the marquess would likely choose the same day as the Royal Wedding!"

"Not that I could compete with the Regent's daughter."

"Of course not, you're ever so much prettier than Princess Charlotte," Diana said, and Cecily's mouth quirked.

"Regardless, you do have a point, my dear," the duchess said. "We must plan the date very carefully, or no one will pay us any attention at all!"

"And we can't have that, can we?" Cecily murmured.

"Gracious, no." The duchess rose, her gown draping about her, and reached again to take Cecily's chin in her hand. "It will work out, child. I trust you will be very happy."

"Yes, Mama." Cecily's eyes gazed back at her, clear and direct. "I expect I shall." She dropped a curtsy as her mother glided out of the room, and then rose, her face determined. She *would* be happy. She would not allow herself to doubt that for a moment.

But, much later, in the early morning hours, Cecily lay in bed, listening drowsily to the sounds of the street vendors making their rounds through Grosvenor Square, and wondering about her life. Had she made the right decision? She hardly knew the marquess; she'd met him only in public and had little real idea what he was like. After yesterday, however, she suspected that he was as much a high stickler as his adherence to fashion implied. If, for example, he knew what she was planning to do this morning, would he approve?

An impish smile spread across Cecily's face, and she threw back the covers, jumping out of bed and running

10

to her wardrobe. There she pulled out some clothes and, after splashing water on her face, hastily began to dress. If her mother could see her, she thought, gazing at herself in the pier glass, she'd likely faint, for there Cecily stood, garbed in an old shirt and a pair of breeches that had once been her brother's. Stuffing her hair up under a soft cap and carrying her boots, she slipped out into the hallway. The servants, even Jem, the groom, who no doubt had Dancer saddled for her by now, and Annie, her maid, would keep her secret. Lady Cecily Randall, the very proper daughter of the Duke of Marlow, preferred riding unescorted and astride.

A brief while later, she was mounted upon Dancer and heading toward the park. The thought of what she was doing, in defiance of the restrictions society placed on young, unmarried girls, made her grin with guilty delight. She wouldn't be able to do this once she was married, but there would, she was certain, be other compensations. Her spirits began to rise, and she broke into song, making Dancer's ears prick back. How could one be depressed on such a fine, spring morning? All would be well. Somehow, she would love the man she married.

It wasn't easy being a rake.

Alexander Darcy, Viscount St. Clair, regarded himself in his shaving mirror, studying the effects of a night spent in the pursuit of pleasure. Dispassionately, he noted the red-rimmed eyes, the pallor to skin usually swarthy and dark, the lines in his forehead that hadn't been there just yesterday. He looked a good deal older than his twenty-nine years, and he felt it, as well. What was it he had done last night? Rubbing his throbbing temples, Alex struggled to remember. Ah, yes. Gambled at Crockford's, had he not, with such devil-may-care abandon that he had won in that exclusive,

11

ruinously high-stakes club, adding to a fortune already ample enough to provide his every need. Gone from there to the arms of Nanette, his current *chere amie,* and it was probably just as well that he remembered little of that encounter. And, drunk too much wine, which was why neither gambling, hell nor mistress was clear in his mind. Better that, though, than the rare self-disgust and depression he now felt, and which he would soon assuage, he hoped, in any of the varied pursuits of a gentleman of leisure. Anything, to keep the emptiness at bay.

He was scowling at his reflection when there was a discreet knock on the door. Parsons, who served him as butler and valet, came in carrying a steaming bowl of water. Without a word he set it down on the washstand; in equal silence, Alex lathered his face and proceeded to shave himself, something of which Parsons heartily disapproved, but which Alex trusted to no man. He had learned in a hard school never to leave his throat, or any other part of himself, unprotected. Including his heart. God knew why, he thought, looking at his reflection again as he wiped away the remaining shaving soap.

"God's teeth, but I look like the devil himself," he muttered.

"The wages of sin, my lord," Parsons said, in a voice as expressionless as his face.

From under his brows Alex gave him a look that would have made a lesser man quail. "Turned preacher now, to match your name?" he said, an edge to his voice, and Parsons' face grew even more wooden. "Oh, hell. Forgive me, Parsons, but you, of all people, should know I cannot abide being preached to."

"No, my lord."

Alex glanced up, and then gave Parsons the sudden, charming smile that so changed his face, giving him the look of a fallen angel. He had disarmed many an adversary with that smile, causing them to forget just

12

how dangerous he could be. Dangerous when he was crossed, with the pistols and swords he used so well, or with his fists, lithe athlete that he was; dangerous in a different way in amorous encounters, with the skilled and subtle lovemaking at which he was equally adept. But he was most dangerous like this, smiling, charming, and yet highly alert, his quick brain analyzing and dissecting everything. Such intelligence had made him invaluable during the late wars with France, which Alex had spent on the Continent, gathering information for England's defense. He had returned home enigmatic, cynical, apparently cold, and yet undeniably charming, a hard man to know, an even harder one to like. Few suspected, however, that beneath the careful facade he showed to the world, Alex was a very lonely man. It was not something he would admit, even to himself.

"My apologies, Parsons," he said, his voice meek. "I am not quite myself this morning." For a moment, he thought it wouldn't work; unfortunately, this *was* himself, the man he'd become, and he sometimes wondered why Parsons put up with it.

Parsons, obviously struggling with himself, gave in. "I expect you have the headache this morning, my lord," he said, going so far as to spread his mouth in the slight curve that passed for a smile.

"A trifle, Parsons, and a good ride should work it out of me." He rose. "I'll want the black riding coat, and inform the stables to saddle Azrael."

"Yes, my lord," Parsons said, his voice wooden again, and turned away to lay out Alex's clothing.

Behind his back, Alex grinned. It wasn't at all to Parsons' liking that his employer rode a horse named for a dark angel, but then, little of what Alex did lately was to Parsons' liking. The comradeship that had served them so well in their past adventures had changed. Parsons had, appropriately enough, turned to religion since their return from the Continent and

13

was now a devout churchgoer; Alex, spending most of his waking hours in raking, was a devout hedonist. Why Parsons stayed with him, God only knew.

A little while later, Alex rode out from the mews near his lodgings, pausing out of long habit to check the street before entering it. Nothing untoward was in sight, however, no soldiers waiting to arrest him, no assassin to perform his deadly deed. No danger at all, in fact. He had left all that behind. He was in England, and it was a fresh spring morning, the start to another aimless day.

With little effort, he steered the huge black stallion down Piccadilly and into the park, riding down the road which later that afternoon would be filled with fine horseflesh and carriages of all descriptions, in the daily promenade of the *ton*. If the weather held. Alex cast a skeptical glance at the sky. So far, this spring had been damp and chill, though today was clear. Perhaps because of that, he wasn't alone in the park; some distance off was a youth, mounted upon a gray, too big for him. Good seat, Alex thought critically, before guiding Azrael down another path. He had no desire to speak with anyone so early in the morning. There would be enough time for conversation in the rest of the day.

Alex's mouth twisted as he let Azrael have his head. It would, most likely, be a day like any other: lounging down St. James's this morning, and perhaps calling in Whites', to catch up on the news of the day; stopping at Gentleman Jackson's for a round or two of boxing, or at Manton's to practice shooting. Visits this afternoon, to acquaintances and friends, and perhaps he would join the promenade of the *ton* through the park. As for the evening — well, he had many events to which he had been invited and which he had no intention of attending. Which, he thought, was perhaps why he was so sought-after. The *ton* prized exclusivity; the more invitations he refused, the more were sent to him, and those hostesses who could claim him as a guest considered it quite a coup, indeed. He doubted people would believe him if he told them that he found such social events genuinely dreary, or that *ton* life was stifling and dull, after the years he'd spent on the Continent. No, he would not be present in any fashionable drawing room tonight. He might, however, pay a visit to Nanette and, in all probability, consume more wine than was good for him. A typical day, and not at all exciting. And that, he thought, was how he wanted it. He had had quite enough of excitement in his life.

He had been riding hard and fast across the grass and now he was drawing near to one of the bridle paths. With the ease and instinct born of years spent in the saddle, he slowed the powerful stallion to a walk, leaning over to pat his neck. A walk to cool the horse out and then it would be home for him, and the start to the day's activities.

Alex turned onto the bridle path and then checked. Ahead of him was the boy he'd seen earlier, riding at a sedate pace and—singing? A younger lad than he'd thought, because the voice drifting back to him was definitely soprano. Unwilling to face such cheerfulness so early in the morning, Alex tugged at the reins, preparing to turn away, when a very odd thing happened. The boy's horse reared. No, not reared, exactly, Alex realized, spurring Azrael forward, but he was certainly on his hind legs and was actually walking. And then, as abruptly as he'd gone up, he came down. All the way down, his forelegs collapsing under him. The boy gave a cry as he lost his balance, his arms flailing wildly. Then, unable to stop himself, he catapulted over the horse's head.

"God's teeth!" Alex muttered. This was just what he needed, an encounter with a youth too young and foolish to control his horse, but he could not leave the boy there if he were hurt. "Are you hurt, lad?" he called, bringing Azrael to a neat stop by the fallen rider and dismounting.

The rider, sitting sprawled on the ground, looked up at Alex and, disconcertingly, laughed, a crystal peal of sound. Golden-brown curls danced about a heart-shaped face, and Alex realized several things at once. The rider's eyes, huge and golden, were the most unusual he had ever seen, and the lashes, the longest. And she was definitely not a boy. She was, instead, one of the most attractive girls it had been his privilege ever to meet, filling out the plain buff breeches and the simple white shirt she wore in a way no boy ever could. His heart lurched in his chest and then returned to its usual place, leaving him feeling odd, disoriented, off-balance, and yet exhilarated. Suddenly, his day no longer looked quite so routine.

Chapter Two

"Good morning!" The girl scrambled to her feet and danced — there was no other word for it, Alex decided — over to her horse, who was standing obediently by, his head down. "Good old Dancer, you can still show us a thing or two, can't you?"

"Dancer?" Leading Azrael, Alex stepped forward.

"Yes. Because he dances, you see." She turned to look at him, her eyes dancing with mirth.

"You could have been hurt."

"Oh, old Dancer's never hurt a soul in his life, have you, boy?" She gave the horse's nose another pat and then stepped away. "Shall we show the gentleman what you can do?" And, to Alex's astonishment, she began to sing, her voice a lilting soprano. The horse's ears pricked up and then he rose, front legs pawing at the air as he turned and caparisoned. As the girl ended the song, he suddenly came down, bending his front legs in the way that had been the girl's undoing, and then rising again.

She looked up at Alex slantwise, mischief sparkling so in her eyes that for the life of him, he was unable to look away. "He does that, you see, to let his rider dismount, only I forgot."

"I haven't seen anything like it since leaving Vienna," Alex said, intrigued in spite of himself.

"Oh, were you at the Congress, sir?"

17

"No. How did you come by him?"

"Papa bought him from the gypsies. Mama saw him one day and had to have him. Not that she would ever do anything so undignified as to actually ride him. Oh, dear, I shouldn't have said that!" She clapped her hand over her mouth. "But he's a good old horse. I just forgot he'd dance if I started singing. And I had to sing, 'tis such a beautiful morning."

"You could have been hurt," Alex said again. Even to his own ears his voice sounded repressive. In spite of her dress, this was no urchin; her voice and bearing spoke of the Quality. "God's teeth, what are you doing riding alone at this hour of the morning?"

The girl looked startled and then let out another laugh, that crystal sound that so disconcerted and attracted him. "I—I am sorry, but you sounded so like my papa then."

The thought of his sounding like anyone's Papa at last awoke Alex's sense of the absurd, long dormant, and the corners of his mouth twitched. "My apologies. I did not wish to sound the tyrant."

"No, you don't look anything like him," she said and then went very still, looking up at him. He opened his mouth to say something, but she had turned away, stooping gracefully to pick up Dancer's reins. How old was she? Sixteen, seventeen? A mere child, but the most enchanting girl he had come across in a long time. And she evidently had no idea of who he was, which was just as well. Girls just out of the schoolroom weren't exactly his style. "I must be getting back."

"May I walk with you? After all"—his lips twitched again—"you never know whom you might meet in the park. Though I'm not sure being seen with me would do your reputation any good," he added to himself, and the black mood that had so briefly lifted descended upon him again.

"Why? Are you someone I shouldn't know?" Her eyes danced. "A rake, perhaps?"

18

"Minx. Tell me who your father is so I may tell him to keep you confined."

"I think not." She fell into step beside him, leading Dancer, and an oddly companionable silence fell between them. For the first time since returning to England, Alex relaxed. "What is your horse's name?"

"Azrael."

"Azrael?" The girl looked toward the black stallion, who had shied away from Dancer's inquiring snuffle. " 'Abash'd the devil stood.' "

Alex turned startled eyes toward her. "You read Milton?"

"Of course. Don't you?"

"Yes, but I'm—"

"A man. Yes, horrid thing for me to confess, I being only a girl, but"—her hand pressed dramatically to her heart—"I do know how to read."

Alex laughed, startling himself. Had anyone else spoken so to him, he would have immediately damped their pretensions by a look from under his brow. "Minx," he said again. "Why do they allow you out of the house so early?"

"They don't know. If I return early enough, no one's the wiser except the grooms."

"Who should know better than to allow you to roam the streets unescorted."

"I'm perfectly safe. Aren't I?"

Alex looked startled, and then grinned ruefully. Here he was, the most notorious rake in all of England, and yet she was, as she had implied, safe with him. He wouldn't dream of touching her and thus spoiling her intriguing mixture of innocence, knowledge and sensuality. *I must be getting old,* he thought. "Nevertheless, you should be getting home, before someone sees you. Besides me."

"And as you don't know who I am, you don't count."

"Who are you?" he asked, impelled by a sudden need to know and the girl shook her head.

19

"Never mind. I don't want to be that girl just now. I just wish to enjoy the day." She flung her head back, gazing up at the canopy of trees arching over them and Alex found himself staring at the clean, pure lines of her throat. The longing to press his lips against her soft white skin was so strong that he took a step away. "The world is so beautiful in the morning," she went on, unaware of the sudden interest she had awakened in him, and after a moment, Alex walked on.

"Of course you find the world a beautiful place," he said, more sourly than he'd intended. "You've never seen anything else."

The girl looked startled, and a look came into her eyes that made him instantly want to call the words back. "I'm sorry you feel that way," she said softly and he realized with chagrin that the look in her eyes was pity. For him! "But I think we have to enjoy what we can, when we can. Otherwise, life is too hard."

"How do you know that?" he demanded, wondering with a sudden surge of angry protectiveness what had happened to her to give her such a fatalistic philosophy. It matched his exactly, but then, he'd come by it in a hard school.

"I'm not blind." She paused. They had come to the Stanhope Gate, and outside waited the world. "I must be going. I dare not be late."

"I suppose not," he said, but he paused, oddly reluctant to end this idyll. "May I see you home?"

"I—" For the first time, the girl appeared flustered. She glanced up at him and then lowered her eyes with a sweep of long lashes. "I think not. But thank you." Setting her booted foot on the stirrup, she swung easily up into the saddle, the curve of her hip in the breeches so bewitching that he wondered how he had ever mistaken her for a boy. "Good day to you, sir," she said and, without a backward glance, rode away.

"Good day," Alex answered, feeling oddly abandoned as he watched her go. Some of the beauty of the day,

20

the bright sunshine, the trilling birds, the gentle breeze, went with her.

Azrael butted his head against Alex's arm. "Yes, Azzie. Home for us, and breakfast. Ah, thought you'd like that." He, too, swung up into his saddle, and glanced down Park Lane in time to see the girl turn onto Upper Grosvenor Street. He could follow her, perhaps, find out where she lived, ensure that she made it home safely, but something held him back. Something about the proud set of her shoulders when she had turned away, something about the incident itself, stopped him. It had been a moment out of time, and already it seemed not quite real. Girls like her simply didn't exist in his world of sophisticated society ladies or willing courtesans. She was not for him.

Still, he wondered as he turned toward his lodgings if he would ever see her again.

Cecily glanced back as she turned onto Upper Grosvenor Street. The man was still there, on horseback now. She wondered for a moment if he meant to follow her, but then he turned away. She wasn't certain whether to be relieved or disappointed.

The street was still quiet, and few paid heed to Cecily as she set Dancer to an easy walk. In the space of just a few moments, her world had changed, though she couldn't say exactly how. She was still herself, and yet, she felt different—felt as if another Cecily, one she had barely acknowledged, even to herself, had suddenly appeared. And it was all because of that man.

Dancer knew the way home, needing no guidance, and so Cecily was free to let her thoughts return to the encounter just past and the moment she had glanced up at the man in reaction to something he had said and realized that he was very handsome, indeed. Not classically handsome, in the way her fiancé was, she amended loyally, but compelling, all the same. There

21

was something about him, about the high, arched cheekbones, the thin, aquiline nose, the mobile lips, held very stiffly, as if he were in pain. He must have been in the war, Cecily thought. Her cousin Peter had had just that same look in his eyes when he'd returned home, invalided out of the army, a pain too deep for words, a terrible weariness. For one brief moment, Cecily had wanted to take the man's head and cradle it against her breasts, comforting him, until she had remembered where she was, who she was. To him, she was likely just a hoyden, escaped from the constraints of the schoolroom and the rules that governed so strictly how a young lady was to behave. An engaged young lady. The man in the park, compelling though he might be, ideal companion that she had felt, in those few moments, that he could be, was not for her. Her life had already been decided for her.

Still, she wondered as she turned Dancer into the stableyard, if she would ever see him again.

"Then, we are decided?" the man said, looking around the table, gray eyes glittering coldly behind the mask he, like every man there, in the otherwise empty tavern, wore. Though the table was round, though there was little to distinguish him from the others, clearly he was the leader of this group. His clothing was dark, plain, but a discerning observer would have noted that the material of it was finer, the cut more precise, than that of anyone else's. He would also have noted the man's hands, slender and white, and yet strong. This was not a man who had had to do much hard labor in his life. Yet from him emanated such supreme self-confidence, such authority, that the others, successful men in their own right, automatically deferred to him. He, after all, was the one who had conceived the conspiracy that had brought them all together. There was also a touch of fear in their respect. No one could meet the hard, gleaming gaze of those eyes for long.

"Aye," the man at his left said at last, in broad Lancashire accents. "Reckon it's the only thing we can do."

"Time we woke up this country," another man said and from the rest of the men came nods and voices raised in agreement, voices that showed the origin of their speakers: Scots, Cornish, Welsh. Only the accent of the first man, the leader, was pure, and that was a source of curiosity to most of the conspirators. No one dared inquire too deeply into his background, however. Their leader had a way of dealing with such insolence.

"Time, indeed," he said now. "Gentlemen, we all know what is happening here. Children starve in the street, soldiers go begging, and trade is ruined. We are Englishmen, gentlemen, and yet any protest we make is looked on as sedition because of this present government. They have had things their own way for too long, with their Corn Laws and their acts of suppression and their taxes. We must strike back! America and France have shown us the way, gentlemen. The time to strike is now!"

"Here, here!" erupted cheers from the other men, and the leader sat back, deeply satisfied. They were his. He had chosen well, indeed: the wealthy merchant from the City whose daughter had married an impoverished nobleman, only to be badly mistreated; the Yorkshire factory owner whose business had nearly been ruined during the late war with America, when he couldn't get the cotton his mills needed; the Devon farmer, suffering from the ruinous effects of the Corn Laws. And the little Cockney, who by his own account had served his nation bravely in the wars with France and had received no compensation for it. The leader's eyes narrowed briefly as they touched on him. Something would have to be done there.

"We will meet again in one month's time to discuss our plans," he said, rising. "At that time, gentlemen, I

23

hope to have a suitable candidate to do the actual job to put before you. I trust you will not be disappointed."

"Who you going to get, guv'nor?" the Cockney said, his eyes a bright, sharp blue behind the mask. "Ain't many would care to be involved in assassination."

A hush fell over the room at the word, spoken openly for the first time, and the leader's left eyelid twitched. "I have my sources. You will not be dissatisfied. Gentlemen? Shall we adjourn? The publican will show you the way out."

The men rose, muttering and shaking each other's hands, and their leader leaned back in his chair, apparently at ease, his steepled fingers just touching his lips as he watched them leave. The publican, who had stayed in the background, had come forward and was leading the men out through a door few would know of, into the dark alleys and streets of London's Whitechapel district. A dangerous place, but these men could handle themselves. He would not have chosen them, else.

The Cockney stopped as he passed by. "Might be I could help you, guv," he said, his smile ingratiating. "I know of some sharpshooters from the army who—"

"I will handle it," the leader said, his voice smooth and urbane, but underlaid with steel.

"Your show, guv," the Cockney said cheerfully, and, nodding his head, went out behind the others.

The leader watched him go, his eyes thoughtful, and then snapped his fingers. From the shadows came another man, masked like the rest, though he had not sat at the table. "My lord?"

"Quiet, you fool!" For the first time that evening, the leader was truly angry, his eyelid twitching furiously, and the other man took a pace back. "How many times must I tell you—ah, well, no harm done. They're gone." He looked down the passageway, where he could just see the Cockney leaving. He wasn't certain, but he thought the man had been watching. All the more reason, then, to do what had to be done. "You know what you must do."

"Yes, my—sir." From his pocket the other man withdrew a long knife, thin-bladed and sharp. The steel winked in the firelight and then he sheathed it again. With a quick bow toward his employer he, too, made his way down the passageway.

Satisfactory. The leader leaned back, savoring the success that was to come, the power that would soon be his. Fortunate, was it not, that he had discovered the true identity of the Cockney? Good though his disguise was, the tale he told of his army service had been his undoing, for the leader had learned through channels of his own that the Cockney had never been in the regiment he had claimed. He had, instead, been in the employ of the Foreign Office on far more clandestine business. A spy, in other words, and it was the leader's experience that once a spy, always a spy. And that could not be tolerated. He would allow nothing, at this late date, to interfere with his plans.

His servant returned, sheathing the stiletto. "Done, sir."

"Good." It was no more than he'd expected. The Cockney would bother them no more. He rose. "Help me out of these damnable clothes," he said, and turned toward the stairs.

Sometime later, Edward Varley, the Marquess of Edgewater, returned downstairs. He was his usual dapper self, attired in an evening coat of royal-blue velvet over a waistcoat of oyster-white satin embroidered with gold and a neckcloth tied in the complicated folds of the *trône d'amour.* Foaming lace at his cuffs disguised the strength of his hands, now holding a walking stick, and a top hat of black silk covered hair that gleamed golden in the dull firelight. No one would ever have identified him as the leader of the conspirators who had just left, except for his eyes, which were still hard, still watchful. Not even the conspirators knew his true identity; those he had recruited himself believed him to be only an impoverished relation of some noble family. And that, the marquess reflected, pulling on his gloves, was the beauty of this whole scheme. Who would ever expect him, a peer of the realm and noted dandy, to be involved in such a thing as revolution?

Edgewater stepped outside and into the nondescript cab his servant had waiting for him; he would later transfer to his own town carriage, much more resplendent and much more notable. No one ever would connect him with tonight's events, or those that would transpire later, until it was too late. All was going splendidly. Best of all, since someone else was financing the plot, it wouldn't cost him a penny.

The marquess leaned back, his hands resting on the golden knob of his ebony walking stick. All would be well. Soon, he would have his revenge.

"That's him." Alex took one last look at the body lying on the dirty wooden table, and then turned away, his face expressionless. All about him was the smell of death, something he would never forget, something he thought he had left behind. For God's sake, this was England, and the war was over. He was entitled to live his life as he saw fit, to try to rebuild his long-lost peace of mind, and not to be plunged again into the nightmare from which there was no awakening.

"I'm sorry." The other man signaled to the morgue attendant that they were through. He was taller than Alex, his dark hair thick and straight, his eyes a burnished silver. In his work with the Foreign Office and now, since the war's end, the Home Office, Oliver, Duke of Bainbridge, had had to perform many distasteful tasks, but few as distasteful as this. A cold fish, he thought, looking at Alex. He had looked at the body of a man who had once been his closest associate and shown not a flicker of emotion. "You knew him well."

26

" 'Alas, poor Yorick,' " Alex muttered as they emerged from St. Bartholomew's Hospital into the murky morning. "He came through the war unscathed, and then gets knifed in a brawl in a Whitechapel tavern, for God's sake."

"Perhaps," Bainbridge said as his coachman jumped to open the carriage door for them.

"Perhaps?" Alex paused in the act of climbing into the carriage, and turned, his gaze penetrating. "Say what you mean, Bainbridge."

"Not here."

Bainbridge gestured again toward the carriage and this time Alex climbed in, his stomach knotting with anger. "Well?"

Bainbridge glanced over, and for a moment Alex imagined he saw sympathy in his eyes. "Come back to Bainbridge House," he suggested. "I'll explain everything there."

"There's more to this, then?"

Bainbridge nodded. "I fear so. But not here, St. Clair."

Alex stared at him a moment, taking his measure, and then nodded. He had been barely awake, and certainly had not recovered from last evening's dissipation, when the summons from the Home Office had come. And he had jumped to answer it, he thought now with disgust, quite as if he had still been in the employ of the government, instead of his own man, and for what? Only to see the body of a man who had once been his closest friend. Alf Barnes, born in the East End but able, somehow, to assume any identity he desired. Had he gone on the stage, his talent would surely have brought him fame and wealth. Instead, he had chosen to use it in a better cause, to help his country. He had saved Alex's life more than once, had survived the horrors of war on the Continent, only to die in England. Ironic, that. Comic, even, in the way the jests the Greek gods had played were comic. Strange,

27

then, that he felt not the slightest desire to laugh.

In his study at Bainbridge House, the Duke called for coffee to be served, and the two men sat in silence until a footman had brought the tray. Alex studied the thick Turkey carpet, the mahogany desk, the gigantic globe that stood in one corner; Bainbridge studied him. "You're probably wondering why I summoned you this morning," he began without preamble.

Alex looked up, and his eyes took on the hooded look they always assumed when he was facing a new, unknown situation. "It had crossed my mind."

"The situation is this." Bainbridge leaned back. "When you returned from the Continent, you resigned from the service. Alf Barnes didn't."

"No war on at the moment that I've noticed," Alex commented mildly, though he was annoyed by the criticism implied by the other man's words.

"No, not with a foreign enemy. The trouble is inside."

Alex took a sip of coffee before answering. "Revolution?"

"It's a possibility. Has been for years, but now, God knows things seem to be getting worse. We're watching matters closely." Bainbridge set down his cup and leaned forward. "We received information—it doesn't matter how—that a new conspiracy was forming with the goal of overthrowing the government. It's not the first, probably won't be the last. What bothers us about this one is that from what we've learned, men of substance are part of it."

"You're taking it seriously, then," Alex commented, wondering yet again what this had to do with him, but intrigued, just the same.

"We have to. These men have power. We decided we needed an agent to infiltrate the group."

"Alf Barnes."

"Exactly. I needn't tell you how adept he was at taking on any rôle he wanted."

28

"No." Alex grinned, the sudden smile that so changed his face. "Once I was wounded behind enemy lines, and Barnes managed, God knows how, to get a French uniform. It got us past the sentries. I almost believed he was French myself."

Bainbridge let the silence continue for a few moments before he spoke. "Barnes managed to infiltrate the conspiracy. He was accepted as a member. Or so he thought."

"You think they killed him."

"I think he was onto something dangerous, and yes, I think they killed him for it. You see, the only piece of information he managed to pass on is that the leader is gentry. Possibly even aristocracy."

"Hell," Alex said softly.

"Exactly. The only other thing Barnes mentioned about the leader is that his left eye twitches when he's angry. If he is the leader."

"I don't follow."

"Apparently he hinted that there was someone above him, that he was only an emissary. It was the leader's identity Barnes was trying to find out."

"And did he?"

"We have reason to believe he did. And that he died for it." Bainbridge paused. "He was a good man."

"A good friend."

Bainbridge glanced sharply at the other man. Alex's head was bent, and his eyes were unfocused. Not such a cold fish after all, Bainbridge thought, and crossed the room to pour out a measure of brandy. "Here."

Alex glanced up, his face for once without its usual mask of wary cynicism, and for a moment his eyes met the other man's. "Thank you," he said, taking the glass, and Bainbridge sat again.

"Several days ago," he went on, "Barnes managed to contact me. He said he thought he knew who the leader was, but he needed proof. He also said that at this next meeting he would find out the aim of the conspiracy. I couldn't call him off after that, of course."

Alex nodded. "Indeed. So you kept him on it."

"Yes. I'm afraid, though, he gave himself away somehow."

"Hell," Alex said again, and drained his brandy. "What does this have to do with me?"

"You can see the situation we're in, St. Clair. We need help."

"My spying days are done."

"The conspirators made one mistake," Bainbridge went on as if Alex hadn't spoken. "Barnes didn't die right away. A watchman found him, and before he died he said a name."

Alex leaned forward, intrigued in spite of himself. "The leader?"

"I don't know. I sincerely hope not." ·

"Who, man? Who?"

Bainbridge looked uncomfortable. "Cecily Randall."

"Who?" Alex said blankly, and Bainbridge's look of discomfort increased.

"The Duke of Marlow's oldest daughter."

Chapter Three

"Marlow's — God's teeth!" Alex slammed his glass down on the table by his side. "You'd have me believe Marlow is implicated in this? Everyone knows he's above reproach."

"So far as we know, he is. His daughter, though — no one knows about her. It wouldn't be the first time a woman has been involved in such a scheme."

Alex's lips twisted in distaste. "She can't be very old."

"She isn't. Marlow has a son at Oxford and his two older daughters are both out."

"So I'm to believe that a chit just out of the schoolroom is involved in some dire plot. I've seen a lot of things, Bainbridge, but this —"

"How often did you know Alf Barnes to be wrong?"

Alex stared at him and then leaned back. "Not often. But, hell." Thoughtfully he stroked his upper lip. "What were his exact words?"

Bainbridge frowned. "I'm not sure I know. Something like, 'Cecily Randall. Ask Cecily Randall.' "

" 'Ask'?" Alex said sharply. "Ask what?"

"God knows. But it's the only clue we have."

"I see." Alex was quiet for a long moment. "Say he was right," he said slowly. "Say this girl does have something to do with this plot. Why tell me?"

"Because you're the only man with the right credentials to investigate her."

"Rubbish. You must have any number of spies—"

"But none with *entree* to the right places," Bainbridge said, his voice almost gentle.

"Most of which I avoid. Consider my reputation, Bainbridge."

"I have."

"Do you seriously believe this girl's mother would allow me near her?"

"Has that stopped you in the past?"

Alex's eyes were hard. "I don't seduce innocents."

"But we don't know that she is innocent. I suggest, merely, that you become friendly with her. Find out who her companions are, who she knows, where she goes. Good God, man, do I really have to tell you what's at stake? If news of this gets out, the government could fall, at the least and that's the last thing we need."

There was a muffled thump at the door and both men started, as if the very conspirators of whom they had been speaking had discovered them. Bainbridge was already striding across the room when the thump was followed by a childish wail, and his face relaxed. He opened the door, stooped, and came back in, a small boy in his arms, knuckling his eyes. "My heir," he said wryly.

"My congratulations, Bainbridge," Alex said, and the child looked up.

"Gobe, Daddy," he demanded.

"Where is your nurse?" Bainbridge asked, but without any anger as he walked across to the giant globe, spinning it, to the child's delight. Alex watched, lips quirked back, feeling distinctly out of place in this domestic scene.

The door opened again and a young woman hurried in, her hair, like liquid sunshine, held back simply by a ribbon. She gave Alex a quick, distracted smile as he rose, and crossed the room. "I'm sorry, Oliver, but you know how fast he runs."

The child turned and bestowed on her a beatific

32

smile. "Gobe, Mommy," he said. "'Merica."

"Yes, pet," she said, reaching for the child, "and perhaps someday you'll go to America. But for now it's back to the nursery for you."

"Sabrina, I don't believe you've met our guest." Bainbridge walked across the room with her, his hand resting possessively at her back. "My wife, Sabrina. The Viscount St. Clair."

Alex inclined his head. "An honor, ma'am."

"How very nice to meet you, sir. Excuse me, but I'm afraid my hands are rather full just now," she said, smiling down at her son, who was busily pulling at her hair ribbon.

"Of course, ma'am." Alex watched as Bainbridge walked with his wife to the door, smiling down at her and the child, a different man from the one who had spoken so seriously of revolution and conspiracies a few moments ago. A most affecting scene, Alex thought sardonically, unaware that just a touch of wistfulness had crept into his eyes. No woman would ever tie *him* to her apron strings like that.

The door closed behind the duchess and Bainbridge returned. "My apologies, St. Clair. The boy is fascinated with the globe." Alex merely inclined his head in reply, his face impassive. "To return to what we were discussing—"

"You wish me to get close to Lady Cecily, if I read you aright," Alex said bluntly and Bainbridge, after a startled glance at him, nodded.

"Exactly. I have as hard a time as you believing she could be involved in such a thing, but I find it harder to believe that Barnes was wrong. She may not be the leader, but she may be able to lead us to him."

"So I am to court her and learn her secrets. I see." Alex rose and his voice when he spoke was flippant. "Who better than a rake to investigate a woman?"

"A man already skilled in intelligence work," Bainbridge corrected quietly, and Alex's mouth twisted.

The entire affair left a sour taste in his mouth. He had thought he had left all this behind, the deception, the treachery, the death and the thought of involving a possibly innocent girl in such matters was distasteful. But Alf Barnes had discovered she was implicated in some way, and Alex had never known him to be wrong. A tiny glow of excitement, one he didn't really wish to acknowledge, sprang into life inside him.

"Very well. I'll do it," he said, and held out his hand. The two men shook hands solemnly, and Alex left the room.

Sabrina met Bainbridge in the hall, and the child reached for his father. "He'll do it, then?"

Bainbridge smiled down at her. Gone were the days when he had mistrusted this girl; his heart and soul were now in her keeping. "Yes. He'll do well, too."

"Poor man," Sabrina said, and Bainbridge looked at her quizzically. "He looked lonely, don't you think?"

"That one?" Bainbridge laughed. "My dear, you're wasting your pity on him."

"Perhaps. But I do hope this does more for him than give him something to do. Well." She looked at her son, who was struggling to get down. "I'd best return him to Nurse." Smiling at her husband, Sabrina reached up for a quick kiss and headed for the stairs.

Outside, Alex clapped his beaver hat upon his head and tucked his walking stick under his arm. His steps were firmer, more purposeful, as he ran down the stairs to the pavement and strode along, already planning his strategy. His first thought at seeing Barnes's body, to drink himself into oblivion, was gone. No more empty days, or even emptier nights; no time, even, for a girl chance-met in the park. At last he had a purpose again, and it might even, in some way, make up for what had happened to him in France. Alf Barnes, he vowed, would not go unavenged.

* * *

Mr. Anthony Carstairs, pink of the *ton*, attired in an evening coat of mulberry velvet, his shirt points so high and so starched that he was in imminent danger of cutting himself if he should so much as turn his head, studied his cousin long and hard through his quizzing glass. "Never thought to see you at Almack's, coz," he said, letting the glass drop. "Not exactly your sort of do. No high flyers here, don't you know."

"Indeed," Alex answered, hiding his intense amusement. Had he not known Tony from boyhood, he would have dismissed him instantly as a worthless fribble, but he knew dandyism was simply a pose he had affected. There was good stuff in him, and that was a great relief to Alex. When he went, Tony would become the ninth Viscount St. Clair. Alex had no doubt the title would be in good hands. Better, perhaps, than his own.

"Nothing to drink but lemonade or orgeat, and nothing to eat but stale cake," Tony went on in his languid drawl, "and cards played for chicken stakes, don't you know."

Alex smiled, so briefly it was almost invisible. In contrast to his cousin, he was dressed in sober black, in the fashion decreed by Brummel, discredited though he now was. His evening coat was of superfine; his breeches of black satin, against which his waistcoat and neckcloth stood out dazzlingly white. The cut of his clothing was impeccable, of course; nothing less would do. It suited him to dress so, inconspicuously, so he thought, unaware that by contrast with the peacock dress of his cousin, he looked all the more elegant, and more than a little mysterious. As Tony had hinted, the Viscount St. Clair rarely appeared in such tame surroundings as Almack's, and his appearance had already occasioned a great deal of speculation. Little was known about the viscount, or where he had spent the last years. He was an enigma, a challenge few ladies wished to resist, with a reputation both scandalous and dangerous. Anxious mamas steered their daughters toward safer prey, while older, more sophisticated ladies eyed him speculatively, wondering just what went on behind that undeniably handsome, enigmatic exterior.

"Then, why are you here, Tony?" he asked.

"To see a goddess."

His tone was so fervent that Alex looked at him. For the first time he realized that Tony's attention had been constantly focused on the door, though he had greeted acquaintances and flirted with the young ladies present. His inner amusement grew. "Who is it this week?"

"Unfair, coz," Tony answered, his energy belying his languid pose. "This time it's real."

"Of course."

"It is! Wait until you see her, and you'll agree. Hair like midnight, face like an angel—"

"You could be a bit more original in your compliments, Tony."

"You wait," Tony promised, "and you'll see. And—there she is!"

"Indeed?" Alex glanced toward the doorway and felt a tiny jolt. A party of four was just entering, two girls, a matronly woman, and a man whose raiment almost rivaled Tony's. But it was on the smaller of the girls that his attention focused. Dressed in a modestly cut gown of gold tissue that made her skin glow, her hair tumbling in artless curls, she looked sweet and innocent, and not nearly so arresting as the tall beauty at her side. The girl from the park. The one he had caught himself thinking about at odd moments, distracting him from the task at hand. A welcome distraction, perhaps, but a dangerous one. With her here, how would he be able to concentrate on the treacherous Lady Cecily?

"An angel," Tony breathed fervently, and for once, Alex was almost inclined to agree.

"But I thought you said her hair was dark," he said,

36

looking at the cluster of golden-brown curls that framed the girl's face. Unfashionable, perhaps, but it suited her admirably.

"Not Lady Cecily, gudgeon," Tony said impatiently. "She's leg-shackled to Edgewater, or as good as. Her sister. Lady Diana."

"Who did you say?" Alex demanded, and Tony, distracted by the odd note in Alex's voice, turned to look at him.

"Lady Diana, the taller one, there—"

"No, the other one."

Tony grinned, destroying completely his pose of bored young man about town. "Never known you to be smitten so fast, coz."

"Damn you, Tony, don't cozen me! What did you say her name is?"

"Lady Cecily, coz." Tony continued to grin, enjoying enormously the spectacle of his normally inscrutable cousin appearing so agitated, and over a female, at that. "Marlow's daughter, don't you know."

"Hell!" The expletive slipped out before Alex could prevent it. Lady Cecily Randall. The woman he was supposed to investigate; the girl whose presence had brought the first stirrings of hope for the future to life within him. *Hell.*

Chapter Four

"There he is! No, don't look," Diana hissed in Cecily's ear as they entered Almack's. "He's looking at us. Oh, just look at him!"

"How can I if you won't let me?" Cecily asked, smiling.

"He is *so* handsome," Diana went on, and Cecily glanced at Edgewater, on her other side, to share her amusement with him. He was, indeed, smiling at Diana, but it was a cruel smile, a mocking smile. Cecily's amusement was replaced by unease.

"Are you talking of that fop over there?" He raised his quizzing glass. "The one who aspires to the dandy set?"

"Oh, don't!" Cecily placed her hand on his arm, and Edgewater looked at her. Something sparked in his eyes, something that made Cecily wish she hadn't been so impulsive as to touch him. She hoped she had imagined it.

"As you wish, my dear." His tone was mild as he dropped the quizzing glass, but Cecily's unease didn't lessen. "And who is that with him? Ah, the notorious St. Clair. Hardly edifying company, and not at all suitable for you, Lady Diana."

"Heavens, no," the Duchess of Marlow said from behind them. "I wonder how he has the nerve to appear here, of all places! What are the patronesses thinking, to allow such as he in?" The duchess shook her head, the feathers of her headdress bobbing. "Diana, love, I can't think what Mr. Carstairs is about to be seen with him."

"His cousin, Mama," Diana protested.

"Oh, dear. I do hope he has the sense not to introduce you to him! Hardly suitable company for you."

"Has he a loose screw?" Cecily asked, and at last looked across the room. The young man with the brown hair swept forward *a là Brutus*, attired in a combination of colors that made her eyes ache, could only be Diana's current flirt, Mr. Carstairs. But the man next to him—Cecily felt a tiny jolt go through her. The notorious Viscount St. Clair. The man she had met riding in the park.

"Cecily, such a question! Oh, dear, where is my vinaigrette? I declare I'll have palpitations if you speak so again."

"I'm sorry, Mama."

"Come, you must make your bow to the patronesses." The duchess turned away from the door. "Cecily, child, please don't fidget; one would think this was your first season."

Cecily hastily stopped herself from smoothing down her gown yet again. "Yes, Mama."

"And Diana, please do behave yourself this evening. Perhaps you'll be allowed to waltz."

"Yes, Mama," Diana murmured, slanting Cecily a mischievous look.

Cecily was too preoccupied with her own thoughts to notice. The Viscount St. Clair. Even she, sheltered though she was, had heard of him. Since his return to England last year, his dissipations had been legendary. Cecily wasn't sure what such activities involved, but she was certain they must have something to do with gambling and drinking, and of course, women. Many women, perhaps? And yet he was obviously respectable enough to be allowed *entree* into so stodgy a place—for so Cecily, for all her surface pleasure, considered it — as Almack's. Nor had he seemed particularly diabolical when she had met him in the park; in fact, he had seemed to like her.

The thought that such as he might actually be interested in her sent a curious sensation down her spine, a frisson of mingled pleasure and alarm. After all, a man known as a rake must have something he used to attract women, and he had certainly been charming that one time they had met, in spite of her appearance. And that, she thought, with a quite uncharacteristic lowering of her spirits, was her problem. Whyever would he be interested in her, when there were other, prettier girls available, such as her sister? Even dressed as she was, in a gown of gold tissue that made her eyes sparkle, she knew she was no beauty. Why should that matter, though? She was engaged, for heaven's sake! She had no right to be thinking of other men when her fiancé was at her side, holding possessively to her arm. And yet — She couldn't resist just one more look at him.

"I say, coz," Tony said, "isn't she an angel? Alex? Don't you agree?"

"Hm?" Alex slowly came out of his shock. It couldn't be. It couldn't. "Who? Oh, of course. Quite lovely, Tony," he replied absently.

Alex's dazed thoughts went on while Tony prattled about his beloved's charms. From bitter experience, he had assumed that any woman involved in such a plot as Bainbridge had outlined would be more sophisticated, knowledgeable, certainly older. Instead, he found himself faced with a girl who couldn't be above twenty, a girl whose fresh innocence shone all over her. A girl he had thought, without really analyzing it, that he might be able to trust.

You should know better, a voice whispered in his mind, and his mouth set in the cynical sneer that was becoming habitual. *Who is there who can be trusted? And who would you rather believe, Alf Barnes or a girl you hardly know?*

Alex's sneer slowly faded and a look almost of sadness came into his eyes. All women were faithless; he had learned that the hard way. Until he knew Lady Cecily better, he had best watch himself. And, he thought, his eyes narrowing, if he learned that she had, indeed, had something to do with Barnes's death, then she would pay.

Cecily, turning for that last look at St. Clair, nearly stumbled. The sky-blue eyes she had already seen in many moods, alarmed, amused, startled, were now slightly narrowed, cold, hard, somehow suspicious. She turned to see where he was looking, and then realized, with another jolt, that he was staring at her.

It was hard to meet that stern gaze, but Cecily was no coward. Her chin slightly raised, she returned his look and had the satisfaction of seeing St. Clair's eyes widen slightly in surprise. For a long moment her gaze held his, and then a smile spread slowly over his face. His eyes warmed again, but in a different way. She could feel the heat of them even here, as they traveled over her body with a look so intimate, so knowing, it was almost tactile. Flushing, flustered, she hastily turned away, clinging just a bit tighter to Edgewater's arm. She felt somehow as if she had been challenged.

"I wish they'd finish speaking with the patronesses," Tony said, fidgeting beside Alex. "When they are settled, let us go across to them. Is she not an angel?"

"Indeed," Alex said, his tone ironic, but it was not of the admittedly lovely Diana that he spoke. Her sister had her own beauty, subtle though it was; it was there in her slender form, in her tousled curls, in the eyes that had gazed boldly back at him, refusing to be intimidated. A beauty too subtle for Tony to appreciate, perhaps, but one that he, a connoisseur of women, found enticing, challenging. He suspected that, young though she was, Lady Cecily would be a worthy opponent. This assignment, distasteful though it had seemed, might just yet prove to be enjoyable.

41

"Lady Diana hasn't been approved to waltz yet," Tony went on, oblivious to his cousin's preoccupation. "Coz, do you think if you asked Lady Jersey?"

In spite of himself, Alex's lips twitched with amusement. Had he himself ever been so young that the thought of dancing with a pretty girl had been so important? "Scared of Lady Jersey, are you?"

"No such thing!" Tony replied indignantly, but at the look Alex gave him, he colored. "She talks so much, coz, and asks so many questions I can't answer that I never know what to say to her. But she likes you."

Alex's lips twitched again. "Rest easy, halfling. I shall accompany you. And then we shall seek out the enchanting Lady Diana." As well as the equally enchanting, and possibly treacherous, Lady Cecily. Alex found he was looking forward to the encounter with an anticipation long absent.

"You're a great gun, Alex. Perhaps we'll find someone here for you tonight."

"Not exactly my style," Alex said dryly, but his eyes flickered toward Cecily, seated now on a gilt chair with her escort bending over her. "Who is that with the Marlow ladies?"

"Don't you know? That's the Marquess of Edgewater."

"Edgewater?" Alex frowned slightly as he and Tony crossed the room, beginning now to be crowded with the cream of the *ton*. "Ah, yes, I place him now. Edward Varley. I knew him at school. Supercilious prig."

"No such thing, Alex!" Tony protested. "He's all the crack, don't you know. Everyone I know wants to be like him."

"Then, everyone you know has lamentable taste. What is he doing with the Marlows?"

"Engaged to Lady Cecily, don't you know."

"Indeed." Alex's eyes narrowed again as he glanced toward Cecily. Engaged, was she? Interesting. In fact, the situation was becoming more intriguing by the moment. He would have to make the acquaintance of the charming Lady Cecily soon. And then he would see.

The encounter with Lady Jersey proved to be as long-winded and as arduous as Tony had predicted, though no one would have guessed Alex's feelings from his face. Scandalous though he was considered to be, he was indeed well-liked by the patronesses of Almack's, most of whom held a soft spot in their hearts for a charming rake. Thus the two men bowed and then strolled away some moments later, Tony dazed with his good fortune. Tonight, at last, he would waltz with his goddess.

Lady Diana appeared equally pleased to see Tony, when he and Alex reached the Marlow party, if her smile and dimples were any indication. "Evening, Your Grace," Tony said, bowing to the duchess, who inclined her head graciously. "Like to present to you my cousin, Viscount St. Clair."

Alex, too, bowed in acknowledgment of the introduction, though he noted, as Tony appeared not to, that the duchess's smile was stiff. Edgewater's greeting was curt, but Diana, as he bowed over her hand, made up for that. Glancing up at him through her lashes, she gave him a mischievous smile that said clearly that she knew of his reputation and found it intriguing. His own lips twitched in response. A definite minx, was the Lady Diana. Tony would have his hands full with her, he thought, and turned to Lady Cecily, whom he had deliberately left for last.

"Lady Cecily," he murmured, bowing over her hand in what was meant to be only a polite gesture. He glanced up as he began to rise, to see her regarding him with those luminous golden eyes of hers. There was neither shyness nor boldness in her gaze, but rather a frank curiosity, and a dawning awareness. His interest in her sharpened, and he held her gaze for what felt like eternity, until Edgewater cleared his throat.

Recollecting himself, Alex rose, releasing her hand, though he could still feel the warmth of her slender fingers, gloved in kid, against his palm. "Charmed," he said, finding the word more meaningless than usual.

Edgewater glared at him. "Lady Cecily and I are recently betrothed," he said, laying a heavy hand on her shoulder.

Cecily's eyes were downcast, but Alex couldn't help but notice her shift under the pressure of her fiancé's hand. "My felicitations," he said smoothly, as the orchestra began to play the first dance of the evening, a cotillion. "I imagine you are engaged for this dance, Lady Cecily?"

"She is dancing with me." Edgewater's tone was smug as he reached for her hand, raising her to her feet.

"Indeed. Are you also engaged for the waltz?"

"Of course, she—"

"No, I am not," Cecily said at the same time, her voice soft, but determined.

"Cecily—" Edgewater began.

"Then, I would be honored if you would dance it with me," Alex said.

Cecily dropped into a brief curtsy. "Certainly, sir."

"Thank you." Alex inclined his head and then turned away, walking across the room to speak with acquaintances.

Cecily watched him go, bemused. Of all the ladies in the room, he had singled her out. It didn't mean anything, of course, and so why did her heart race at the thought of waltzing with him?

"Cecily, you won't waltz with that man," the duchess said. "Will you?"

Cecily glanced up. "I can hardly refuse now, Mama."

"I don't approve," Edgewater said on her other side. "You know not what manner of man St. Clair is."

"Oh, surely, sir, one dance won't hurt."

"He is charming," Diana said.

The duchess shot her a look. "Oh, dear. I don't want

you having anything to do with him either, Diana," she said. "Oh, very well, there is nothing we can do about this. But, oh, your reputation! I do hope it will not suffer for this."

"No, Mama. Please, sir, should we not join the sets? Everyone is looking at us," Cecily said.

"You should have thought of that before." Edgewater was frowning heavily as he led her onto the floor. "I cannot approve of your waltzing with him," he went on as they joined a set just forming. "He isn't a suitable partner for you."

"I promise nothing will happen, sir," Cecily said, laying her hand briefly on his arm and smiling at the other couples. She well understood that what she had done was somewhat scandalous; she also knew that continuing to discuss it before the avid ears of the other dancers would only make matters worse. What she didn't at all understand was why she had agreed to dance—to waltz, of all things!—with St. Clair, why her pulse should race at the thought. Perhaps, she thought prosaically, she was coming down with a fever.

She knew, though, it was something more than that when St. Clair came to claim his waltz. It was hard not to shiver a bit when he took her hand, leading her onto the floor. It was hard not to be aware of his shoulder where her hand rested on it, broader and more strongly muscled than Edgewater's, or the warmth of his hand at her waist. It was even harder to meet his aquamarine eyes, looking at her with an expression she couldn't quite fathom, not the earlier coldness, but a mixture of warmth and confusion, as if he, too, were puzzled by his impulse in asking her to waltz. And that was strange. Surely he had waltzed with many women in his time. Many beautiful women. Cecily had long ago accepted her shortcomings, but suddenly she wished she were beautiful, for him.

Alex, too, was very aware of the girl in his arms. As he had expected, she was light on her feet, her slender body supple and graceful beneath his hands. She was smaller than he'd realized, barely reaching to his chin, and yet she moved with him as if waltzing with him were the most natural thing in the world. Some of her curls had come loose from the ribbon which bound them, he noticed, but rather than looking untidy, she appeared instead charmingly disheveled, and somehow endearing. Not his usual type of woman at all, and yet—"You are very beautiful," he murmured, his voice husky and her eyes, which had been avoiding him, flew to his, startled at first, and then laughing.

"Oh, fustian!" she exclaimed, her smile wide. "I'm no beauty, sir. At least not next to my sister."

"Your sister is not here," he said, and twirled her in a step that left her breathless. "Allow me to know what I am talking about."

"Of course. You are, after all, a famous rake."

Alex choked, and missed a step. "God's teeth, where did you hear that?"

"From my mother." Her eyes were candid. "Is it true?"

"This is not a proper subject for us to be discussing," he said repressively.

"Fustian. Now you sound like my fiancé."

He looked down at her averted head, and a strange tenderness filled him. "Does he scold you, little one?"

"Only after I agreed to waltz with you." The mischievous sparkle danced in her eyes. "Am I in such danger, then?"

"No." He whirled her around again; it was the only way he knew to silence her, if only for the moment. What did he do now? He had planned a campaign of slow seduction, hoping to get close to her and thus learn her secrets. Instead, her artless comments had completely disarmed him, as perhaps they had been meant to. Was she really so innocent as she seemed? "Surely you're not disappointed," he said lightly.

"Such a question, sir!" She raised laughing eyes to

him. "However I answer that is an insult, either to you or to me."

"So it is." He grinned down at her. "I salute you, ma'am. You're very quick."

"Fustian," she said again, but she was smiling. This was not at all the type of flirtation she was accustomed to, but she was enjoying it. If he were this charming to every lady, she could well understand how he had come by his reputation. "I am only surprised that you would risk your reputation by coming to such a place as Almack's."

Alex returned to earth with a thud. For a few moments, he had forgotten the purpose of this meeting. Now it returned. To be captivated by her was dangerous. The last time he had let himself forget his mission in the presence of an attractive woman, it had been a deadly mistake.

"Indeed," he said, his voice so cool that Cecily looked up quickly. "Even a rake desires a change now and again."

"I see." She couldn't help the note of bewilderment in her voice. One moment he had been smiling, teasing, charming; the next, coldly indifferent. What had she said amiss? Surely nothing that was insulting. If only she could think of a way to make amends—but what would it signify if she did? She was nothing to him, only a girl chance-met in the park. And he was nothing to her. After all, she *was* engaged. There was no need for her to fall into the mopes over this. She would hold her head high and smile, and not let anyone see how hurt and confused she was.

The magic had gone out of the waltz. In silence, they finished; in equal silence, they walked back to where the duchess sat, Cecily's hand resting lightly on his arm, Alex's face turned away. She curtsied; he bowed. Then he was gone, leaving her to stare after him, a puzzled frown creasing her brow and her thoughts so chaotic that she barely heard her mother's scolding. It had been one of the most unusual, somehow significant, dances of her life, but it was, after all, only a dance. He was only a man. Her life was planned for her, and it would go on. She would manage quite well without him. Likely she would never see him again.

The Marquess of Edgewater was not pleased. When he had agreed to escort the Marlow ladies to Almack's, he had done so with the idea of setting the seal of respectability on his forthcoming marriage. Not that that was necessary, of course, he being who he was, but he was quite proud of himself for having caught such a prize, the daughter of one of England's premier peers. For a time it had seemed he would have little luck finding a suitable mate; he found most women vain and shallow, and had never really minded that he had little luck with the opposite sex. He had been angling long and hard for Lady Cecily, however. So long, and so hard, that when she had finally agreed to his suit, he had wanted to shout the news to the world. That was not his way, however. He had found it best, always, to work in secret.

A smile flickered across Edgewater's face. The fools, all of them, bowing and scraping to him tonight because he had deigned to grace Almack's with his presence, and because of his recent betrothal. If they only knew what he had planned for them — but they didn't, and that made the secret that much more delicious. It was high time they had their comfortable lives shaken up, and he was just the man to do it.

Lost in thought, Edgewater continued to disrobe, handing his clothing to Simpkins, his valet, until he was sitting in front of the fire, wearing a magnificent brocade dressing gown, with a glass of brandy and water at his side. Ordinarily he was abstemious, preferring at all times to keep a clear head, but tonight called for celebration. He had done it. At long last, he had been accepted by society as one of their own, and because it had taken his engagement to do it, rather than his own merits, his coming revenge would be all the sweeter. Oh, yes, they would pay. All of them.

All his life, it seemed, he had been on the outside, looking in: in the village where he had been raised, where his aristocratic background had prevented him from mingling with other boys his age, though his family was as poor as any of theirs—Ted the toad, they had called him, a name that still rankled; at Eton, where, as a King's scholar, he had suffered untold abuse from those more fortunate than he, and had taken refuge in his studies. It had become a point of pride with him that his mind was so much quicker than so many others'; his nature so quick to spot slurs and slow, yet steady, to repay them. It was at Eton that he had realized that he was superior to everyone else, save in the matters of money and rank. He grew quick to find and exploit others' weaknesses; he learned that a vituperative tongue was a weapon to be wielded well, and that if people didn't like him, having them fear him was nearly as good. Soon he had gathered around him a coterie of admirers, holding them by respect and, quite frankly, fear of his ready ridicule. Oh, yes, he was indeed a superior being. Those things he lacked, money and power, would someday come.

And they had, the money first, through means he found prudent never to discuss. Rank had come unexpectedly, when his despised uncle and cousin, who had always looked down on him for the lowliness of his circumstances, had been killed in the same carriage accident. He was a marquess, ranking only below a duke, and his accession to power should have been sweet. It was sweet, but something was missing. He wanted more, and so over the past years, he had gradually conceived his plans, choosing his confederates carefully and biding his time, until the circumstances were right. Now the time was nearly here, and at last, he would have all the power he could desire.

So long as nothing went wrong. Ordinarily Edgewater had no doubts about the effectiveness of his plans; but he had already made one mistake, and tonight he had realized that an unknown element had entered in. Marriage to a high-ranking member of the aristocracy was important to his plans; to Lady Cecily, doubly important, for she had witnessed his one mistake, though he doubted she realized it. Until this evening, she had seemed an eminently sensible choice. A bit too given to levity, perhaps, but docile and biddable. He had little doubt that she would be a suitable wife.

Or, rather, he'd had little doubt. Cecily had not shown herself to be so docile when it had come to waltzing with St. Clair. A small matter, perhaps, but Edgewater had learned that the small matters were the ones most likely to trip one up. He would have to watch her carefully, and learn her weaknesses, to use them against her if necessary. As for St. Clair—

A sneer marred Edgewater's handsome countenance. St. Clair. An idler, the type of person Edgewater most despised. What else did he do but spend his days in the pursuit of his own pleasure, ignoring those who were in need of so much more? When the time came, Edgewater would take great pleasure in eliminating such as he.

Until that time, though, St. Clair would bear watching. There had been something about him tonight when he had asked Cecily for the waltz, something challenging about his eyes. There was, in fact, a hint of steel underneath the idle exterior, and that concerned him. Not, however, very much. As he had with other opponents, Edgewater would learn the man's weaknesses, and exploit them. Only then would he be prepared to best him, and best him, he would.

Smiling grimly, Edgewater drained his glass and then rose to prepare for bed. Oh, yes, he would win that fight. He would have to. Nothing must interfere with his plans.

"She doesn't seem to do nothing out of the ordinary, sir," Parsons said, raising his tankard of porter. Sitting sprawled across the table from him, a nearly empty glass of brandy before him, Alex thoughtfully stroked his upper lip, a habit remaining from the days when he had once sported a mustache as a disguise. "She goes shopping with her mother or sister, driving with Edgewater, and to the usual affairs at night. There's nothing different about her."

"There has to be." A week after Almack's, and he was no closer to learning the elusive Lady Cecily's secrets, though he had tried. He had spoken with acquaintances in the *ton;* all had had nothing but praise for her. He had even attended some of the affairs he so detested, to his hostesses' delight and mystification, only to watch Cecily. Though he never approached her, even he had to admit that her behavior appeared above reproach. Now Parsons, whom he'd set to watch the Marlow household, was reporting the same thing.

"There has to be something," he repeated. "Barnes was a good man. If he said she's involved, she's involved."

Parsons nodded. He, too, had known and trusted Alf Barnes, and wanted every bit as much as Alex to find his killers. He was beginning to have his doubts, however, as to how to do so. "The housemaid I, uh—"

"Romanced," Alex supplied, with a little smile.

"Became acquainted with," Parsons said, frowning. "She says the same thing, sir. Lady Cecily isn't doing anything wrong. Look, sir." Parsons leaned forward, a strand of his hair falling lankly over his forehead. "Barnes was dying. Who knows what he was thinking? Maybe he saw Lady Cecily and fell for her—"

"Become a romantic as well as religious, Parsons?" Alex inquired and Parsons' face went stiff. "My apolo-

51

gies, but I think Barnes knew something about her. Something important."

"Then, you tell me what it is, sir." Parsons spread his hands in defeat. "I can't find nothing wrong with her."

"No." Alex stroked his upper lip again. "There is one thing. Does she still ride out alone in the morning?"

Parsons frowned. "Haven't heard nothing about that, sir."

"I met her, you see, riding in the park alone. Before I knew who she was."

"Sir, do you think—"

"That she's meeting someone there? It's possible." Idly he turned his glass around. "Though she didn't look as if she were doing so that day. Still, we can't discount it. It seems to be the only thing we know she does out of the usual." He rose with sudden energy. "I must be getting ready if I'm to be at Lady Sefton's do. This is a bother, Parsons."

"Yes, sir." Parsons followed Alex into his bed chamber, to lay out the clothes Alex would be wearing this evening.

"I've done many things for my country, but I never thought I'd have to attend assemblies and routs for it," he went on, sounding so disgruntled that Parsons smiled.

"I have information that Lady Cecily will be there, sir."

"Ah, yes, your little housemaid. Let us hope the lady does something soon, Parsons. This is getting tiresome."

"Yes, sir," Parsons said, smiling again. "By the by, sir, you had a caller while you were out this afternoon."

Alex, standing in front of the mirror to tie his neckcloth, looked up, his eyes wary. "Who was it, Parsons?"

"A young person, sir." Parsons' face took on the look of distaste he produced so well. "Wearing, I might say, a very heavy scent. Attar of roses, I believe."

"Nanette. Hell." Alex's nimble fingers went on tying

the neckcloth. His mistress, whom he hadn't visited in over a week. Since, in fact, that evening at Almack's. Odd, that he felt no desire to see her again. "I'll have to do something about her. What would you suggest, Parsons?"

"I'm sure I couldn't say, sir." Parsons held up Alex's evening coat of dark-blue velvet and Alex shrugged into it. "The, er, girl, would probably prefer something expensive."

"No, she's no lady, is she?" Alex said absently, picking through his jewel box until he found a sapphire stick pin. Thrusting it through the folds of his neckcloth, he stepped back from the mirror to study the result. "Complete to a shade, wouldn't you say, Parsons? Will I do?"

"Admirably, sir. What should I say if she comes again?"

"I'll handle it, Parsons. There was a diamond bracelet she was speaking of."

"Very expensive, sir."

"Her *congé*, Parsons," Alex said, surprising himself. Until this moment, he hadn't realized that he planned to break with Nanette. "Does that satisfy you?"

Parsons set himself to smoothing the slight wrinkles that dared mar the fit of Alex's coat across the shoulders. "It's not for me to say, sir."

"Liar."

"If you say so, sir. Will you be late tonight?"

"No." Alex picked up his gloves and hat and strolled toward the door. "Not if I'm to ride early tomorrow."

"I understand, sir. I'll continue to keep watch, then?"

"I think for tonight you can let it be. Tomorrow — well, we'll see."

Chapter Five

It was tomorrow. Cecily opened eyes still heavy with sleep and looked to where the sun peeked in through the open curtains. A perfect morning for riding, in fact, after all the recent dismal weather, and yet all she wanted to do was turn over and pull her pillow over her head, shutting out the world. Last week everything had looked so easy, so planned, so safe. Now, though nothing was different on the surface, everything had changed. *She* had changed, and she wasn't certain how.

Sometime later she rode into the park, attired in her boys' clothes. A little distance ahead, a man waited astride a black stallion, and she recognized him with a little shock. St. Clair. Somehow, seeing him here was inevitable.

He waited until she reached him. They walked their horses together in silence, heading toward the Serpentine and crossing the bridge, aware of each other in a way they hadn't been the other morning. "I didn't really expect to see you here," Alex said finally. "I thought that now you're engaged, you wouldn't do this sort of thing anymore."

"I was already engaged the other morning, sir." Cecily stripped off the glove of York tan and brandished her hand toward him.

"This is the ring he gave you?"

"Yes."

"Indeed. Among other things, he is a skint."

"He is not! I think it's lovely." Cecily wheeled away, spurring Dancer forward, past the Chelsea Water reservoir and through the flower avenue, just now beginning to bloom. Alex caught up with her easily, riding a few paces behind her. By God, but she could ride, with more spirit than he would have expected had he known her only as the proper Lady Cecily. There was more to her than met the eye. She would, he told himself, bear watching.

Cecily was aware of his presence beside her again, but not by so much as a turn of her head did she acknowledge him. What did he want with her? Before last week she hadn't known him; now he seemed to be everywhere she was. When she was dancing, or conversing with someone, or simply listening to the music, she would look up to see his piercing blue gaze fixed thoughtfully on her. It wasn't the look of a lover, or a man interested in dalliance; whatever his reasons, he hadn't even approached her since last week. Which was probably just as well, considering what had happened after their waltz at Almack's.

Thinking about it made her smile. She had been scolded again by her mother and her fiancé, and even quizzed by her father, who usually left such matters to his wife. She had endured questions and sidelong glances from society matrons eager to spread scandal, and she had been watched closely ever since, to see what other mad starts she would get up to. It should have bothered her, as it appeared to bother her mother, but somehow she couldn't take it seriously. What had she done, after all, but dance just once with a man who had asked her? A handsome man, true, a charming man who intrigued her, but who meant nothing, really, to her. At least, she didn't think he did. What was wrong with that? If it became known that she was riding with him now, unchaperoned, then she really would be in the suds.

She cast him a sidelong look. His eyes were unfocused, staring ahead, and so she could look her fill. He looked tired, older than she had expected, and the weary look she had noticed before was back in his eyes, which were bracketed with lines. He was only a man. Oh, certainly he was handsome; certainly she had been charmed by him at Almack's, but she preferred him like this, approachable, even vulnerable. It was a side of him she suspected few were allowed to see.

As if he sensed her eyes on him, Alex turned to look at her, and their gazes held for a moment while, without meaning to, they slowed their mounts. Cecily endured that searching blue gaze for only a moment, and then leaned forward to pat Dancer on the neck. "I didn't think rakes rose this early, sir," she said.

Alex gave an appreciative chuckle. "And what of ladies of fashion?"

"I'm hardly that at the moment, sir."

"On the contrary." Alex's gaze traveled slowly over her. "I rather like that outfit on you."

"Fustian," she said, moving a few paces forward, but her cheeks were pink.

"You're different in it," he went on. "More relaxed. Perhaps the real Lady Cecily?"

His words mirrored so closely what she had just thought about him that she turned toward him, startled. "I'm not certain there's a hidden part of me, if that's what you're implying. I am what you see, sir."

"Are you?" He brought Azrael to a halt and leaned over to pull a bunch of lilacs from a bush. "Here. This becomes you."

To her fury, Cecily could feel herself blushing again, and she brought the flowers to her face to cover her reaction.

"I like it when you blush. Your skin turns a golden rosy color."

" 'Tis sallow. Mama sometimes despairs of me. She says she doesn't know how I came to be her daughter."

"No, you're not at all like her. Thank God."

There was no answer to that. Cecily rode on, silent, wondering yet again what he wanted of her. Surely he didn't really think her attractive, and yet his attention to her was what was making her feel so unsettled lately. She wished he'd leave her alone; she wished he'd never go.

"When are you marrying?"

"The end of June."

"Next month. Edgewater must be eager to claim you."

Cecily turned, a retort ready, and then thought better of it. "We wish to marry before everyone leaves town."

"Oh, is that it? And what were you really going to say?"

"I was going to tell you it's none of your affair, if you must know."

"I suppose it isn't, but that never stopped me before."

That made Cecily look at him again. What, really, did she know of him? Only his reputation, that his prowess with women, as well as at cards and sport, was legendary. Everything else was shrouded in mystery. "Why do you care?"

"How did you meet Edgewater?" he asked—as if she hadn't spoken.

"The usual way. Why do you care?" she asked again.

"Because I don't think he's the man for you." What did she see in him, anyway, that useless fribble of a man?

Cecily tossed her head, a mannerism that worked quite well for her sister, but that she had never tried before. "He and I suit quite well."

"Indeed. So you don't love him."

"I didn't say that!"

"You didn't have to. I suppose it should be expected."

She turned to look at him, with her clear golden eyes that made him feel, uncomfortably, that she could see right through him. "You don't believe in love."

"No sensible person believes in love."

Cecily stopped. Unaware, Alex went on a few paces. Had no one ever loved him, then? But he had his choice of women; he could have anyone he wanted. And perhaps that, she thought with dawning wisdom, was part of the problem.

Alex turned in the saddle. "Is aught wrong?"

"Hm? No." She walked the few paces to meet him, and then stopped, her eyes searching his face. "Poor rake," she said softly, and reached out with gentle fingers to touch his face.

Alex jerked back. "God's teeth, madam! What do you think you are about?"

"Nothing." Cecily withdrew her hand and glanced away. "I must be getting home, before I'm missed."

"So soon?" he said, before he could stop himself. Belatedly he had realized that he hadn't come here to talk with her, pleasant though it had been. No, he had come to spy on her. The word left a bitter taste in his mouth. To spy on a girl he was beginning to think might be involved only peripherally, if at all, in nefarious doings; to spy on an innocent. At least, he hoped she was innocent.

"I'm flattered, sir," she said, her voice light, "but the sun is rising higher, and I dare not be caught."

"No, of course not." Alex's voice sounded normal as he turned Azrael to walk with her. He didn't want her to go. He wanted her to stay, and to see whom she met. No, that wasn't true. He wanted her to stay

58

with him. "You'd best go," he said abruptly.

"Yes." Cecily managed to keep her hurt at his brusque tone out of her voice. He was nothing to her. Why should she care? "And will I see you tonight at whatever affair I attend?" she said airily.

"I doubt it." Alex suddenly reached a decision. This girl was no more guilty of fomenting revolution than he was. He didn't know why Barnes had said her name; perhaps he never would. One thing he did know, though. She did not have the duplicity in her to appear as she did, now and at the same time work toward her country's undoing, unless she were a superb actress. No, she was innocent, and that meant that his task was done. He would report to Bainbridge and go back to his own life, forgetting about her. He would have to. She was dangerous, this little one, in a way few other women ever had been. If anyone could make him trust again, she could, and he had learned, long ago, never to trust anyone. Not even sweet, innocent girls with luminous golden eyes. "I've grown rather tired of the social round. The grasping debutantes and their doting mamas, and the people who have nothing better to do than to gossip and cut up one's reputation."

"I see." Cecily's eyes suddenly sparkled with mischief. "We can safely assume, then, that you aren't hanging out for a wife."

"God's teeth, no! And where did you learn cant?"

"From my brother." She tossed her head again, pleased that he wasn't interested in any other young lady. "Then, perhaps I'll see you riding."

"I don't think so. I find rising so early fatigues me," he said sounding bored. It was best to make the break now and to make it clean, he thought, before he made the mistake of turning to look at her.

The hurt in her eyes was more than he could bear. Before he could stop himself, Alex reached over and touched her cheek. "Have a good life with your suitable marquess, little one," he said, and set Azrael to the gallop, riding away before he could do anything else stupid. Like reaching for her hand, or pulling her off her horse into an embrace and—

God's teeth! It was better this way. He would go on with his life and forget he'd ever met her. He would have to. She was engaged to someone else.

Cecily's vision blurred as she watched him ride away. It had to be the sun, risen above the treetops now, and shining directly into her face, that was making her eyes water; why should she cry? Her life was perfect. She had money, position, and a match that, if not the most romantic, was suitable. There was no room in her life for a rake with hurt eyes and a wounded soul. No, she was much better off without him. She was glad he had said good-bye, she thought, turning Dancer toward home. Very glad.

She felt blue-deviled throughout the day, though, even when her fiancé came by in the afternoon to escort her to Hatchard's. Not believing in self-pity, Cecily was thoroughly disgusted with herself by the time she came downstairs to meet the marquess, attired in a walking dress of pale green, with a spencer of deeper green over it. Her high-crowned bonnet of Leghorn straw was trimmed to match her spencer. For once her appearance was impeccable; not a curl was out of place, not a ribbon twisted, and a smile of delight was pasted to her lips as she held out her hand. With every appearance of equal delight, the marquess bent over it, and involuntarily Cecily remembered another man bowing just so, a man with darker hair, whose touch had quite burned through her gloves—

"You are looking lovely this afternoon, Cecily," the marquess said, and Cecily looked up. Ridiculous to be thinking of another man when she had such a handsome fiancé paying her court. Today Edgewater was

60

attired in a coat of pearl-gray superfine, which nearly matched his eyes. Watchful eyes, Cecily noticed, and detached. A little cool, not at all like the warm blue gaze she had felt on her this morning and would never feel again.

"A fine afternoon for a walk," Edgewater went on, tucking her arm through his proprietorially and leading her toward the door. Cecily mentally shook herself. She would have to forget St. Clair and concentrate instead on her fiancé. St. Clair was not for her, even if he were at all interested in her. Which he wasn't, she told herself firmly. She was a very lucky girl to be engaged to a man who was not only handsome, but was one of the leaders of the *ton*. With him, her future was assured.

And so, to ease a conscience that felt uncomfortable, if not actually guilty, she set herself to be charming as they strolled together down the street, her maid trailing behind to act as chaperone. She told Edgewater of her life at Marlow, the huge estate just north of London, which she missed. She entertained him with stories of people met at various soirees, routs, and balls, using her natural gift for mimicry to bring them to life. She even told him about Dancer, which earned her a look from him under raised eyebrows.

"A dancing horse? Forgive me, my dear, if I find that a trifle hard to believe," Edgewater said, though he smiled.

"But 'tis true, my lord. Perhaps we might go riding some day, and I'll show you. He dances if I sing."

Edgewater took a moment, frowning, to flick away an infinitesimal speck of lint that had dared to land on his sleeve. "I trust that no wife of mine would do anything so undignified."

Cecily, encouraged by the slight smile that accompanied those daunting words, went on, heedless. "But it is above all things great, my lord.

61

He's vastly entertaining."

"Like a circus, which is for children. You are not a child, my dear."

"No, I am not," Cecily said, her voice more subdued.

"And if I should wish to see such a thing, I would go to Astley's. Though that is a little below us, my dear, and not worth the money."

As good as anything I've seen at Astley's. The words from a long-ago encounter in the park with a handsome man riding a black stallion came back to her, and she pushed them away. "I do enjoy Astley's," she said, almost defiantly, "but perhaps not so much as I did as a child."

"Of course not." Edgewater doffed his hat at a passing acquaintance. "You are no longer a child, Cecily, but a young woman. A lovely young woman, I might add." This last was added in such an absent tone of voice that Cecily's own eyebrows rose. "Such behavior is beneath you."

"I hope I'll always be able to laugh and enjoy myself, sir, no matter what my age. My grandmother Marlow, the dowager duchess, was unable to come to London with us because of ill health, but she is one of the most cheerful, amusing people I know! But, there, I don't want you thinking I am light-minded, sir," she went on as they turned onto Piccadilly. "Several years ago my father started a school on the estate for the children of the tenants, and I've become very interested in it. I even persuaded Papa to let the village children attend. I enjoy working with the children and helping them to learn to read and write."

The patronizing smile had left Edgewater's face. "Another thing that you will not be doing as my wife, I trust."

Cecily stopped. "But why not?"

"Come, Cecily, we are creating a scene." He

tugged on her arm. "Because it won't be a suitable activity for you."

"Not suitable! But, sir, you're interested in the plight of the poor! Why cannot I be?"

"Because you are to be my wife, and I won't have you exposed to such influences." He reached past her to open the door of Hatchard's. "Come, my dear, we shall discuss this at another time."

"We certainly shall," Cecily murmured, her cheeks pink and her stomach churning with a combination of anger and dismay. What did he expect of her as his wife? That she would be a docile helpmeet only, who never spoke her mind? She had hoped for better things from married life, that she would at last be free to talk as herself, to be herself, without receiving a scolding from a disapproving parent.

"M'lord Edgewater! Good day to you!" a voice boomed, and both Edgewater and Cecily turned. Coming toward them was a rotund, genial-faced man, his clothing, though of good quality, not the best, his huge hand outstretched. "Remember me? Josiah Worley, sir. There's much we must needs discuss."

"Is there?" Edgewater said in such icy tones that Cecily glanced up at him, startled. His eyes were hard and cold, and his left eyelid twitched. "I believe not. I bid you good day." And with that he ushered Cecily into the book shop, leaving the other man standing spluttering on the pavement.

"Heavens!" Cecily had recovered her poise. "Edward, whoever in the world was that?"

"A Cit," he said curtly. "Beneath your notice."

Cecily peeped through the panes of Hatchard's front window to see the man, his face mottled with anger. "He looks prosperous enough." Her eyes danced as she turned back. "Edward, don't tell me you actually engage in trade!"

The look Edgewater gave her was enough to freeze

her where she stood. "I suggest you select your books, my dear," he said, mildly enough.

"Yes, Edward," Cecily murmured, bewildered, and turned away, her mind whirling with all that had happened. Edgewater, however, seemed his usual urbane self. Proclaiming that he wasn't much interested in reading, he followed Cecily down the aisles, occasionally complaining about the fees she would spend on such claptrap as the scary Gothic romances which were all the rage, and which she enjoyed. For her part, Cecily was preoccupied. How best to go about convincing Edgewater that she could actually help him in his work, if he would allow her? At the moment, she had no answer to that question.

They emerged from Hatchard's into a day grown overcast and chilly. Edgewater signaled for a hackney, his face showing his distaste at having to ride in such a pedestrian vehicle. Holding his hand out to Cecily, he was just about to help her in when a voice spoke behind them.

"Please, sir, can't you help a poor man?"

Cecily turned and saw a man huddled against the building, the tatters of a once-proud uniform hanging about him. Like many soldiers at war's end, he apparently had not been able to find work, and he looked unwell. "Oh, the poor man! Edward, do please help him."

Edgewater spared the man no more than a glance. "I'll not waste my money on such as he. He should find work."

"But he can't! He's ill. Oh, very well." She fumbled in her reticule. "If you won't—"

"Cecily, I forbid you to give him anything. You are only encouraging him."

"Here, sir." Cecily held out a coin. "Little enough, I know, but I hope it will get you a hot meal at least."

"God bless you, miss," the man said reaching for her

hand as if to kiss it. Before he could do so, however, Edgewater's walking stick came smartly down on his wrist, making him yelp and pull back.

"Get away from the lady, or I'll have the watch on you." Edgewater's face was set in a cold sneer.

"Edward," Cecily protested again.

"Be quiet. And if you don't stop bothering good people, I'll see you sent to gaol."

The man's eyes, burning now with hatred, went from Edgewater to Cecily. "God bless you, miss," he said again, "and God help you, too. I pity you." With that, he turned and, with great dignity, hobbled away.

"Pity you! Of all the damned nerve—"

"Edward." Cecily caught at his arm, noting the bunching of muscles in an arm that she'd never thought particularly strong before. "Let him go. He can't do anything to you."

"He is an insolent cur, and should learn to mend his manners!" Edgewater turned back, his eyelid twitching furiously. "That he should dare to pity you, when you are engaged to the Marquess of Edgewater!"

"I'm sure that's not what he meant," Cecily said soothingly. "Come, it is raining harder. You don't wish the rain to spot your coat."

"What? No, of course not, my dear, you are absolutely right." Edgewater's face relaxed as he turned to help Cecily in, and though he was a genial companion on she ride back to Marlow House, Cecily could not relax. She didn't think she'd ever forget the way he had looked when he had grown angry at the beggar, and she devoutly hoped that she, herself, would never inspire such anger. What, she wondered, had happened to Edgewater's much-vaunted concern for the poor?

At Marlow House Cecily turned to Edgewater with relief, holding her hand out to him. What she needed now was time, to sort through her conflicting emotions and consider some way to deal with this unexpected side of her intended. Instead, Edgewater took her arm in the same possessive grip and walked into the house with her, though she had not invited him.

"Good afternoon, Timms," she said, smiling at the butler. "Are my mother and sister returned yet?"

"No, my lady." Timms's face, which no one had ever seen smile, remained wooden. "They are still shopping, I believe."

"Oh." She turned toward Edgewater. "Then, sir—"

"Are you not going to invite me up to the drawing room, Cecily?" Edgewater said, smiling, with just a hint of challenge in his eyes.

Cecily glanced at Timms. It would not be proper to receive Edgewater alone, even though he was her fiancé, but at the same time, she didn't wish to argue the matter here. Timms, for all his appearance of detachment, was, as she well knew, an avid gossip. "Of course, sir," she said finally, and turned toward the stairs, not speaking further until they were alone in the drawing room. "But you know this is not at all proper."

"Isn't it?" There was a funny little smile on his face, making her just the slightest bit uneasy. "But we are betrothed, Cecily. Surely no one would object if we spent some time together? I rarely get to see you alone."

"But, sir," she protested as he slipped his arms about her waist.

"Do you know, Cecily, you are really quite attractive." He sounded a bit surprised as he studied her face, so closely and with such a detached manner that she wanted to turn her head away. "It is fortunate you know which colors to choose, otherwise you'd look sallow."

"How flattering, sir," she said lightly, while against her will, she heard another voice, a deeper voice, tell-

66

ing her that her skin was a delightful rosy gold. *Oh, go away!* she thought. *Go away, St. Clair, and leave me in peace!*

"I am fortunate to have found you," Edgewater went on, as if unaware of her reaction. "I think we will deal very well together, indeed."

His head bent toward her, the scent of the sandalwood cologne he always wore almost suffocating her. *Oh, heavens, he's going to kiss me!* In spite of her confusion, in spite of her distaste for his earlier actions, she couldn't suppress the little spurt of excitement that went through her. She had never been kissed before. Prompted by curiosity, Cecily raised her face and let his lips meet hers. And—nothing happened.

She had closed her eyes as his head bent, but now she opened one again, peering cautiously at his face, so close, wearing a rapt expression. The pressure of his lips on hers increased, but still she felt nothing, only the sensation of flesh touching flesh. What was so wonderful about this? Where was the union of souls she had been led to expect from the books she read? Why didn't she feel the slightest desire to swoon? Instead, she glanced quickly toward the ormolu clock ticking on the mantle, wondering when this would be over, wondering when he would leave.

Edgewater at last broke the kiss, to her vast relief. Now she would be free. "Ah, Cecily," he murmured, and to her horror, his lips descended again. This time, however, they were open, and she recoiled from the feeling of his tongue probing against her closed mouth. Panic filled her, and she struggled harder, until that cool little voice inside her suggested another way. Standing perfectly still, she let herself go stiff in his arms, her eyes open, her lips resolutely closed, and finally, at last, he released her.

Cecily stepped back, barely resisting the urge to scrub her hand over her lips, and then looked up at him, fearing what she would see. Would he be disgusted at her lack of response, or angry that she had tried to pull away?

What she saw in his eyes startled her. It was a curious expression, composed of calculation, satisfaction, and, oddly, triumph. With a little shock she realized that he had been aware of her feelings, and that he didn't care. A chill went through her at the thought.

"I must be leaving," he said, smoothly reaching for her hand. She let him raise it to his lips, though what had always been only a polite gesture before now made her want to snatch her hand back, and then dropped a brief curtsy to him. And then he was gone, leaving her standing alone, confused, bewildered, and more than a little frightened.

Early the following afternoon, dressed in the darkest, drabbest clothing she owned, Cecily slipped down the back stairs of Marlow House, hoping that once again her luck would hold and she would manage to leave unremarked. She breathed a sigh of relief when the side door of the house had closed behind her, with no one the wiser. If her luck held, she would be able to return equally unremarked. Her parents would be certain to disapprove of what she was about to do.

Jem pushed himself away from the brick wall of the house as Cecily came out, tugging at his forelock. A long-time groom for the Marlow family, Jem was one of the few witnesses to behavior in Cecily, that others might label "fast." It was he who saddled Dancer for her in the early mornings; he it was who escorted her on this bi-weekly excursion, though he knew that if he were caught it would mean his position. Such was his admiration, and affection, for Lady Cecily, and such his knowledge of her character, which could be stubborn, that he had set himself up as her protector, staying close by her side.

"The hackney's just around the corner, my lady," he said falling into step beside her. "No trouble getting out?"

"No, none," she said serenely. "They all believe I have the headache and am resting. Pray check that there is no one on the street, Jem."

Jem stepped forward while she waited behind, but he saw no one more menacing than a man, apparently dozing in the afternoon sun, leaning against a tree across the street. Signaling to Cecily, he led her to the waiting hackney and helped her in, and they were off.

Had Jem looked back, he would have seen the man who had been leaning against the tree jump into frantic action. *Damn!* Parsons thought, though he tried to censor even his thoughts against such oaths. Here he had promised Lord St. Clair he'd keep an eye on the Marlow girl, and the first sign she gave of doing something suspicious, he was caught napping. Breaking into a run, he rounded the corner in time to see her hackney drive away.

"Damn!" Fortunately there was another hackney in sight down the street, and he ran toward it, signaling frantically. Pointing toward the other cab, now nearly out of sight, he gasped out instructions and then collapsed onto the seat. Lord St. Clair would have his hide if he let Lady Cecily get away.

He grew increasingly perplexed, and increasingly suspicious, as the ride progressed. At first he had thought that Lady Cecily was merely going shopping, or perhaps meeting someone clandestinely, but as the hackneys proceeded through the fashionable areas of town and into neighborhoods growing increasingly seedy, his suspicion grew. Something was up here, something St. Clair would want to know about. When he had a chance, he would go to his employer and warn him.

Lady Cecily's hackney finally stopped before a gray, grim building, deep in the heart of Whitechapel. She appeared not to notice the refuse littering the street, the men standing in doorways watching, the urchins begging or jeering, as she proceeded up the stairs and into the building. The hackney stayed behind. Parsons took off his hat and scratched his head. What now? Mentally he cursed himself for not finding help to watch the girl. Should he stay and see what she did, or go warn St. Clair?

Parsons made up his mind. St. Clair had to know. Thumping on the roof of the carriage, he leaned out the window. "Piccadilly," he said, and settled back, feeling vindicated and confident. They'd catch Lady Cecily at her game at last.

Chapter Six

"I do wish I could come here more often," Cecily said, setting down the thick earthenware mug on the scarred, scraped table in the cramped sitting room. Not by word or gesture did she indicate that neither the mug, nor the weak tea it contained, was what she was accustomed to. "The children are so eager to learn."

"You done wonders with them, m'lady." The woman sitting across from Cecily, matron of the orphanage in which they sat, took a healthy gulp of tea, her little finger crooked in what she thought was the proper way to hold the cup. "A shame, it is, that more people like you don't take an interest."

"I know." Cecily sighed. "I've spoken about it with Papa, but he thinks we need complete reform. I do see his point." She set down the mug, empty, to her relief. "How much good can one school do, after all? But if just a few children learn," she said earnestly, leaning forward, "then perhaps they can have a better life. I wish I could do more."

"You do good work now. Though I do wish, m'lady, you wouldn't bring them no sweets. Spoils them, it does."

Cecily looked guilty. "I know, it was very bad of me. But if it makes the children willing to come to the schoolroom, then it's worth it." She sighed. "Unfortunately, once the season is over, I won't be coming here anymore. I am to marry next month."

Matron set down her mug, an almost comical look of dismay on her face. "Oh, m'lady, then who will help? The children miss you now. Jenny Driver already goes to sleep with her primer every night."

Cecily smiled. "I know. It's a shame, isn't it, that Jenny's father couldn't keep her? But my fiancé is interested in the poor. I'm hoping I can convince him to open some real schools, so the children can really learn." The tall case clock in the corner struck the half hour and Cecily rose. "I must be going, before I am missed. I'll return in two weeks, if I can."

"God bless you, m'lady." Matron grasped Cecily's hand in her own work-roughened one. "I wish there was more like you."

"And I wish there were more matrons like you who actually care about the children. When I think of the other orphanages I've visited, what the conditions were like." She shuddered. "No one should have to live like that."

"If more like you would do something, m'lady, maybe things would change."

Cecily smiled and, after saying her good-byes, walked out into the hall. Jem was waiting there, leaning against the wall, a look of unease on his face. He straightened when he saw her. "Trouble, my lady."

Cecily looked up from pulling on her gloves. "Oh?"

"Yes. The hackney wouldn't wait."

"Oh. I see."

"I told you this would happen," he burst out, with the familiarity of an old retainer. "It's as much as our lives are worth to be here, my lady. If anything happens to you, I don't want to think what the duke will do—"

"Nonsense, Jem, nothing is going to happen." Cecily felt in her reticule for the silver-handled pistol she always carried on these expeditions; she was not so heedless as Jem thought. "You have your cudgel?"

"Yes, my lady."

"Then, we shall just have to make it through the best we can."

"Yes, my lady," Jem said, and opened the door for her, not knowing whether to be appalled by her foolhardiness, or impressed by her courage.

They paused at the top of the steps before heading down, scanning the area. No one appeared to pay any attention to them; Jem, however, knew they had been remarked from the moment they had entered the slum, and that they would be lucky to leave without incident. "Onward, Jem," Cecily murmured, and they set off.

Both were quiet as they made their way down the muddy, unpaved street, carefully avoiding the trench running down the center where water, and who knew what else, drained. Again they appeared to pass unnoticed, and though Jem had an itchy feeling in his back, as if a million eyes were watching, even he began to feel that they might make it through unscathed. A look at Lady Cecily's set face and squared shoulders told him that she was as aware of the danger as he, which he found oddly reassuring. Lady Cecily had bottom, he'd say that for her. No milk and water miss, she, but a real game 'un. Jem's determination to get her safely out of this increased, and he clutched his cudgel tighter. "We're being watched, my lady."

"I know we are," Cecily said, apparently serene. "Just keep walking. And please don't call me 'my lady.' I'd rather no one know who I am."

"Yes, my—miss." Not that it would matter, he thought gloomily, if they were accosted, though he could see her point; she feared being held for ransom. Privately, he thought that was the least likely thing to happen. A young lady of quality straying into these parts was putting herself into danger more severe than that.

The street took a twist, and ahead of them they could see the traffic of Whitechapel High Street. For the first time, Jem began to hope that they might actually escape. "Almost there, miss," he said and at that moment, two men stopped in front of them, blocking their way.

"Where is she?" Alex demanded, starting up from the chair where he had been passing the time, reading.

"Whitechapel," Parsons gasped. He had run up several flights of stairs, knowing St. Clair had to know of this.

"Where Barnes got it. Hell, Parsons, she's in this up to her neck!" Alex strode into his study and came out carrying his pistols. "Where was she going?"

"A big building, I didn't stop to look. She had her groom with her."

"Hell, when I get my hands on her," Alex muttered, shoving the pistols into the pockets of his greatcoat and heading for the door. Parsons prudently held his tongue. Beneath St. Clair's very real anger at whoever had killed Alf Barnes lay something else, and Parsons had no desire to stir it to life. "Hell, man, are you coming?"

"Yes, sir." Parsons clattered down the stairs behind him. "The hackney's waiting."

"Good."

The driver looked mutinous at the idea of being asked to drive to Whitechapel again, but the pile of coins Alex shoved at him apparently convinced him. They rode in tense, tight silence, neither speaking, until the hackney turned off Whitechapel High Street onto a twisting narrow lane, and came to an abrupt stop.

74

"Is this it?" Alex demanded, looking out.

"No." Parsons craned his head out the window. "There's some sort of fight ahead—crikey, it's Lady Cecily!"

"Hell!" Alex jumped to his feet and sprang out, tossing more coins to the driver. "If you know what's good for you, you'll stay right here."

"Yes, guv," the startled driver said, and took off his cap to scratch his head through unwashed hair. Quality sure did get up to some queer doings sometimes.

Cecily looked up at the two very large men who blocked her way, aand who were grinning evily at her, and swallowed, hard. Jem was right. She'd landed them in the suds this time.

One of the ruffians grinned, displaying teeth rotted and stumped. "Well, well, what have we 'ere? A pretty little chicken."

Cecily drew herself to her full height, wishing that she were taller. "Let us pass."

The ruffian chuckled. " 'Ear that? The lady wants us to let her pass."

"I hear." The other ruffian's grin was just as evil. "Got spirit, this one. Mother Carey'll like her."

Cecily's blood froze. She had heard of the infamous Mother Carey, who lured young girls to her brothel, never letting them out again. She tried to protest, but all that came from her throat, suddenly dry, was a strangled sound.

"And," the first ruffian, the larger of the two and evidently the leader, went on, "we'll get a good price for her, or my name's not Joe Driver."

Cecily looked up. "Joe Driver? You're not Jenny Driver's father, are you?"

The ruffian's eyes narrowed and he leaned forward. " 'Ere, and what if I am?"

"Miss," Jem said uneasily.

"Jenny speaks of you all the time, Mr. Driver," Cecily said, not budging an inch. "I don't think she'd be so proud of you if she knew what you were doing."

Joe's look of suspicion hadn't abated. "How do yer know my daughter?" he demanded.

"Why, I teach her. I've been teaching her to read."

Joe looked startled. "Yer not Jenny's Miss Cecily."

"Yes, I am. She's a bright little girl. You must be very proud of her."

"Aye, that I am." Joe's face softened. "It's been hard, her mam being gone and all, but I do wot I can."

"I'm sure you do." Cecily nodded understandingly. "You want the best for your daughter. I'm sure you wouldn't want her going to Mother Carey's."

"Hell, no, miss, that I wouldn't," he said forcefully. "Hell of a life. But wot's there going to be for my Jenny? Yer tell me that."

"I've already told Matron that when Jenny's old enough I'll help her find something. Perhaps she could apprentice in a shop."

"My Jenny, in a fine shop." Joe's eyes glowed for a moment, and then faded. "Now, don't yer think yer can go fooling Joe Driver. Things like that don't happen to people like us."

"I say we just take 'em, Joe," the other ruffian said, and Jem again moved uneasily.

Cecily stood her ground. Inside she was feeling a strange exhilaration, knowing she was in danger and yet feeling more alive than she ever had. "I give you my word, sir," she said, laying her hand on Jem's arm to keep him from surging forward in her defense. "Jenny will have a better life."

" 'Ere, Joe, 'adn't we better be takin' these two—"

"Shut yer trap!" Joe rounded on him furiously. "Can't yer see this is my Jenny's Miss Cecily? We can't harm her." He turned back to Cecily. "And wot yer doing in these parts on foot, miss, I don't know, but yer got to get out of 'ere."

Cecily smiled, and Joe blinked at the sudden brilliance of it. "I know that. So if you'll please let us pass—"

"I'll do better'n that." Joe swept off his cap, holding it against his chest. " 'Twould be my pleasure to escort you out, miss. Won't no one hurt yer with Joe Driver around, that I'll warrant."

"Why, thank you, Mr. Driver. I would be honored." Without hesitating, Cecily placed her hand on the filthy sleeve he held out to her, and at that moment a voice spoke ahead of them.

"Unhand the lady, sir."

Cecily's eyes widened. "St. Clair!" she exclaimed, taking in both the sight of him and his pistol, held almost negligently in his hand. "This isn't how it appears—"

"Get to the hackney, Cecily," Alex ordered crisply, aware that the crowd of interested onlookers had grown bigger. If he didn't get her out of this soon, there was likely to be a riot.

" 'Ere, who do yer think yer are?" Joe demanded, his voice truculent again, and Cecily tightened her grip on his arm.

"It's all right, Mr. Driver, I know him."

"Cecily," Alex said.

"If you or Jenny ever need anything, tell Matron. I'll do what I can, I promise," Cecily said.

"Yer a true lady, miss," Joe said, grinning, and briefly touched her shoulder. "Best you go with the gennulman now."

"Get your hands off her!" Alex roared, filled with a rage he didn't understand. The menacing gesture of his pistols appeared to be all that was needed to set the crowd, until now watching mostly in silence, into action. Alex looked startled as the group surged forward, shouting threats against him for menacing one of their own.

"Go, miss!" Jem shouted, pushing Cecily by the shoulders. She stumbled, and Jem, as aware of the danger as Joe, grabbed her arm. "Go while you can!"

"The hackney's leaving!" Parsons shouted.

Alex turned. "Hell! Cecily!" he yelled.

"Come on, my lady!" Jem grabbed Cecily's arm, and pulled her forward, swinging his cudgel from left to right, just as the mob reached them.

"But Mr. Driver," she protested.

"He'll take care of himself! Come on!"

Cecily let out a shriek as someone grabbed her other arm and she looked up to see Alex. "You little fool," he growled. "Come on, let's get out of here." They set off at a run after the departing hackney, the mob in hot pursuit. Cecily stumbled again on the slippery cobblestones, falling this time, and the men dragged her to her feet, pulling her along with them. She could hardly get her footing and at any moment expected blows to fall upon her back. But there, at last, was the hackney. Alex shoved Cecily inside and crowded in with the others, and they fell back against the seats with a jerk as the hackney started up at a run. The noise swelled as the mob followed, throwing rocks and mud, and then faded, as the hackney rocked onto Whitechapel High Street. They were safe.

Cecily passed a shaky hand over her face. Only now, with all danger behind them, could she admit how frightened she had been when she had seen that mob pouring toward her. Reaction washed over her in giddy waves as she thought of what could have happened, not just to her, but to people she cared about. To St. Clair. *Oh, nonsense,* she chided herself. She had, she admitted reluctantly, been very lucky, and very foolish. Next time she ventured to the orphanage, she would make sure of the hackney driver's loyalty first.

With her decision made, Cecily relaxed, and glanced over at St. Clair to thank him for his gallant, if misguided, concern for her safety. To her surprise he was glaring at her from under his brows. "You have quite recovered?"

"Yes, thank you," Cecily said, bewildered, "but—"

"Good. Because I have some things I wish to say to you, miss."

"Excuse me, sir, but you shouldn't speak to Lady Cecily like that," Jem began.

"Be quiet. We'll get to your part in this later. Well, miss? Did you enjoy acting like a peahen and putting yourself into danger?"

Any gratitude Cecily might have felt disappeared in a blaze of anger so intense, and so unusual to her, that it startled her. "Who do you think you are?" she demanded. "You've no right to scold me so."

"Oh, haven't I! After I nearly got killed rescuing you—"

"Whose fault was that? I was doing quite well—"

"With that mob?"

"I was safe! Weren't we, Jem?"

"Yes," Jem said, somewhat reluctantly. "We were. But if we hadn't met up with Mr. Driver—"

"And don't think I don't know what Mr. Driver's really like, Jem. But he wouldn't have let us come to any harm."

"Who is this Mr. Driver?" Alex said, biting each word off.

"The man you threatened, sir."

"The man *I* threatened?"

"Yes!" She faced him with a gaze as cool as his own. "We were doing quite well without you, sir. There was no need for you to interfere in what wasn't your business." And what was he doing in such a neighborhood, anyway? Perhaps visiting his mistress. A most lowering thought, though Cecily wasn't quite sure why it should be.

"I see," Alex said, his voice very quiet. Seated beside him, Parsons could feel the rage emanating from him. He'd seen his master in this mood before and it surprised him that St. Clair wasn't letting his rage go. What surprised him even more, however, was the way the young lady was reacting. Parsons looked from one to the other interestedly. Not only was she not afraid of St. Clair, but she was actually standing up to him. Parsons leaned back, thoughtful. If what he suspected was happening, it could complicate matters considerably, though he'd never before known his master to be interested in a young innocent.

Alex broke the tense silence by reaching up to pound on the roof. After a moment, the driver looked in the window, starting to expostulate about his recent experiences, and Alex held up a hand. "Spare us. You will be well recompensed. In the meantime, you may bring us to—" His gaze turned to Cecily, and his brow knotted.

"What?" Cecily said puzzled.

"Lord, my lady, you can't go home looking like that," Jem said, and Cecily glanced down. Her pelisse was covered with mud, and worse, there was a rent in her frock, making her look more disheveled than usual. Why, oh, why must she always look so mussed when she was with St. Clair? Dismayed, she looked up at him, and he returned her gaze without expression.

"Piccadilly," he said to the driver.

"Sir, is that wise?" Parsons said, and he and Alex exchanged a long look. Some kind of wordless communication seemed to pass between them before Alex turned back to Cecily.

"Your servant is right. You cannot go home looking like that, though God knows you should, and face the consequences of your actions."

Cecily put up her chin. "I was doing nothing

80

wrong, sir. And where are you taking me?"

"To my lodgings. Oh, don't worry," he said, at her startled look. "You'll be perfectly safe. We will contrive it so that your reputation is not ruined."

"I see." Mischief sparked in her eyes. "And what of your reputation, sir? If such kindness becomes known, no one will believe you a rake anymore."

"Be quiet, Cecily," he said tiredly. Cecily subsided, after glancing toward Parsons. St. Clair's servant, she supposed. Now, why was he looking at her with such interest?

The hackney pulled up into the stable yard of the building where Alex lived. After making sure no one was about, they smuggled Cecily upstairs, her bonnet pulled well down over her face to disguise her. Cecily couldn't prevent the little thrill of excitement that went through her, at this extension of her adventure, and at actually being in the apartments of such an infamous rake. Not just any rake, though. Somehow she knew she was safe here. Any danger St. Clair posed her would come from another direction.

Parsons showed her into a sparsely furnished bedroom and, after laying out a dressing gown for her, took away her pelisse to clean. She would mend her frock herself, she assumed, glancing about the room. At first she thought it was Parsons' own chamber, so bare was it, but a glance at the books on the bedside table proved her wrong. The flyleaf of each was signed with "Alexander Darcy," in a strong, bold hand. So this was his room, his most private place, the only place, perhaps, where he could be himself. Curious, Cecily turned 'round slowly, determined to learn all she could about him.

The furnishings were of good quality, but plain. The four-poster mahogany bed was without bed curtains, and the dark green drapes hanging at the window were simple, with neither pelmet or cornice. The

81

top of the dresser was neat to the point of starkness, holding only a highly polished box, as well as some silver-backed brushes. No pictures hung on the wall; no carpet was laid on the wide board floor. Except for the books and the brushes, the room was completely devoid of any personal touches. Cecily's heart ached. Who would ever have expected that a man so given to the pursuit of pleasure would live in such Spartan surroundings?

Swallowing an absurd lump that threatened to choke her, Cecily unhooked her gown and tossed it on the bed. The dressing gown Parsons had left for her made her giggle. In contrast to the plain furniture, it was a splendid affair of crimson brocade, so large it nearly wrapped around her twice. *His* dressing gown, she thought, rolling up the sleeves and tying the sash in a tight knot. His, and it held his scent. She turned her head into the lapel, breathing it in, clean and refreshing after Edgewater's cloying sandalwood. If anyone were to see her now, wearing St. Clair's clothes, her reputation would be ruined for sure. Somehow the thought bothered her not at all.

Opening the door, she stepped into the sitting room. To her relief, it was empty. Like the bedroom it, too, was plainly furnished. London's most notorious rake appeared to live in a small, cramped apartment, with only one servant to look after him. She wondered why.

Parsons came in carrying a tray, from which rose a fragrant steam. Tea! Cecily was suddenly ravenous, and she smiled up at Parsons as he set the tray down on a table next to a comfortable-looking armchair. "Thank you, Parsons. You must find all of this strange goings-on."

"Not at all, my lady," Parsons said his face wooden, his eyes averted.

Cecily couldn't resist the impulse to tease, though

she wasn't certain where it came from. Nor did she understand why she was so enjoying an experience that should surely make a proper young miss swoon. Had there always been a more forward, adventurous girl hiding under her practical exterior? "Then, it is usual to have strange females in the viscount's sitting room?"

"No, miss, it ain't!" Parsons straightened with more than necessary energy. "For all they say of him, the viscount's a good man."

"I know he is, Parsons." Her voice was soft. "Forgive my impertinence."

"It's all right, my lady." Parsons' tone was wooden again. "But if I was you, I wouldn't tease him. He's in a rare taking. He really was worried for you." He paused. "I haven't seen him like that often."

"Have you been with him long, Parsons?"

"More years than I care to remember. And—"

"Is everything settled, Parsons?" Alex paused in the doorway and then strolled in, apparently at ease, though Cecily had only to looked at his squared shoulders and his set face to know that he was still angry.

"Yes, my lord."

"Then, you may leave us."

Parsons hesitated. "It ain't right, my lord—"

"Leave us, Parsons. And none of your Bible-thumping disapproval, either."

"Yes, my lord. I'll get you a needle and thread, my lady," Parsons said, and left, his face expressionless.

Alex turned toward his unwelcome guest. Somewhat to his surprise, she was gazing at him unwaveringly, the straightness of her glance distracting him a little from the fetching picture she made in his dressing gown. It was much too big for her, of course, and wrapped in its folds, she looked absurdly young and absurdly small, the bones of her wrists tiny and delicate, the line of her neck slender and pure. His gaze softened. "Well?"

"That wasn't necessary, sir," she said. "He cares about you."

"Spare me such caring," he said, his voice clipped, and sprawled into the armchair facing her. "Now, miss. You will tell me why you were in that slum."

Cecily took a sip of tea before answering. "No, I don't think I will. I might," she went on quickly, "if you were to ask me, but the only man who has any right to speak to me so is my father."

"Who would not be best pleased with you just now," he shot back.

"No, he wouldn't. But he won't learn of it. Will he?"

"I believe that's up to you." His gaze softened again. "What were you doing there, Cecily? Don't you realize how dangerous it was?"

"Of course I do. And I might add that I wasn't in any danger until you interfered."

"Interfered!" Rage rose within him again at this description of what he felt had been quite an heroic effort.

"I admit it looked bad," she said candidly, "but once I found out that one of the men was the father of a child I teach, everything was fine."

"A child you teach." Alex's brow knotted. "Where?"

Cecily looked surprised. "Why, at the orphanage, of course. No, you wouldn't know that. You see, I go to the orphanage to teach some of the children to read and write." She set her cup on the tray. "You won't tell, will you?"

"I should," Alex said slowly, testing her words for truth. Unless she was an extraordinarily fine actress, she sounded sincere. "It's not safe. Yes, I know, you knew one of the men. But suppose you didn't? Have you thought about what could happen to you?"

"If I hadn't, I certainly would have found out today." Ill at ease under his searching gaze, she fidgeted with the sash of the dressing gown. "Please don't tell. The children need so much. Papa lets me help at the school at Marlow, but if he finds out about this, he'll forbid me to go anymore."

"As well he should. God's teeth, Cecily, why does it have to be you?"

"Who else will do it? Sir, something has to be done for those poor people." She leaned forward, unmindful of the way the dressing gown gaped open at her throat. "They have nothing, and most of the time it's not even their fault! Someone has to help, and it should be us. We have so much, it doesn't seem fair sometimes."

Alex leaned back, tearing his gaze away from the soft, enticing skin the dressing gown revealed. "You really care about this."

"I do."

Alex rose and paced over to the mantle, his fingers stroking his upper lip. A fine actress, or an honest girl. Which?

"Haven't you ever felt that way?" she went on. "Hasn't there ever been anything you believed in so much that you would do anything for it?"

"Once," Alex murmured, remembering a time when he, too, had been so foolishly idealistic, eager to serve his country in any way possible.

"What happened?"

"I came up against reality." The reality of spying, of a world peopled by strangers one automatically feared, friends one didn't dare trust. He had no reason to believe anything had changed. "As you nearly did today."

"As I already have," she said, and Alex's startled gaze swung toward her. "I've always known there was danger involved. I thought it was worth it." She looked down at her hands. "I think I'm not the proper miss everyone thinks I am."

Alex sat down again. "Does your fiancé know

85

about this?"

"No." She frowned. "And I don't know what he'd think if he did. Yesterday we saw a soldier, maimed in the war and—well, never mind. But I do hope he'll let me continue helping the poor in some way."

Alex leaned forward, his hands clasped between his knees. The room was so small that his face was scant inches from hers. "Maybe he's not the right man for you."

"Maybe he's not," Cecily agreed, mesmerized by his intent blue gaze. "What would you do, sir?"

"If?"

"If you had a wife who did something you didn't approve."

He sat back, grinning. "Judging by today, lose my temper. And then I hope I'd calm down enough to listen to her reasons."

"You're a most unusual rake."

"Am I?" He was leaning very close, so close that she could see the blue vividness of his eyes, smell his fresh, unique scent, feel the strength and warmth emanating from him.

"Yes. You think about people."

"I know." His smile was self-deprecating and totally charming. "A terrible habit, I know."

"I don't think so." She searched his face. "I think you care a great deal more than you let on."

"Do you?" He caught her hand in his and studied it. "You bite your nails."

Cecily's fingers clenched. "Yes, I cannot seem to stop."

"I had a mustache once. Sometimes I still reached up to touch it." Laying her hand down, he reached out to tuck an errant curl behind her ear, letting the silky strands flow between his fingers. Cecily's eyes briefly closed against the sensations his touch evoked. "I think about you, you know."

Her eyes opened. "Do you? Why?"

"Because you are a most unusual girl. A beautiful girl." Because she had reached him as no one had in a very long time. Innocent she might be, but not naive; young, but strong in her own way, and caring. She almost made him believe in life again.

"I'm not beautiful," she protested softly.

"Of course you are. Rakes know these things."

Her eyes sparkled with the mischievous laughter he was coming to like very much. "Oh, pardon me. I meant no insult."

"None taken." His eyes went of their own volition to her lips, soft and full and slightly parted. Somewhere in his mind an alarm bell began ringing and though he had always obeyed this signal of danger before, this time he ignored it. He knew only that this girl was bringing him back to life, and he no longer wanted to fight it. Engaged or not, conspirator or not, she drew him to her in a way he could not fathom. For the moment, she was his.

"Cecily," he murmured, and brought his lips down on hers.

Chapter Seven

Heavens! Two kisses in two days! Cecily thought, before Alex's lips met hers, blotting out all other concerns save him. Her hands came up of their own accord to clutch his shoulders, and her head tilted to accommodate him while a sweet, aching sensation began to spread through her. Mindlessly she pressed up against him and felt his arms go about her, pulling her close against him as the kiss lengthened, deepened. His mouth opened over hers, and this time there was no revulsion. This time her mouth opened in response, and when she felt his tongue touch hers, she melted against him. There was no time; there was no place. There was only now, only him, as much a part of her as she was of him, together, inseparable, forever.

Alex lifted his head and gazed down at Cecily's flushed cheeks, her closed eyes, her lips, swollen from his kisses, parted invitingly. Almost he took up the invitation and the challenge that they offered, but that little alarm bell jangled in his head again. God's teeth, what was he doing? He was supposed to be investigating her for possible involvement in a dangerous conspiracy; he had just found her in a suspicious place, a place where no girl of her station should be. No matter that her explanation was plausible. Without proof, he couldn't accept it. He'd gotten soft, that's what had happened. He'd lost his instinct for survival, the edge that had kept him alive in a dangerous world, a world no less dangerous now that he was in England. Until he knew better, Cecily was the enemy, a woman engaged to one man, yet kissing another. And he had thought about trusting her? He must be mad.

Cecily's eyes fluttered open, and then closed again. She didn't want to leave this new world she had found; she wanted to stay, safe and warm, in his arms forever. She wanted him to kiss her again. She tightened her grip about his neck and lifted her face, nestling against him confidingly. When nothing happened, she opened her eyes again. Alex was regarding her coolly, his eyes slightly narrowed, his lips held tight. "Is that how you kiss your fiancé?" he said.

Cecily recoiled. "Wh-what?"

"Did you enjoy kissing a rake? God, you like to play with fire, don't you?"

Cecily stared at him in bewilderment as he strode around the room. "I wasn't playing!"

A mocking smile spread across Alex's face. "But I was." Cecily recoiled again. "My dear, I can have any woman I want. As I believe I just proved."

Cecily rose abruptly, her torn frock falling unnoticed to the floor. "I think I want to go home."

"By all means, my dear." Alex made her a mock bow. "Parsons will see to your clothes." And with that he turned and strode away, into his study, so that he would no longer have to see the hurt, blind look in her eyes. It was better for her that it end this way, and absolutely necessary for him. She saw a side of him that didn't exist anymore, if it ever had. If he gave in to his impulses and crushed her against him, kissing her, keeping her safe from the dangerous world outside, he would end by hurting her. He was not the man she thought.

Parsons came into the study a little while later to see Alex standing by the mantel, staring into the fire. "They're gone, sir."

"I know. I heard." Alex's tone was clipped, and Parsons turned away. He knew his master well in this mood, and knew enough to avoid him. There was, however, one thing that needed saying.

"Sir," he said, and Alex looked at him from beneath his brows. "You got a problem."

Surprisingly, Alex did not rip up at him. "I know, Parsons." He sighed and kicked at the fender. "God's teeth, I know." Bending his head, he stared into the fire again, not acknowledging Parsons as he left the room. He had a problem, indeed. What did he do now?

"Cece!" Diana bounced into the bedchamber where Cecily was lying upon her bed. "Oh, wait until you see the bonnet I bought; it is a Kendal bonnet, like Princess Charlotte's, and it is the most charming thing! Is your headache gone? Heavens, why are you wearing that old rag?"

Cecily put her hand over her eyes. She didn't know how she had made it home from St. Clair's lodgings. Nor did she know, or care, if anyone had seen her enter the house. A blessed numbness had wrapped around her, sparing her, for now, the pain of rejection. "Diana, do go away."

"Heavens, someone is in the mopes today!" Diana bounced down upon the bed, swinging her legs up and wrapping her arms around her knees in a most unladylike manner. "We had the most fun today. We met Mr. Carstairs, oh, and Lord Edgewater, too. He asked for you specifically, and when we told him you were ill, he seemed quite concerned—"

90

"Diana," Cecily interrupted, leaning up on her elbow, "have you ever been kissed?"

"What?" Diana stared at her. "Of course not, silly, I'm not fast! Oh, of course there was Jack Waverly, but that hardly counts; I was only ten at the time. Why?" Diana's eyes became disconcertingly shrewd. "Who's been kissing you? Oh, no, don't tell me! Edgewater! Oh, Cece, it's so romantic! What was it like? Tell me everything!"

"It wasn't much, Diana." Cecily laid her hand over her eyes again. Diana, for all her surface silliness, could be shrewd when she wished to be, and could usually detect Cecily's falsehoods. "I don't know why the novel writers make so much of it." *But I do,* she thought, turning her head into the pillow. *I do, and that's the problem.*

"Cecily, are you feeling quite the thing?" Diana's voice was filled with real concern. "You've gone all pale."

"No, my headache is worse."

"Poor Cece. You should take a sleeping draught. I'll just go tell Annie to prepare one for you, shall I?"

"Yes, thank you," Cecily mumbled, glad to be left alone again. Sleep would be welcome, to release her, if only for a time, from the memory of the last hour. She had been an utter fool. How could she live with herself now?

She covered her eyes again, as if to shut out the memories, but they were there, tantalizing, seductive, painful. She had been kissed and had quite willingly kissed back, a man known to be a rake, a man to whom the kiss had meant nothing. What was worse, she had actually liked it, until the moment when she had opened her eyes and had faced hard reality. The kiss had meant nothing to St. Clair. He had for some reason of his own quite callously used her, and she had allowed it. Had allowed him liberties, in fact, that had revolted her with her fiancé. Good Lord, how could she ever face Edgewater again, when she preferred the kiss of another man to his?

Confused, she rolled into a tight ball, her pillow over her head. It had been foolish of her to ask advice of Diana, but then, who could she ask? Certainly not her mother. How could she explain that she had somehow turned from a proper young lady into a wanton woman, and with the wrong man? She didn't understand it herself. Apparently there were depths in her, unknown places she'd never realized existed. How she was going to deal with that knowledge, she didn't know.

One thing was certain, she thought, sitting up. Devastating though this was, she wasn't going to hide from the world. Not unless St. Clair chose to disclose her behavior. Though her feelings toward him at the moment were decidedly hostile, even she doubted he'd do such a thing. No, she would keep her shame to herself, consider it a lesson hard-learned, and go on from there. The adventurous Cecily would be put aside; the very proper Lady Cecily would take her place. She would live her life as she had planned. And never, never, would she forgive St. Clair.

It was hell being sober.

Alex stropped his razor in front of his shaving mirror. His eyes were clear; his skin firm, with healthy color. The face that looked back at him, however, held the same contempt it had when he had been at his most dissolute. In the past few weeks, he had given up his former pasttimes with nary a trace of regret. He had bid his mistress farewell, neither lost nor won at cards and remained remarkably abstemious. What he had done instead, though, made those activities pale in comparison. He was sick to death of it, sick to his soul, and with all his heart he wished for a better life. What he lacked was the knowledge to achieve it.

"God's teeth, but I look like hell," he muttered, lathering his face.

"You been through hell, sir, if I may say so," Parsons said, laying out the biscuit-colored pantaloons and the coat of green superfine that Alex would wear that day.

"No, you may not say so." Alex's voice was absent as he scraped the lather off his cheeks.

"No, sir. But you have been, all the same."

Alex wiped the razor on a towel and looked at Parsons in the mirror, his eyes keen. "So how do you suggest I get out of it, Parsons?"

"You could try praying, sir. Or," he said over Alex's snort of derision, "you could try believing in something. Not everyone is treacherous or a liar."

"Prove it."

"Lady Cecily isn't."

"Ha. She's a woman, isn't she? Women and treachery are inextricably linked, Parsons."

"No, sir, not this one." Parsons stood his ground as Alex raised the towel to wipe the remaining lather from his face. "This isn't France. You care for Lady Cecily—"

"The devil I do!"

"—and it was an orphanage she went to. Matron there speaks highly of her."

Alex laid down the towel and turned to glare at him. "Just what are you trying to say, Parsons?"

"I think you're wrong about her, sir. Just because she wants to help the poor doesn't mean she wants revolution, neither. I don't think Lady Cecily's in-

93

volved in anything."

"Nor do I," Alex said, and as he did so, a great weight lifted from his heart. He didn't believe her guilty. *I* am *going soft,* he thought, without censure. He had learned to trust his instincts. In spite of all evidence to the contrary, they were telling him that he could trust Cecily. And that he had wronged her badly.

Alex frowned as he pulled his shirt over his head and began the complicated business of tying his neckcloth. He had indeed wronged her, and how he would ever make amends, he didn't know. He wanted to try, though, and the first step would be to inform the Home Office of her innocence. Then he would see.

Alex's heart was light as he stepped out for Bainbridge House. For the first time in many a year, he could see hope for the future. His mood didn't darken, even when he was shown into Bainbridge's study and Bainbridge, his face sober, rose to greet him. "I'm glad you've come," Bainbridge said as they settled into comfortable leather armchairs in front of the fire. "There have been some new developments."

"Have there?" Alex crossed his legs, quite at ease. No matter what he learned today, he was determined not to allow it to affect him. His days of spying were done. It was time to seek another life, with, perhaps, a girl with honey-hued curls and golden eyes, who was an intriguing mixture of innocence and sensuality. It was time to move on. "Before you tell me, however, I'd like to tell you the results of my investigation."

"So soon?" Bainbridge raised an eyebrow.

"We rakes work fast," Alex said, with his charming, self-deprecating smile. "I am convinced Lady Cecily is innocent."

"Are you?"

"Yes." Alex went on, ignoring Bainbridge's frown. "I've had her followed, and she does nothing out of the ordinary. Little out of the ordinary, I should say. She does visit an orphanage to teach the children to read. I'd appreciate it, by the by, if you'd keep that to yourself."

"Are you certain that is where she goes?"

"Positive. I've had Parsons following her. He confirmed it. Why?" he asked, belatedly struck by the serious look in Bainbridge's eyes. "Do you know aught else of her?"

"I told you there have been new developments." Bainbridge rose and crossed to the mantel, his fist to his mouth. "Damn, this is hard. You've fallen for the girl, haven't you?"

"Devil a bit," Alex said cheerfully. "But I will admit I'm no longer objective where she's concerned. If you wish to continue your investigation, you'll have to find someone else. Not that it will do you any good. She's innocent."

"We have a good idea what the aim of the conspiracy is," Bainbridge said abruptly.

"Oh?"

"We've heard from other sources that someone is searching for a sharpshooter, and is offering a good sum of money."

Alex went very still. "God's teeth. Assassination."

"It looks that way."

"How do you know it's the same conspiracy?"

"Because of the name of the person asking." Bainbridge sat again, his eyes grave. "It's a man. We have a description of him. He's said to be about forty, short, balding on top. His nose apparently was broken at one time. Otherwise, there's little remarkable about him. Except his name." Bainbridge paused. "He goes by the name of Randall."

Chapter Eight

Alex jerked back as if he had been shot. "Coincidence."

"Perhaps. We don't think so." Bainbridge's voice was crisp. "Obviously Barnes knew something about Lady Cecily. Why else would he have said her name?"

"Damn it, I don't believe it!" Alex rose and began to pace the room. "She's innocent. I'd stake my life on it."

"You may already have," Bainbridge said and went on as Alex turned. "What was she doing in Whitechapel yesterday?"

"I told you. She teaches children at the orphanage."

"All the time? I'm sorry, St. Clair. It looks like Lady Cecily is in this up to her pretty little neck."

"Hell!" Alex pounded the mantle with his fist. "Hell." It couldn't be. Someone so innocent, so sweet, simply couldn't be involved in such a nasty business, no matter the evidence. He knew it, deep in his bones. But—appearances sometimes lied. No, correct that, usually lied. He had been deceived before, and he had quickly learned his lesson. Trust no one. It was the only way to survive. How had a slip of a girl with huge golden eyes and disheveled curls managed to make him forget that hard-won lesson?

"Did the man find his sharpshooter?" Alex said, his voice hard.

"We don't know." Bainbridge sounded chagrined. "A man followed him, but evidently Randall was aware of him and managed to get away."

"Hell."

Bainbridge regarded him sympathetically. "I am sorry, St. Clair."

"For what?" Alex's voice was clipped.

"To be the one to tell you. As you can see, we have to go on with the investigation. But I agree that you're no longer the man to do so—"

"Oh, no. I have a score to settle with that young lady."

"It's not wise—".

"And who do you have to replace me? Three weeks ago, you told me I was the only man who could do the job. 'Who better than a rake?' " he quoted bitterly.

"We'd find someone. Come, St. Clair, you admit yourself you're not objective about this."

"I will be. If there is anything to find out about her, you may be certain I will find it."

Bainbridge studied Alex's grim face and then nodded. He still had serious misgivings, but St. Clair had a point. Who else was there who could do this job as well? "Very well. I needn't tell you how serious this is. With all the riots lately, the country's ready to go up, and the assassination of the right figure could set it off."

Alex nodded; he knew, of course, of the recent riots over low wages and high prices in Suffolk and Cambridgeshire. "No idea who the target might be?"

"None. Unfortunately, we still know little about the members of the conspiracy, but our man who learned about Randall overheard something else. There's to be another meeting of the conspirators,

Thursday next."

"Daytime? At night?"

"At night, I would think. It's to be somewhere in Richmond."

"Richmond, Thursday next." Alex frowned. "Now, why does that sound familiar?"

"Lady Radcliffe is having a rout at her home there. We've been invited."

"So have I. And"—he stared at Bainbridge—"so has Lady Cecily."

The two men regarded each other for a long moment. "Well, then," Bainbridge said at last. "It looks like you'll be going to Richmond."

"Yes." Alex's voice was grim. "I'll go." And he would learn, once and for all, what the beautiful, devious Lady Cecily was up to.

"Cece!" Diana burst into Cecily's room. *"He's downstairs!"*

Cecily lifted her head from the book in which she had immersed herself, forgetting, at least for a time, the events of the past few days. "Who's downstairs, Diana?"

"Edgewater! And he doesn't show it, he's too much the gentleman, but he's angry."

"Angry?" Cecily frowned, and then clapped her hand to her mouth. "Oh, no! I promised to go driving with him this afternoon and I forgot!"

"Forgot!" Diana stared at her sister as she hurried to her wardrobe. "However could you forget?"

"Ring for Annie, please?" Cecily twisted around to unhook her dress. "I thought you liked Mr. Carstairs."

"He's a child. Here, Cece, stand still; I'll do that for you." Diana's fingers went to work on the long row of hooks at the back of Cecily's frock, while

98

Cecily fidgeted. "Honestly, Cece, the way you act about Edgewater—if you weren't engaged to him, I think I'd toss my hat at him."

"You're welcome to," Cecily said, her voice muffled as she pulled the frock over her head.

"Cecily!"

"I'm funning! Hand me the apricot muslin, please, Di? Oh, this hair!" She stared at herself in the mirror. "Why can't it be all sleek and smooth like yours?"

"If you only knew what I'd give for curly hair. That color's good on you."

"Thank you. Help me with my hair, Di; I don't want to keep him waiting much longer."

"But he expects it." Diana stood behind Cecily as she sat at her dressing table. "Men know they always have to wait for us. And they usually think it's worth it, too."

"Well, I think it's unfair," Cecily said. "I do like what you do with hair."

"Yes, perhaps I should become a lady's maid." Diana tied the ribbon, binding Cecily's hair into an attractive cascade of curls. "You don't understand men, Cece," she went on, more seriously. "They expect us to act a certain way."

"Shatterbrained and silly? No, thank you." Cecily pulled on the spencer of deeper peach that went with the frock and set her bonnet on her head. "There, complete to a shade! And you, Di, have more common sense than you like to let on."

"Yes, of course I do. That's how I know how to handle men."

"You're hopeless!" Cecily tugged on her gloves. "I must fly. Thank you." She kissed her sister quickly on the cheek and then ran out of the room. By the time she reached the drawing room, to see her mother and her betrothed, she was flushed and breathless. Another man might have commented on the glow on her cheeks or the brightness in her eyes. Edgewater merely raised his quizzing glass and inspected her slowly from head to foot, in that hateful way that always made her want to squirm.

The quizzing glass dropped. "I do like a lady who is well turned-out," he commented, and Cecily glanced down. Her ensemble was perfectly unexceptionable, the frock demure and well cut, the spencer trimmed with velvet, the ribbons of her bonnet dyed to match. What, then? Oh, no, her shoes! She had been in such a hurry that she had left on her old half-boots. Their scuffed toes now peeked out from under the vandyked hem of her frock.

"Oh, well," she murmured, raising eyes merry with amusement to Edgewater. He was regarding her blankly. Her heart fell. However was she to manage with a man who had no sense of humor? "If you will just wait, sir, I'll change into something more suitable."

"It is of no moment," he said turning and replacing the quizzing glass in his pocket with a snap that told her it was of very great moment indeed. Cecily's heart sank lower, before her spirit rebelled against such foolishness. Lord St. Clair would have laughed, or at least smiled, she thought, conjuring up the image defiantly, and suppressing the urge to stick her tongue out at her betrothed's back.

The incident dimmed any pleasure she might have taken in the outing as Edgewater tooled his high-perch phaeton at a sedate pace toward the park. "Your team is well matched, sir," she commented, though privately she thought the pair of blacks had more flash than go, as her brother might have said. Never would she have said so, however. One did not criticize a gentleman's judgment of horseflesh.

"Yes, they are quite acceptable," he said in his

bored drawl. "Blacks always are."

Cecily glanced up at him slantwise, an unconsciously flirtatious gesture. Did nothing ever excite him? Did he never laugh, or smile, or even lose his temper? "Have you put them through their paces yet?"

"Such a thing would not be seemly here in town, my dear."

"Oh, fustian!" Cecily exclaimed as he turned into the park. "People go at a gallop all the time."

"But not I. It is vulgar. And I do hope, my dear, that you will moderate your language once we are wed."

"Excuse me?"

"For you to use such a word as 'fustian' simply isn't proper. But do not fear, such deficiencies can be corrected and do not make you in any way ineligible."

"Th-thank you, my lord," Cecily stammered, so astonished that she was speechless. Deficiency! If he thought her language were improper, what else would he wish changed? Cecily felt, suddenly, as if she were suffocating under the weight of his expectations. If he wished her to behave just so, when would she ever find the chance to be just Cecily?

Not wishing to incur more criticism, Cecily spoke little on the remainder of the drive, except to greet friends and acquaintances. She smiled and nodded to the Duke of York when he condescended to smile at her; at Lady Cowper and Lady Sefton, a formidable combination, driving in an open landau; and even the Prince Regent, who was riding with his friend Sir Benjamin Bloomfield. If she kept looking for one man, a dark-haired man with eyes as blue and as deep as the sea, she kept that to herself. *He* was not the answer to her problem. She would have to find a way to accommodate herself to her future

101

husband's wishes, or—end the engagement.

Cecily pushed that thought quite out of her mind as they set off toward her home. A most ineligible idea. To break the engagement would mean she would be labeled a jilt. No, she would behave as expected. She would marry the handsome marquess and be happy.

And then Edgewater accompanied her to the drawing room and kissed her again.

The duchess, reclining on a chaise longue in her sitting room, smiled when Cecily shyly poked her head around the door. "Come in, child and give your mama a kiss," she said, waving her hand.

Cecily crossed the deep pile, cream and rose rug hesitantly, feeling, as always, a little inadequate in this atmosphere of overwhelming femininity with its frills and furbelows. "I'm not disturbing you, am I, Mama?"

"Gracious, no, I hope I always have time for my daughters! I was just reading a novel. That nasty Caroline Lamb, imagine writing a book such as this, and about people she calls friends! Most vulgar of her. But, there, you won't want to hear about that," she said, hastily pushing the volume down beside her, and settling her hands in her lap. "Oh, dear, Cecily, you've been biting your nails again."

Cecily quickly tucked her fingers against her palms. "I do try, Mama," she said, dropping into a graceful heap on the floor, her back to the chaise longue. She longed to lean her head back and feel her mother's comforting fingers touch her hair, but she knew better.

"Gracious, Cecily, I begin to despair of you! To sit on the floor when there are perfectly good chairs—"

"Please, Mama, don't scold me."

The duchess's brow furrowed. "Very well, child, but you know I'm only thinking of you. What the marquess would think, were he to see you like this!"

"My lord doesn't approve much of what I do these days."

Cecily's confusion and unhappiness at last penetrated the duchess's self-absorption. "Is something wrong, child?" she asked in a voice more gentle than Cecily had ever heard her use before.

"Yes. No. I don't know." This time she did lean her head back. "Mama." Cecily twisted around to look at her. "Do you love Papa?"

"Gracious, child, such a question!" The duchess fidgeted with her negligee of soft pink chiffon, arranging it more securely over her knees, and then sent Cecily a glance that was unexpectedly keen. "What is it, child? What is troubling you?"

Cecily turned away. "Edgewater kissed me."

"Ah. I see."

"And I didn't like it." *But I did like it when another man kissed me,* she thought and went hastily on. "Is it always so unpleasant?"

"Kissing? Why, no, I never found it so. But it isn't exactly as the books would have you believe, is it?"

"No." Not with her fiancé, anyway. "But I didn't mean just kissing," she stammered, her face red. "I meant —"

"Child, you'll be expected to do your duty as a wife. You must produce heirs, you know."

"I know." With Edgewater, duty it would be. But with St. Clair—now *that* was an ineligible thought! "Is it so unpleasant?"

The duchess fidgeted with her negligee again. "This is a most improper conversation, Cecily. When the time comes, you may be certain I'll tell you what you need to know."

"But, Mama," she protested, and then fell silent.

103

How could she explain that that time was now? She was horrified by her reactions to her future husband; baffled by what she felt for another man. Kissing him had been more than just pleasant. It had been—well, she couldn't exactly describe the feeling. All she knew was that she was confused. "Mama, I don't think I want to marry Edgewater."

"Not want to marry him?" The duchess stared at her. "But he is a perfectly proper husband for you, child. Besides, the settlements have been signed, I'm sure. It's much too late for you to change your mind." Looking at Cecily's bent head, the duchess reached out a hand, as if to touch her, and then withdrew it. "I suppose I should rise. I have been lazy quite long enough. Please ring for Quimby."

Cecily rose and crossed the room, tugging on the bellpull to summon her mother's dresser. "Mama." She raised her chin. "I mean it. I really don't want to marry him."

"Nonsense, child." The duchess sat at her dressing table and began pulling pins out of her hair. "Of course you'll marry him. We'll have no more of this foolishness, now."

"But, Mama—"

"This is quite normal, Cecily," she went on, brushing her hair, "though I'd expect it more of your sister than of you. You have so little sensibility."

"I don't understand."

The duchess laid down the brush and looked at Cecily in the mirror. "Child, all girls feel this way before they marry. Nervous, and frightened. I know I did."

"You did, Mama? But you were marrying Papa."

"A man I didn't know very well, child. A man my parents chose for me. Thank heavens we do things better in these days! At least you have a chance to become familiar with your husband. I never did," she added, with so much resentment that Cecily could only stare.

"I think—Mama, I think it's more than nervousness."

"Don't be silly, Cecily. Ah, Quimby, here you are. Draw my bath for me. Now, enough of this." The duchess rose and put her arm around Cecily's shoulders. "Of course you're nervous. Marriage is a frightening step. But I assure you it will work out well. And we'll have no more talk of breaking the engagement." She paused. "Will we?"

Cecily's head was bent. "No, Mama."

"Good. Now, you must hurry, child, and start preparing if you wish to be ready for the theater tonight."

"Yes, Mama." Cecily left the room, no more comforted than she had been earlier and vastly more confused. The view of marriage that had briefly opened up to her was frightening. She had always thought her parents dealt well together; never would she have guessed at her mother's unhappiness. Would she herself feel the same in twenty years' time?

It was just all so confusing! Cecily paced back and forth in her room, gnawing at her thumbnail. The kiss of one man caused her nothing but revulsion, while the touch, even the very gaze, of another man was enough to set her pulse to racing. He was totally unsuitable for her, and yet, with him somehow she felt complete. Why, then, was she marrying someone else?

Cecily stopped, staring at her reflection. She *didn't* have to marry Edgewater! If she were, indeed, the proper, practical Lady Cecily everyone believed her to be, she would go through with the marriage, but she wasn't. The adventurous side of her that had so recently surfaced, that she had tried to stifle, would not be denied. What did it matter what people would say should she break the engagement? It was her life! She was the one who would have to live with Edgewater, and she was the one who would be unhappy should the marriage fail. It was her life. She had control of it.

Cecily gazed at herself, and then nodded at the decision she had made. One more chance. That was all she would allow Edgewater. And then she would be free to live her life as she saw fit. The future was hers.

Alex was in a foul temper as he strode into Joseph Manton's gun shop. Not that he needed a new set of pistols, but the exercise of loading, aiming, firing, precisely suited him today. If he did nothing else to work off his mood, he might very well end by killing someone.

Several days had passed since he had caught Cecily in Whitechapel, several days which, to his surprise, had turned out to be lonely and bleak. His solitary rides in the park were no longer enlivened by the company of a girl ridiculously attired, riding a most ridiculous horse. Nor did he spend his evenings in her presence, frequenting the *ton* events he had, in the past, found so stifling, but which, recently, he had anticipated. He had, instead, gone back to his old routine. With Parsons, displeased at this turn of events, to keep an eye on Cecily, Alex had returned to his gambling and drinking, though he wondered how, in the past, he had managed to survive the way he felt in the mornings. Last evening, he had even visited his former mistress, who had not yet found a new protector, only to leave after a few moments. What he had ever seen in her overblown charms perplexed him; why he had no desire for her perplexed him even more.

On the advice of the gunsmith, Alex chose a pair of pistols with mahogany grips, sighting down the barrels of each and nodding in approval. "I'll try these," he said, and walked into the back of the shop, where Manton had set up a shooting gallery. Today the gallery was empty, save for Alex, and so he was able to shoot in peace, with Manton himself giving advice, until the tinkle of the bell on the shop door announced that another customer had come in.

Alex raised his pistol again and fired, coming close enough to the center of the target to both satisfy and frustrate him. His months of living for pleasure had dulled his skills; once he would have been able to hit the center every time, with lightning quick reflexes. Now that he had reentered the dangerous world of espionage, he might very well need those skills. He was not going to be caught off-guard again, as he so nearly had been by the unexpectedly seductive Lady Cecily.

His lips were set in a grim line, his arm raised to fire, when another man came to stand at his side, his coat removed for the exercise of shooting. "St. Clair," Edgewater said coolly, loading his pistol.

"Edgewater." Alex nodded in acknowledgment, and fired. The shot went wide.

Edgewater peered at the target in apparent perplexity. "I thought you were said to be a dead shot, dear boy."

"This pistol pulls to the right," Alex said curtly.

Edgewater nodded. "Of course. When wrong, always blame the instrument, not yourself," he said, and raised his pistol. Without even seeming to aim, he fired a shot dead center into the target. "There. That is how it is done, dear boy."

Alex calmly reloaded his pistol. He would not allow Edgewater to annoy him, though he had never liked the man, or his cool air of arrogant superiority. What Cecily saw in him—but he wouldn't think of that now. "Fine shooting." He sighted down the barrel and, this time, correcting for the pistol's slight tendency to aim right, hit the target in the center. "And so, I believe, is that."

Edgewater shrugged. "A mere trifle, dear boy." His second shot was placed precisely an inch above the first; his third, an inch below. "Ah, I see I haven't lost my touch. A shame you've let your skills grow rusty, dear boy."

Alex sent him a brilliant, cold-eyed smile. "And what skills are those, dear boy?" he said, laying ironic stress on the last two words and having the immense satisfaction of seeing Edgewater's nostrils flare with sudden anger.

"Shooting, of course," Edgewater said after a moment. "What else?"

"Shooting. I see. But I must tell you, Edgewater," he raised the pistol, aiming, "that I am as good a swordsman as ever." He fired and the hole in the center of his target grew larger. "Ah, capital. Which, I believe, you never were."

"Come fence me a time and find out."

"Fencing? Who is speaking of fencing?" Alex's smile was friendly, pleasant, but also mocking. "Your little fiancé never looks happy with you." Edgewater's shot went wide. "An unfortunate shot, sir."

"I have some words of warning for you, St. Clair," Edgewater said, the drawl gone from his voice. "Cecily Randall is mine. Keep away from her."

"Tch, tch, bad *ton* to bandy a lady's name about in such a way." Alex reloaded the pistol, hiding his grin. He was hugely enjoying this encounter, although until this moment he hadn't realized how much he disliked Edgewater. "Is she displeased with your performance?"

Edgewater's face had grown very red, and the lid of his left eye twitched. "Just what are you implying, St. Clair?"

"Why, nothing, sir. I'll take this one," he said, turning to the gunsmith. "The other one does pull to the right."

"Yes, my lord," Manton said.

"I demand satisfaction for that," Edgewater said as if the gunsmith weren't present.

"Gentlemen, please—"

"A duel?" Alex pretended to yawn, though an alarm bell was jangling in his head. "How tedious. You might spoil your clothes, sir."

"Not a duel." The look Edgewater shot him was contemptuous. "A shooting match. Right here, right now. Or have you gotten too soft, playing with the ladies?"

"At least they allow me—"

"Right here, right now." Edgewater's voice was low and intense, and the tic in his eyelid was more pronounced. "Or I will meet you in the field."

"Indeed?" Alex turned again to the gunsmith, who still looked alarmed. "Will you referee, sir? Best three out of five, Edgewater. Agreed?"

"Agreed. Manton, set up new targets."

"Very well. But you may want to relax. I don't know how you'll be able to shoot with your eyelid twitching." As Alex spoke, the ghost of a memory came to him. Something important, but as he tried to grasp at it, it faded away. Whatever it was, it made him look sharply at his opponent. Edgewater wasn't looking at him, but was instead studying the new target Manton had set up, his arm extended. The hand that held the gun looked strong and capable, for all its whiteness; the muscles of his arm stood out hard and corded. No idle dandy, he, though he cultivated the pose of it. Alex wondered

109

why. "We wouldn't want your pistol to pull to the side."

"Don't worry about me," Edgewater said curtly. "Worry about yourself."

"Oh, I am, sir." Alex's voice was grim. It had somehow become essential that he best this man, if only at shooting. Edgewater had won Cecily; damned if Alex were going to allow him to win this, as well.

So it was with great annoyance that a few moments later, he found himself congratulating Edgewater on five perfect shots. His own shooting had been respectable; four of the five had hit the center, with only the last going wide. The worst part of it was that it was his own fault. Though he had tried to keep his temper under control, something about his opponent bothered him, so much that it had affected his shooting. It surely couldn't have anything to do with Lady Cecily. Of course not.

"Congratulations." Alex's face was expressionless as he held out his hand to the other man.

"Thank you." With the aid of the gunsmith's assistant, Edgewater struggled into his morning coat of swallowtail blue, a color that nearly made Alex's lips curl in disdain. "Must go along, you know," he said, his voice a drawl again. "I'm promised to Lady Cecily for the afternoon."

"Are you." Alex's voice was as expressionless as his face.

"Yes." Edgewater paused by the doorway. "I need hardly remind you, dear boy, to keep away from her, do I?"

Alex glanced up from straightening his cuffs, having shrugged himself into his own coat, and his eyes met Edgewater's, cool, hard, watchful. Again the alarm bells went off in his head. There was danger here, though he didn't know why. Edgewater was a

110

useless fribble, a man-milliner. For a moment that elusive memory returned to haunt him, and then was gone.

Curtly Alex nodded and Edgewater left, looking smug. Alex followed a little later, after completing the purchase of one of the pistols, returning to his lodgings in as foul a mood as he had left them. Parsons took one look at his face and retreated into the kitchen, there to prepare his lordship's luncheon. Moodily Alex sank into an armchair drawn up before the empty fireplace, stretching his legs out and stroking his upper lip. A most unprofitable morning, and it had nothing to do with the lost shooting match. He had allowed Edgewater to get to him, and all because the man was engaged to Cecily.

"Hell," he muttered. Why should that matter to him? He had no desire to marry Cecily, or anyone. In fact, in keeping with his reputation, it would be better if Cecily were married. He did not seduce young innocents.

The thought of Cecily married left a sour taste in his mouth; the thought that it would be to Edgewater made his stomach turn. Hell, of all the men she could have chosen, why him? He was nothing, a dandy concerned only about his appearance and his place in society, and yet — Alex frowned, remembering the disquieting impression he'd received that there was more to Edgewater than appeared on the surface, something hard, something possibly even cruel. He had learned to judge men quickly, and his instincts were telling him that he was right about this. Edgewater very carefully kept his real self hidden from the world. The question was, why?

Frowning, he stroked his upper lip again, staring sightlessly into the fireplace. The frustrating part about this situation was that he could do nothing about it. Cecily meant nothing to him; she couldn't.

111

His only concern with her was investigating her link to the conspiracy. He could not allow himself to be concerned about her, or her forthcoming marriage. Nor could he allow himself to waste time, or energy, on Edgewater. He'd dismiss him from his thoughts. Still, Alex grinned, Edgewater hadn't had it all his own way that morning. Alex had managed to annoy him enough that his left eyelid had started twitching.

Of a sudden, the memory that had been haunting him came back, the Duke of Bainbridge's voice repeating words Alf Barnes had said. "The only other thing Barnes mentioned about the leader is that his left eyelid twitches when he's angry."

"God's teeth!" Alex sat bolt upright, stunned by the memory and the startling conclusion he had reached. God's teeth, was Edgewater the leader of the conspiracy?

Chapter Nine

Parsons appeared in the doorway, wiping his hands on a towel. "My lord?" he said, frowning as he watched Alex stride back and forth. "Is something amiss?"

"What? No." Alex stopped, resting his hands on the back of the armchair. "You have someone watching Lady Cecily."

"Yes, sir, I—"

"Good. Keep him there. I want you to find out everything you can about the Marquess of Edgewater."

"A marquess? Sir, surely he wouldn't be involved—"

"I don't know, Parsons. Call it a hunch, but I think he may be. And I think," he added, softly, "that he's bigger game than we expected to find."

"I'll do what I can, sir." Parsons bowed. "Luncheon will be ready in a few moments."

"Yes, yes." Alex waved his hand impatiently and began pacing once more. Cecily and Edgewater. Why hadn't he seen it sooner? A young girl like Cecily would not be able to move freely about without causing suspicion, but if Edgewater were her accomplice—yes, it all dovetailed neatly. He still wasn't certain what Cecily's rôle in the conspiracy was; he doubted she was its leader. Involved in it she was, though, and so was her fiancé, which explained that apparently unsuitable betrothal. If they thought they

113

had eluded detection, they would soon learn differently. At the ball in Richmond, one or the other of them would surely slip away to attend the meeting of the conspirators that would be held near there.

Alex smiled, a grim, unpleasant smile. Oh, yes, he would go to Richmond, and he would keep his eyes open. And then he would learn, once and for all, just what Lady Cecily was up to.

"Diana, you look perfectly lovely," the duchess of Marlow burbled as her two daughters entered the drawing room. "And so do you, Cecily."

"Thank you, Mama." Cecily rose from her curtsy to see her fiancé regarding her through his quizzing glass. When she married him—if she married him—she would do what she could to break him of that odious habit.

"Charming," Edgewater pronounced, secreting the quizzing glass in his pocket. "That particular color suits you. I do believe, however, that you should let your hair grow."

"Cecily detests long hair," Diana said cheerfully, reaching up to touch her own elegant chignon and preening under the marquess' admiring glance.

Cecily looked on with a mixture of amusement and chagrin. She knew she was looking particularly well tonight, having taken extra care with her toilette. Her gown of aqua watered silk with its lace overdress and sash of silver ribbon fitted her perfectly. Slippers dyed to match were just visible beneath the newly fashionable longer skirt, a lace shawl was draped becomingly over her arms, and a matching silver ribbon bound up her curls. Pearls of excellent quality were about her throat, and in her hand she carried a daintily embroidered fan. Not a hair was out of place; not a detail of her dress was amiss. In short, she looked perfectly well, and she was annoyed with her fiancé for his unwarranted criticism. As if he should talk, with the shoulders of his coat that she had discovered were padded when he had pulled her against him. St. Clair's certainly weren't padded. And Edgewater's shirt points were so ridiculously high he was in danger of cutting himself if he so much as turned his head, she thought, hastily pulling her mind away from the dangerous topic of Lord St. Clair. The marquess was treading a very thin line. All she needed was one more incident, and she would break the engagement, regardless of society's reaction.

"My carriage awaits," Edgewater said, holding out his arm, encased in peacock-blue velvet, to her. She rested her hand on it lightly. At least his arm was muscular, if not as strongly so as someone else's she could think of. *Stop it, Cecily!*

"Thank you, sir." She gave him a brief smile, settling herself on the cut-velvet squabs of his carriage with unshakable equanimity. She was tired of letting others dictate her fate. It was her life. Tonight she would, if necessary, take it firmly into her own hands.

The Radcliffe ballroom in Richmond was already crowded when the Marlow party made its entrance. Candles sparkled in the myriad chandeliers and sconces lining the walls, and the air was heady with the perfumes of the spring flowers set in tubs about the rooms and the heavier scents worn by the ladies. "Oh, Cece, just look at everyone!" Diana said. This was all still new enough to her to elicit breathless admiration, though ordinarily she cultivated the mask of boredom considered so essential in society life. "I just know this will be a wonderful evening."

"Yes," Cecily murmured absently, for, in all the movement and confusion of people, her gaze had been caught, and held, by just one man's. St. Clair, standing across the room with Lady Wentworth, long known as one of his flirts, gazed at Cecily without the hint of a smile. Cecily returned the look, hiding behind her own cool expression; the impact he had on her, and the hurt of seeing him with another woman, particularly one so beautiful. He was no dandy; his evening coat of black velvet and breeches of white satin were faultless, but not out of the ordinary. Nor was he the most handsome man present. She found it difficult, though, to look away. Then he turned, and the moment was broken.

Alex stared at Cecily for one more moment, and then, inclining his head, returned his attention to Lady Wentworth, who was chattering vivaciously and hadn't appeared to notice his lapse in manners. Out of the corner of his eye, however, he watched Cecily as she progressed into the room, greeting friends, her elbow held possessively by Edgewater. Alex's hand gripped his crystal flute of champagne so hard it was in imminent danger of shattering as an emotion so primal in its force that it shook him went through him. Damn him! He didn't have to hold on to her in quite that way, nor look at her with that supercilious gaze that announced to the world that she was his possession, and only that. There was so much more to Cecily. Couldn't the man see that?

Murmuring something to Lady Wentworth, he bowed and then turned away, making his way with apparent aimlessness across the room, until he was near the Marlow party. *Stay away,* a voice warned in his head. Cecily was dangerous to him, in some fashion he hadn't yet defined, and yet he couldn't resist her lure. Besides, he told himself, he needed to keep watch on her if the conspirators were indeed to meet. And then he would be free of her.

"Good evening, Your Grace," he said, bowing to the duchess, and saw Cecily, turned slightly away from him, start. "Lady Cecily, Lady Diana. And—

Edgewater, is it?"

"Good evening, St. Clair," Edgewater returned urbanely enough, though his left eyelid twitched once or twice. "How unexpected to see you here tonight. I'd have thought this kind of—affair was too tame for you."

"Perhaps I am reforming," he said lightly, watching Cecily without appearing to. She had not missed Edgewater's double entendre, he noticed. Nor, by the stiff way she held herself, had she forgotten, or forgiven, what had transpired between them when last they met. Just as well. "You look particularly well this evening, Lady Cecily."

"Thank you, sir." Cecily kept her eyes resolutely on her fan, which she kept opening and closing.

"Why, Cecily, dear, I believe I see Lady Jersey across the room," the duchess said, barely glancing at Alex. "Come, children, we must make our bow to her. Good evening, sir."

Alex inclined his head. "Good evening. Cecily," he added under his breath, and had the satisfaction of seeing her shoulders stiffen, just for a moment. Then, quite as if he weren't there, she walked away.

"So, St. Clair." Edgewater's smile was urbanity itself, but his voice was edged with ice. "What do you here tonight?"

"I thought I might find events—interesting," he said, facing the other man directly.

Edgewater's eyes narrowed a trifle, and then he gave a wintry smile. "Quite. But don't forget, dear boy, what I told you the other day. Lady Cecily is mine."

"Does she think so?"

"She had better." Edgewater's voice was soft. "Keep away from her, St. Clair, or I won't answer for the consequences."

Alex flicked a contemptuous eye over the other man's peacock-blue coat, his pale-blue satin knee breeches, his embroidered waistcoat, and elaborately stifled a yawn. "Indeed," he said, and turned away, holding back a grin.

His sense of triumph faded, however, sometime later as he watched Edgewater lead Cecily out for the first waltz. Something inside him clenched; something inside ached at the memory of her in his arms, waltzing at Almack's, returning his kiss so sweetly in his lodgings. And so innocently. He'd lay a wager by her untutored response that she'd never been kissed before that day, at least not like that, and that filled him with an inordinate amount of pleasure. Though he didn't know why it should. Young girls just out of the schoolroom bored him, with their ignorance and inexperience. And yet —

She looked so lovely tonight, with a subtle beauty that drew one's eyes away from the more obvious charms of the ladies he usually pursued. The color of her gown became her, and its décolletage, though modest, was just low enough to show that though slender, she was very much a woman. And that, he realized with a jolt, was exactly what she was. Not the engaging hoyden, clad in boy's clothes and riding a dancing horse; not the earnest reformer, concerned about the welfare of the poor. Not even the young girl who always looked the slightest bit untidy. She was a woman, and in more than just the externals. There was something in the way she held herself, something in her demeanor, that told him she had reached a decision, that she had suddenly grown up. Alex's gaze sharpened. His instincts in coming here had been right. Something indeed was about to happen. The question was, what?

"Has Lord St. Clair been bothering you?" Edgewater asked, and Cecily started.

"No," she murmured, but her eyes didn't meet his.

"I do not like seeing him hang around you, Cecily."

118

"I don't let him hang around—"

"If he bothers you, you are to tell me."

Cecily raised startled eyes to him. "Sir, you wouldn't duel with him!"

"Don't worry, my dear." Edgewater's smile was smug as he tightened his hold about her waist. Cecily resisted, but then gave in. "I am accounted quite a good shot, you know."

Cecily shuddered. But was St. Clair as good?

"You are cold, my dear?" Edgewater's voice was solicitous.

"What? Oh, no. Actually, I'm finding it a trifle warm."

"The price one pays for attending such sad crushes. Everyone is here tonight. And they see that you are with me."

"Yes," Cecily said faintly, wondering at the odd note of triumph in his voice.

"Come, my dear." Edgewater took her arm as the waltz ended and turned her toward the terrace doors "I believe you'd do well with some air."

"Sir, I cannot—"

"Come, Cecily we are engaged, are we not? No one will say anything if we go out just for a few moments." His smile was winning, but his hand on her back was firm. Time was passing alarmingly. If he didn't leave the ballroom soon, and with Cecily to give him an excuse, he would be late for the meeting. And that wouldn't do; it might lead some of his fellow conspirators to mutiny against his leadership. "Come," he said again, grasping her arm tighter, and Cecily had no choice but to obey.

Alex had been keeping watch on Cecily and Edgewater throughout the waltz, but toward the end his attention had been diverted by Sally Jersey, who tapped him on the arm with her fan. "There you are, St. Clair. I'm surprised to see you here tonight. Not exactly your kind of do, I'd have said."

119

Alex gave her his most charming smile and looked away from Cecily, though he cursed the necessity of it. Lady Jersey's ironic nickname of "Silence" was well-earned; he had already shown interest in Cecily at Almack's, and if Lady Jersey learned that that interest had continued, then the fat would be in the fire indeed. By tomorrow, the gossip would be all over town. "Perhaps I've decided to become respectable at last, ma'am," he said lightly.

"Oh, fiddle! There's nothing more boring than a reformed rake. Unless," she said archly, "there's someone in particular you wish to reform for?"

"Why, Lady Jersey," he said, sounding greatly surprised, "how could anyone else compare with you?"

"Oh, fiddle!" she said again, but her pink cheeks showed that his flattery had pleased her. Taking his arm, she began to stroll about the ballroom with him, talking at great length about the ball and the people present. Alex made polite replies whenever she paused to take a breath, all the time searching the ballroom for Cecily. He couldn't see her—there! There she was, looking up at Edgewater and appearing less than pleased. What was the man saying to her, Alex wondered, shaken again by that primal emotion. Damn the man! If he hurt Cecily, he would pay.

Lady Jersey caught his attention again, so he had no choice but to look at her. It wasn't until the waltz had ended that he at last had a chance to scan the ballroom again. It didn't bother him at first that he couldn't see Cecily, though earlier his gaze had homed in on her. The room was crowded, after all, and she was not very tall. But when his search went on for several moments and he still could not find her he became, at first, concerned, and then alarmed. Hell! Both she and Edgewater were gone. Because of his inattention, he'd let them get away. God knew what they were up to.

Hell! He turned to make his excuses to Lady Jersey, no longer caring if she speculated on his reason, and was relieved to see that she was already deep in conversation with someone else. With a perfunctory bow, he took his leave, making every effort to appear casual as he made his way across the crowded ballroom. Where were they? If they were, indeed, going to a meeting of the conspiracy, then they would have had to go outdoors. Into the garden, probably, and that alarmed him. If it was Edgewater who was involved more than Cecily, as he had come to believe, then she might very well be in danger.

In the days since his suspicions had fallen on Edgewater, he'd learned a few things about the man. On the surface he was, indeed, the dandy that he appeared. Underneath, however, lay a very different man. A man who, for example, was deeply interested in politics and had been known to attend the House of Lords regularly. Unusual, perhaps, but commendable, Alex thought sardonically. What really interested him was how Edgewater conducted himself in that august body. Professedly Tory, in the heat of debate over such issues as parliamentary reform or Catholic emancipation, he had been known to say things that bordered on the radical. Strange interests for a man who claimed to be concerned only with the cut of his coat. Why pretend? Alex wondered. Why should Edgewater need to cover his real convictions? The only reason Alex could think of was that he was attempting to divert suspicion. Certainly he was a more likely candidate for conspiracy than Cecily ever had been, though he couldn't discount her completely. But if Edgewater hurt her—

His thoughts lent urgency to his pursuit and he ceased being polite as he pushed his way across the room, ceased greeting people or excusing his apparent rudeness. Something was going on here, and he had to find out what it was. The future of his country, and his own happiness, might very well depend on it.

At last he reached the doors leading to the terrace. Belated caution made him glance around, but no one appeared to be attending to him. Good. If he could avoid gossip about this, so much the better. Taking a deep breath, he stepped out onto the dimly lighted terrace. The fresh evening air felt good after the heat and the mingling of odors within. Moving aimlessly, as if bored with events within, Alex glanced about the terrace. Several other people were here, couples conversing or taking advantage of a few stolen moments alone. None of them were Cecily or Edgewater. No matter how hard he looked, they were nowhere in sight.

Hell! Moving purposefully, forgetting his languid pose, Alex strode across the terrace and ran down the marble stairs into the garden, the scents of damp earth and lilacs enveloping him. He'd find them, he told himself grimly, not caring to analyze the urgency or the panic that drove him on. He'd find them, if it was the last thing he did.

Once on the terrace, Cecily took a deep, grateful breath of the lilac-scented air. It was certainly much more pleasant here than it had been in the crowded, stuffy ballroom. They were also not as alone as she had feared. Other couples were taking advantage of the terrace and the mildness of the evening and though few appeared to pay heed to her, Cecily was glad of their presence. She was glad not to be alone with her fiancé.

Edgewater frowned. "I didn't expect we'd have such a crowd out here," he muttered.

"A crowd, sir?" Cecily gestured toward the others, smiling slightly. The widely spaced lanterns left pockets of shade that gave the illusion of privacy.

122

"Nearly everyone is still within doors."

"Still, I had hoped to speak to you in private." He took her arm again. "Come. Let us go into the garden."

"What?" Cecily stood her ground, though Edgewater was pulling on her arm. The garden was even more sparsely lighted than the terrace, with only an occasional torch to give any light. A romantic spot for a tryst, but that was the last thing she wanted with this man. "Why, sir, that would be most improper," she said flirtatiously, tapping him on the arm with her fan.

Edgewater raised chilly gray eyes to her. "Never hit me again," he said with calm, icy finality.

"I do beg your pardon, sir, but it was the merest tap."

"I would speak with you, Cecily." He pulled at her arm again, catching her off guard, so that she stumbled. "Come, or do you wish to make a scene?"

"No, of course not," Cecily said, though her resentment of him was increasing by leaps and bounds. In the past week, confused as she had been, she had alternated between going ahead with the engagement, and being certain it would never work. Now, at last, she knew her own mind; his casual use of his greater strength and his complete disregard of her preferences, not to mention her reputation, had decided her. No longer was the issue what she had thought it was, that she could not marry one man while confused about her feelings for another. She had no desire to marry this man at all. "Actually, there's something I wish to talk to you about, though I'd rather not do it here—"

"We'll be private enough here." Edgewater pulled her off the path into a bower heavily scented with lilacs and a fleeting memory came to her: St. Clair, handing her a bunch of lilacs, telling her they became her. She couldn't remember ever receiving a

123

sincere compliment from her fiancé. "Now, at last, we can be alone," he said.

Cecily eluded the arm he would have slipped about her waist and went to sit on the bench whose white paint gleamed dully in the faint light. A trellis arched overhead, completing the illusion that they were completely alone. "I mustn't stay long—"

"Ah, Cecily." He sat close beside her, and before she could protest his arms were about her, hauling her against his chest. Caught off balance, she threw up her hands to protect herself, only to make contact with his shoulders. "It seems an age since we were alone."

"It was yesterday, sir. Please unhand me."

"Ah, Cecily, don't be coy." She felt his breath hot against her throat as he bent to kiss her beneath her ear, and her struggles increased. "That's it, my dear, fight me. It will make it all the sweeter when you at last give in."

"I—" Her words were cut off as his mouth came down on hers in a hard, bruising kiss. "Won't. I won't!" she gasped.

"Of course you'll give in. It's inevitable, my dear. Ah, for someone who is so thin, you're all woman, aren't you?"

"Stop it!" Futilely she pushed at his hand fumbling at her bodice, and he caught her wrist, holding it behind her. "Please, let me go—"

"Give in to me, Cecily. You want to, you know you do."

"No!" Badly frightened now, knowing she was fighting for her soul, she twisted her head, eluding his kiss. "No! I won't give in. I don't wish to marry you, sir."

Edgewater went quite still, though he didn't loosen his grip. "I don't believe I heard you aright, Cecily. Of course you want to marry me."

"No. I don't—"

"And the sooner, the better," he went on relentlessly. "I intend to secure a special license. Soon we will be man and wife—"

"No! I'll never marry you, you—toad!"

"A toad, is it?" Edgewater's voice had gone dangerously quiet. "A toad? No one calls me a toad, madam!" His hands gripped her shoulders, hard. "No one, do you hear? Now you will marry me, I'll make certain of that. And you'll pay."

"No!" Cecily pushed against his chest, just as his painful grip on her shoulders loosened, and twisted free. There was a tearing sound, as of fabric being rent, but she couldn't stop to assess the damage. Without a backward glance, she took to her heels and ran toward the house and safety.

Edgewater started to his feet, took a few steps forward, and then stopped. Damnation! That hadn't gone at all as he had planned. It was all her fault, the little jade. If she hadn't encouraged him before, he wouldn't have attempted what he had. And she had called him a toad. His hands clenched into fists at that, the ultimate insult. No one called him toad, not since his boyhood days in the village. He had since learned there were other ways of getting revenge beyond fighting openly. Cecily would realize that herself, quite soon. He would make certain of that.

In the dim light he pulled out his watch, and frowned. No time to go after her now; it was nearly time to meet with the members of his conspiracy. Pulling a mask from his pocket and reaching up into the trellis for the domino he had secreted there earlier, he cloaked himself in his disguise. Cecily had served her purpose, allowing him to leave the ball on a quite reasonable pretext. On her, now, would rest the burden of why she had been in the gardens, at night, apparently alone. Served her right, he thought, and stepped out onto the path, the folds of the domino swirling around him. She would soon learn the consequences of spurning his advances. And, his satisfaction increasing with the thought, it would be his pleasure to teach her.

Edgewater walked down the path toward his destination, his face grim and yet smug, his mind determined. Nothing would stop him now.

And, near the bower, a shadow detached itself from the foliage and followed noiselessly behind.

The path was dark, but Cecily headed unerringly toward safety, somehow avoiding branches of trees that seemed to reach out to grab her, roots that rose to trip. She knew only that she had to reach the house, and never — never! — did she want Edgewater to set hands on her again. He had hurt her, and not only hadn't he cared, he had expected her to like it! A shudder went through her, making her knees go weak, almost making her crumple to the ground, but sheer willpower held her up, kept her going. She didn't care about the scandal, about the plans that had been made. All she wanted was never to have to see him again, and to be safe.

She rounded a turn in the path and there, still some distance ahead, was the house, the brilliant glow of its light spilling out onto terrace and garden, the strains of a country dance reaching her distantly. Edgewater wouldn't dare accost her now, so close, she was thinking, when of a sudden a man appeared before her on the path.

She gave a little cry, but even as she did so she recognized him, knew him with every fiber of her body. Alex. Safety. Without thought, Cecily ran straight into his arms.

Chapter Ten

Alex rocked back as Cecily hurled herself against him. "God's teeth! Cecily—"

"Hide me!" She clutched at his lapels. "Don't let him find me."

"Edgewater?" He looked over her shoulder, but there was no sign of the other man.

"Please! Don't let him find me. Please!"

A ruse, that was what this was. He forced himself to think, past her soft, rounded body pressed against his, past the fragrance of lilacs that rose from her hair, past the warmth of her breath on his neck. He wanted nothing more than to put his arms around her and hold her close, promising her safety, promising her—what? Whatever it was, he couldn't afford it. He had not come to Richmond to hold a dangerously attractive woman in his arms, pleasant though it might be. "Where is he?" he rasped, holding her away from him.

"I—don't know." Cecily shuddered in his grasp. "I thought he was behind me, but—"

"He's not," Alex said calmly, stepping away, determined to learn what was behind this. Only then did he take in her appearance, and his breath hissed out through his teeth. "God's teeth, Cecily, what did he do to you?"

"He—" Cecily glanced down and saw for the first

time that her bodice was torn. With a little moan of mortification, of protest, she put her hands up to her face. "Oh, no."

"What did he do to you?" Alex's hands on her arms were as urgent as his voice. He could see other signs now of what she had been through: her disordered hair; the bruises that stood out starkly on her shoulders; and, most telling of all, her eyes, huge, dark, blank with shock. This was no ruse. "Tell me. What did he do to you?"

"He—he wouldn't let me go, and I struggled, I really did—"

"Did he hurt you?" he demanded, rage getting the better of him, and she recoiled. He forced himself to relax, making his voice gentle and patient. "Cecily. Did he ravish you?"

"N-no. B-but he tried, and if I hadn't got away—oh, Alex, I was so scared!"

"Hush, Cecily, hush." He drew her close against him, wrapping his arms about her, rocking her back and forth. "You're safe, little one. I've got you now. Nothing's going to hurt you." Slowly he backed up until he was leaning against a tree. With any luck, they would be seen neither from the terrace nor the house. The last thing Cecily needed just now was to have a scandal break about her.

"If he comes after me—"

"He won't." Alex's voice was unintentionally grim. As outrageous as Edgewater's behavior toward Cecily had been, Alex suspected it had been intended to cover some deeper, darker purpose. He couldn't go after Edgewater to find the evidence he so badly needed, not with Cecily shivering in his arms. Alex, who let nothing get in the way of his work or his pleasure, was at last putting something else first. "If he does, he'll have me to deal with."

Cecily's hold on his lapels tightened. "When I was running, so scared, all I could think of was getting someplace safe, and then I saw you, and I knew I was safe."

"Did you, little one?" His fingers smoothed her hair comfortingly, feeling her curls soft and silky under his caress. She felt so good in his arms, so right. "I'll keep you safe, I promise." *My darling*, he almost added, and just as nearly dropped a kiss on those soft, luxuriant curls. God's teeth, what was wrong with him? "What we'll have to do now is get you home."

"But—" Cecily pulled back and looked at him, the blank look gone from her eyes. "I thought, if I could get back into the house, I could fix my gown—"

"Little fool," he said tenderly. "Someone would be bound to see you, and you'd be in the suds for sure. This is too interesting a titbit for the gossips to ignore. You'd have to marry Edgewater then."

Cecily's hands flew to her face. "No!"

"Or me." At that, she looked at him through her fingers. "The scandal, you know. Did you come in your own carriage?"

"No, Edgewater brought us. Oh, dear, how we're to get home—"

"With me, of course. I'll find your mother and sister—"

"You won't tell them!"

"No, little one, I'll think of something. The important thing now is to get you to my carriage." Slowly, reluctantly, he let his arms drop. "Are you feeling more the thing?"

"Yes, but I must look a sight."

Alex's teeth gleamed briefly in the moonlight. "It has been my experience that when a woman begins to worry about her appearance, she is recovering."

"Your vast experience, sir?"

"Indeed. Come, little one." He took her arm. "We'll go find my carriage."

Sometime later, Alex's carriage drew up in front of

Marlow House. "I can't thank you enough, sir," the duchess said effusively, clasping Alex's hand between hers. "To think that Cecily took such a bad fall! Well, I always have thought that Lady Radcliffe's gardens weren't well-enough lighted. I'm just grateful you were there, sir, to help my dear daughter. Think of the scandal if anyone had seen her!"

"Indeed," Alex murmured, glancing over at Cecily, who had sat, quiet and pale, during the ride home.

"And if she had been seen with you, sir! No offense, of course, but your reputation—"

Alex's lips twitched. "Of course, madam. After you." He indicated the open door of the carriage. Alex's inclination was to stay within, now that he'd seen them safely home. Cecily needed rest, not an endless recounting of her adventures tonight. The duchess, however, would have none of it. Nothing would do but that he come inside and receive the duke's gratitude. At that, it had been Cecily's lips that had twitched. Alex found he was rather looking forward to meeting the redoubtable duke of Marlow.

The duke was sitting in the drawing room, comfortably ensconced before the fire with a book and a glass of brandy, when his wife and daughters trooped in. He rose to greet them after only one brief, regretful glance at his book. "You're home early," he commented. "Was the ball not to your liking?"

"The ball was wonderful," Diana said. "But Cecily—"

"Cecily had a mishap," the duchess broke in, frowning at her younger daughter. "You know how clumsy she can be, Marlow. Fortunately Lord St. Clair was there to help. I don't know what we would have done without him."

"I see." Marlow took in Cecily's appearance in one quick, comprehensive glance and then smiled. "Go to bed, puss. I'll talk to you in the morning."

"Yes, Papa," Cecily whispered. Both girls dropped brief curtsies and then left, shepherded out by their mother. Marlow watched them go, frowning thoughtfully, and then turned to Alex, who stood near the door, apparently at ease. In reality, he was wondering how the duke would feel about his daughter having been rescued by a rake.

"St. Clair," the duke said easily, extending his hand. "I don't believe I've had the honor, though I knew your father. A fine man."

"Yes, Your Grace, he was," Alex said.

"Please, sit. Care for a brandy?"

"Yes, thank you." Alex chose an armchair across from the duke and watched as he poured the brandy. Marlow was a spare, mild-looking man, not above medium height, with fair hair thinning at the top, and none of the airs one would expect from a man in his exalted position. A modest man, in fact. Alex, however, was not deceived, and he eyed his host carefully as he sat down again.

"Who was it?" Marlow asked, without preamble.

"Edgewater," Alex answered, equally terse, after recovering from his momentary surprise.

"That man-milliner? I'd not have thought it."

"There's more to him than one would think." Alex took a sip from his glass, aware that the duke was watching him keenly. "Fine brandy, Your Grace."

"Thank you. What is your interest in all this, St. Clair?"

"I happened to be there when your daughter needed help."

Marlow's eyes, the same golden color as Cecily's, held his. "I see," he said finally, and Alex wondered just what it was the duke did see. "Wellington spoke well of you, I understand," he went on, apparently at a tangent. "Said that without the work that you and others like you did, we might well have lost the war."

"I was just doing my job." Alex gazed into his

131

glass, acutely uncomfortable with this turn in the conversation. There was nothing so very heroic in what he had done.

"I see. Still, it makes me wonder why you were in the Radcliffe garden. Watching my daughter? Or—someone else?"

Alex looked up at that, to see Marlow regarding him shrewdly. A dangerous opponent, he thought, and, he would wager, an even better ally. "I can't tell you, sir," he said frankly. "Except that it might be a good idea to keep Cecily—Lady Cecily—away from Edgewater."

"Like that, is it?"

Alex's face was very innocent. "Like what, sir?"

"Nothing." Marlow rose, extending his hand. "We are in your debt, St. Clair. Be certain that I won't forget it."

"I'm glad I was there, sir. Lady Cecily is a fine girl."

"So she is. The best of all my children, between you and me. So it is fair to say that you like her?"

"I hardly know her, sir. I do have a great deal of respect for her. She's very special, if you don't mind my saying so. She'll need someone more special than Edgewater."

"Quite." Marlow's eyes twinkled with the same mischievous sparkle that Alex had often seen in Cecily's. "Am I to take it, then, that you would like to pay your addresses to her?"

Alex looked startled. "I, sir?"

"Yes, you. I never liked Edgewater, but Cecily seemed to have her heart set on him. However, I think you would be good for her."

"It's not something I've thought of," Alex said slowly, but the memory of Cecily in his arms this evening gave the lie to his words. It felt good. It felt right. "However—"

"However, it's early days yet. No need to say anything to Cecily just yet."

"No. She'll need time to recover from tonight. Sir." Alex turned in the doorway, his shoulders squared. "You've surely heard of my reputation. What makes you believe I'd be suitable for your daughter?"

Marlow eyed him for a long moment without speaking. "I made a mistake, allowing her to become engaged to Edgewater," he said finally. "I don't make the same mistake twice. Besides," he added, grinning suddenly, "my reputation wasn't much better when I was young."

"You, sir?" Alex said grinning.

"Yes, I. You'll be better for her than Edgewater."

The smile faded from Alex's face. "Sir, it will be best if you handle Edgewater carefully. He's a dangerous man."

Marlow's face darkened. "Frankly, I'd like to take a horsewhip to him."

"I wouldn't advise it, sir. Be assured he'll pay for this. Other people are watching him."

The duke eyed him keenly. "Like that, is it?"

"Possibly. And that's all I can say, sir. Except— keep him away from Cecily."

"You may be certain I will," Marlow said grimly. "Thank you, St. Clair, for your help."

"You're welcome, sir. Good evening," Alex answered and, bemused by the evening's events, made his way home. God's teeth! He was practically engaged. How had that happened?

The old cottage, tucked deep into the woods bordering the Radcliffe estate, looked completely abandoned. Tiles had fallen from the roof, the weatherboarding badly needed a coat of whitewash and the shutters were tightly closed. Not tightly enough, however. Age and weather had warped one of them, so that from it streamed a narrow, golden beam of light, showing that on this night at least, the cottage was not deserted. Parsons, creeping closer with great care, wondered how Lord Edgewater had known of it. A smart man, the marquess. Inclined to think himself above everybody, too, and that could make him careless. Like now, not realizing that the same chink in the shutter that let out light would also allow someone to listen in.

"Gentlemen, there is no longer time for such squeamishness!" Edgewater's voice, Parsons knew it well by now, as he knew a great many things about the man. He wondered how Lord St. Clair had known enough to set watch on Edgewater, but he no longer shook his head over it. St. Clair had an instinct for such things; 'twas what had made him so invaluable in the service of his country.

"I don't like it, that's all." Another voice, Cornish by the sound of it. Parsons carefully put his eye to the chink. Aye, a fine group of traitors. He wished he had more men here, so that each could be followed, though that would increase his own chances of being discovered. Best now to watch each man carefully, cloaked and masked though they were.

"Our aim was decided long ago." Edgewater again, his voice edged with ice. "If you want out, I'm sure we can find a way to manage it."

"And have the same thing happen to us that did to the Cockney?" Another voice, with the accents of London. A Cit, Parsons thought. "Oh, yes, I have my sources, too. I heard of his end."

"Our leader thought it was necessary," Edgewater said smoothly and let the silence build. "The Cockney, it seems, was a spy."

Uproar. Parsons couldn't help grinning at the reaction of the men inside, their voices raised in panic and outrage, though he at last had the proof that the conspiracy had been behind Barnes's death.

"Gentlemen!" Edgewater brought the flat of his

hand down on the table, hard. "Obviously we have not been discovered, or we would not be here now, would we?"

Slowly, the hubbub faded. "Aye," said another man finally. "I've not had no one watching me."

"Or I," another chimed in, and other voices agreed. True enough, Parsons thought, but by tomorrow, they would be watched. By their accents, he could tell that most of the men had traveled great distances to come to this meeting. It would be easy enough to check the local inns, see which had a man from Lancashire staying there, which a man from Wales, and identify the conspirators accordingly. A widespread plot, encompassing all of Britain, apparently. Parsons felt the same surge of satisfaction and excitement he'd experienced in previous assignments, when the long, tedious hours of watching and following had at last begun to pay off. They'd clean up this nest of vipers, see if they didn't!

Inside the cottage the noise had abated, and the men were now discussing their plans as if this were any ordinary meeting at business. "I have, as I promised you, found a man to do the job. No, I did not bring him here tonight," Edgewater went on, as if forestalling any protest, "for your own protection. This way, gentlemen, none of you will have knowledge that is dangerous to you, should our man, by any chance, fail." A murmur went around the table at that. "You may be certain that our leader approves of him."

"When do we get to meet this leader?" one man demanded.

"Not until our plot is complete, gentlemen. I may tell you, though, that he is very pleased with all of you, and your plans for your area. Be assured that you will be rewarded when our plot succeeds." He paused. "Amply rewarded."

"We had better be."

"Now, gentlemen, you know what you are to do. In two weeks, our plot will be set into motion. Let us toast to our success!"

"Hear, hear!" came from around the table as tankards were raised, and Parsons pulled back, stunned. The assassination, if such were to occur, would take place a fortnight hence and would be followed by revolution, unless they could learn more about this plot. *Who is the target?* he thought, willing Edgewater to speak. *Say who the target is!*

Edgewater said nothing, but only sat, watching the others, a little smile on his face as he toyed with his own tankard, a smile of satisfaction and something else. Derision. Aye, Parsons thought sourly, the marquess did consider himself above most men. Not the kind of man to defer to anyone, not even the mysterious leader of the conspiracy.

Now *that* was an interesting idea. Parsons pulled back as the men rose from the table, lest anyone glance toward the window and see him. If the marquess of Edgewater was taking orders from anyone, Parsons thought, he'd eat his hat!

The night was growing old, but still Alex sat by his fire, the glass of brandy beside him untouched. Until Parsons returned with news of his night's work, Alex would not go to bed. It was not, however, thoughts of the conspiracy that kept him awake, but instead the memory of a slender, softly rounded form pressed trustingly against him. A most interesting evening, he thought, stretching, and turned his head as the door opened.

"Got him, sir." Parsons looked tired but satisfied as he fell into a chair facing Alex.

"Edgewater, as we thought?" Alex said, but his voice sounded abstracted.

"Aye, sir. I followed him, like you said, and he

went to as pretty a den of villains as I've seen this age." Quickly he went on to outline what had happened, and the conclusions he had reached and Alex listened, with that same abstracted air.

"So you think Edgewater is the leader, do you?" he said, when Parsons had finished.

"Aye, sir, I'd say he has to be."

"I agree. But we need proof, Parsons." He fell silent. " 'Ask Cecily Randall.' "

"Sir?"

"Nothing. Any idea who the other members might be?"

"None yet, sir. I set some men to checking the local inns, and I followed the Cit home. We'll know soon enough."

"I hope so, Parsons. Two weeks." He stroked his upper lip. "Should give us enough time, if we can only get proof."

"We will, sir." Parsons frowned, troubled by Alex's lack of interest in the affair. "Sir? Is aught wrong?"

"Hm? Oh, nothing, Parsons, nothing." He smiled. "Except that I appear to have become engaged."

"Sir?"

"To Lady Cecily," he added.

"And high time, too!"

Chapter Eleven

"Cecily! Oh, my dear child!" The duchess bustled into Cecily's room, and Cecily glanced up from the window seat, a book opened, but unread, upon her lap.

"Whatever is it, Mama?"

"It is Marlow, my love. I've just been told he wants to see you." The duchess grasped Cecily's hands. "It must be about last night, child. Oh, why I ever let St. Clair accompany us home—"

"He was a perfect gentleman, Mama, and he was very kind to us." Cecily freed her hands and went over to her mirror. For once, she looked perfectly acceptable, with her hair neat and her morning gown of white muslin with a blue satin sash uncrumpled. She had chosen the gown because of its high neckline and long sleeves, to cover her bruises, which she had discovered with horror. She had been lucky to escape from Edgewater without any greater harm.

"But he is sure to be upset, child." The duchess, clad in her dressing gown, sank down upon the edge of Cecily's bed, a sure sign of her agitation. Few were allowed to see her *en dishabille*. "I do hope he does not punish you too severely."

Cecily bent to kiss her cheek. "Papa and I understand each other, Mama."

"How do you handle it?" The duchess's eyes were as

blue and as candid as a child's, and Cecily bit back a smile. The duke was ordinarily even-tempered, but even she had to admit that his rare rages could be spectacular. It was no wonder Mama and Diana sometimes went in fear of him. "He positively makes me quake when he is angry!"

"Don't worry, Mama. I shall survive, I am certain."

"I always said you should have been a boy, Cecily, the way you deal with these things."

"I know. Shocking, isn't it, Mama, that I am so lacking in sensibility?" She placed another quick kiss on her cheek. "Don't fret. I'd best not keep Papa waiting any longer."

"Oh, no, that would never do!" The duchess watched Cecily go. She knew allowing St. Clair to accompany them home last evening had been a mistake, she knew it!

In the hallway downstairs Cecily hesitated, and then knocked on the door of the duke's study. If her father truly were angry, then an uncomfortable interview lay ahead of her. The duke, however, seated at his desk going over estate papers, looked up and smiled at her when she came in. When she rose from her brief curtsy, he was there, lightly holding her arms. Cecily stood still under his scrutiny, until he nodded, a short, sharp nod of satisfaction. "You'll do," he said gesturing toward a chair and perching on the edge of his desk. "You're quite recovered from last night?"

"Yes, sir, my headache is gone," Cecily said.

"Headache? Oh, yes, the excuse you used to leave the Radcliffes'. And what of the bruises?" Cecily's hand flew to her shoulder. "I noticed them last evening, Cecily."

"Oh."

The duke eyed her keenly. "Edgewater?"

"How do you know?"

"St. Clair told me."

Cecily peeped up at him through her lashes.

139

"You're not angry, sir?"

"Not with you. No, not with St. Clair, either. I am, however, angry at myself for letting you become engaged to Edgewater without finding out more about the man."

"I didn't know him as well as I thought, either." She looked down at her hands. "He scares me, Papa."

"I can well imagine." The duke's tone was dry. "Do you wish to end the engagement?"

"Oh, yes!" Cecily's head came up, and then dropped again. "But, sir, the scandal—"

"Hang the scandal! I'll not have one of my children hurt. If you wish to break the engagement, then it is broken."

Cecily's eyes closed with relief. "Oh, thank you, Papa. I was beginning quite to dread marrying him."

"Why didn't you come to me sooner, then?" He paused. "Afraid I'd be angry?"

"No, not that. I'm not afraid of you, Papa." She smiled at him. "But, I was so confused. Everyone seemed to think the marquess was such a good catch, that I was certain he must be, too, and that I was wrong about him. Then when I met someone else . . ."

Her voice trailed off, and she looked away, her face pink. Marlow let the silence lengthen before speaking again. "Well, I won't ask what you were doing in the garden with him. It's just lucky for you that St. Clair was there."

"Yes," she whispered, looking at her hands again so that she didn't see the smile that fleeted across the duke's face.

"Your reputation won't suffer from this. St. Clair is an honorable man. He won't speak of last night."

Cecily looked up. "But sir, I thought that he was—"

"What?" he prompted.

"A rake."

"So what if he is?"

140

"But—"

"At least he has never ruined a young girl's reputation." He leaned forward. "What do you expect of him, Cecily? He is a man. But a good man, for all that. If I had to have someone on my side in a fight, I could do worse than him."

Cecily frowned. "Are you saying, Papa, that you wouldn't object if I saw him? At social events, and such, of course."

"I'd rather see you with him than with Edgewater. At least I know I can trust St. Clair with you."

Cecily dropped her eyes to her hands again. No, that wasn't strictly true—but he had had a chance to take advantage of her, and had foregone it. "I'm confused, Papa. I thought I knew my own mind and—"

"You have time, Cecily. Am I pressing you to marry now?"

"No, but you've said that you won't allow Diana to marry until I do."

"For Diana's own good," he said smiling. "Can you imagine whom she would choose, were she to marry now? I'd like her to gain some maturity before she makes that choice."

"Oh. I never thought of that. But, Papa."

"What?"

"How am I to tell—him?"

"I'll deal with Edgewater," the duke, said smiling grimly. "In fact, it will give me a great deal of pleasure to do so."

"St. Clair said much the same thing."

"He and I agree on many things. Now." He rose. "We won't bother your mother with this. All she needs to know is that you have decided that you and Edgewater won't suit."

"I'll likely be thought a jilt."

"I doubt it will hurt your reputation." He stopped by the door, holding her by the arms again. "I want to see you settled, Cecily, but there is no hurry. Take your time, enjoy the season. When you are ready, you'll know." He bent and placed a brief kiss on her forehead. "You know I want only what is best for you."

"Yes, Papa," she said, and impulsively threw her arms about his neck. He hesitated, as if in surprise, and then hugged her, making her feel safe, as he had when she was a child. But she was no longer a little girl, and it was not only in his arms now that she found safety. She had been right in thinking that one of the two men in her life was wrong for her; her mistake had been in thinking that Edgewater was the right one. "Thank you, Papa." She kissed his cheek and, after dropping another brief curtsy, left for her room. She had a deal of thinking to do. How, for example, was she to get a certain rake to pay attention to her?

Edgewater stomped down the stairs of Marlow House, his eyes almost black with rage as he approached his phaeton. "I shall walk," he said in clipped tones to his groom, and strode away, his walking stick swinging angrily from side to side. Never in his life had he met with such insult. To be told that he—he!—the marquess of Edgewater, was not good enough to marry the daughter of the duke of Marlow was an insult so grave that he felt he might never recover from it. What was worse was that it had been delivered in such a casual, offhand way, as if the duke considered himself to be superior to Edgewater.

The marquess' hand gripped the knob of his walking stick so hard that his knuckles turned white. Damn, he was inferior to no one, not even a duke! Was he not wealthy, handsome, popular? And had he not worked hard to make certain of all these things? He was *Edgewater*, for God's sake, one of the prize catches on the marriage mart! Who was Marlow, to say him nay? And why? All because the Marlow chit had turned missish.

Until now, everything had been going smoothly. Too smoothly, perhaps? While all his plans were in train and looked to have a fair chance of meeting with success, they now faced a new threat. By his marriage, Edgewater had hoped to consolidate his position, and to silence a potentially deadly witness against him. For, though she did not know it, Cecily was in possession of some dangerous information about him. In the unlikely event that things went wrong, a wife could not testify against her husband.

He had reached Park Lane and now walked along it, heading toward Piccadilly, though he was aware of neither his surroundings nor his direction. He would not fail. He hadn't gotten where he was by letting one setback stop him. There were other ways. And there was no reason to delay his plans. He would carry the day, with or without an aristocratic bride. And though it was his very superiority that would see him through, though he was confident of his success, he knew quite well that small details could pose a threat. Cecily was now one of those small details. Somehow, he would have to deal with her.

Edgewater smiled again, a cold smile, a deadly smile. Oh, yes. He would, indeed, deal with Lady Cecily Randall.

Very early the next morning, Alex sat mounted upon Azrael, at the head of Upper Grosvenor Street, looking down toward Grosvenor Square. He doubted that Cecily had ridden yesterday, but today, she likely would. What mattered was that she not ride alone. After the events of the other evening, she could very well be in danger.

Frowning, he bent forward to pat Azrael, who was restive. How much did Cecily know about what was going on? He was almost convinced that she was inno-

143

cent, almost convinced that Edgewater was the leader of the conspiracy, but—there was always that "but." Something about her had awakened Alf Barnes's suspicions. Until he knew what that was, he could not be easy in his mind about her.

He glanced up and saw a slender figure on a large gray horse ride down the street. His patience had been rewarded. Alex waited, fighting the urge to canter toward her. He studied her face as she neared, looking for signs that the events of the other evening still affected her, but instead seeing only a sweet serenity. Relief flooded him. She was all right. It was up to him to make sure she stayed that way.

Dancer nickered, and Cecily, lost in her thoughts, looked up to see a rider standing motionless at the top of the street, at Park Lane. For a moment fear flooded through her, but even as it did she recognized him. St. Clair. The fear was replaced by joy unexpected. "Good morning, sir," she called as she neared, and he at last walked Azrael over to her. "What do you here this morning?"

"Waiting for you." Alex waited until she was abreast of him, and then turned Azrael so that he could walk with her.

She tossed her head. "How very flattering, I'm sure."

Alex grinned. "Trying to imitate your sister? It's not working."

"I know." She flashed him a quick, rueful smile. "I don't know how she does it. She can look at a man, bat her eyelashes once or twice, and instantly he's her slave! When I try it, someone invariably asks if I have something in my eye. Of course," she added, "it doesn't hurt that she's beautiful."

"If you like the type."

"Tall, raven-haired, blue-eyed?"

"You sound like my cousin when he was infatuated with her," Alex said, sounding amused.

"But not you, sir?"

"No. Not me." Alex caught her gaze, and held it. "I find lately that my tastes are changing."

His eyes held such a peculiar expression that Cecily had to look away, her cheeks reddening. "Oh," she said, knowing how inadequate it sounded, but unable to think of anything else. He had looked at her almost as if he cared about her. "Why are you here?" she asked, making her voice brisk and setting Dancer to a faster gait, through the Grosvenor Gate into the park.

"To make sure you'd suffered no harm from the other evening." Alex's voice was equally brisk as he caught up with her. "And to make sure you stay that way."

Cecily sent him an inquiring glance. "Why shouldn't I?"

"Because I don't trust Edgewater."

"But I am not engaged to him anymore. Come on, Dancer, let's have a gallop," she said, and was off before Alex could protest.

"Hell," he muttered, and dug his heels in, catching up with her easily. By God, but she could ride, he thought, admiring her trim figure sitting erect in the saddle. He wondered how she managed on a side-saddle, and decided that he much preferred seeing her this way, in the breeches that set off her slender curves so well.

"Pax," he called across to her. "Do you think we might slow down?"

"Why?" she called back, not looking at him.

"So we could talk."

"Talk, sir?" The quick glance she sent him was so full of mischief that he found himself checking Azrael involuntarily.

"Minx," he muttered, bringing Azrael to a stop. "Very well, boy, we'll let her run her fidgets out. And then we'll see." He sat calmly, patting Azrael's neck and in a few moments his confidence in Cecily's curiosity was rewarded. The big gray gelding turned and

145

headed back toward him.

Cecily's golden eyes were questioning as she reached him again. Sometime during her gallop she had lost her cap, and her curls tumbled about her face in riotous disarray. With her cheeks flushed and her eyes bright, she looked as if someone had been making love to her. As if he had been making love to her. He pushed the thought away. "Decided to settle down now, have you?" he said mildly.

"You needn't talk to me as if I were a child," she said, riding past him.

"You needn't act like one." Alex turned to walk with her, and after a moment she glanced over at him.

"I am sorry, sir. I was confined to the house yesterday — my mother's idea — and I thought I would go mad! It feels wonderful to be out again. To be free," she added softly.

"You're glad the engagement is broken, then?"

Cecily glanced at him, surprised that he had guessed her meaning. "Yes. I daresay it's heartless of me" — she tossed her head again — "but I quite enjoy being a jilt." She gave him the same flirtatious smile she had seen Diana use, and was not at all chagrined to see him grinning at her. "In fact, I think I might set up as a jilt, and leave a trail of broken hearts behind me."

"Can't."

"Why not? After all, I had the nerve to dismiss someone so eligible as Edgewater."

"You're too tender-hearted. Before you know it, you'd be feeling so sorry for any man you jilted you'd likely become engaged to him again out of pity. And then you wouldn't be branded a jilt. Only fickle."

Cecily stopped, a frown creasing her brow, and Alex looked back at her inquiringly. "Do you think me fickle, sir?"

"No," he answered seriously, aware that she was no longer flirting or teasing. "I think you chose the wrong man and realized it in time." *Thank God.* "Why, in God's name, did you choose him in the first place?"

"I don't know." Cecily's brow knotted again. "I suppose I was flattered—he is very handsome, you know, and quite good *ton*. And he seemed to feel the same way I do, about helping the poor."

"Does he?" Alex asked, casually, letting Azrael stop and graze as Dancer was doing. That was interesting. It accorded with what he had learned of the man, that his politics tended toward the radical, though he tried to disguise such leanings.

"Yes. But, it's funny." Her frown deepened. "The more I came to know him, the less handsome he looked to me. And I don't think he really cares about the poor at all. I don't think he cares about anybody. He seems to look down on everybody. I don't think he likes himself very much."

"Indeed? I'd have said the opposite."

"No, because, you see, why else would he need to feel himself so above others? I knew someone like that once, the vicar's daughter in Marlow. She thought everyone was beneath her. Papa explained that the only way she could feel good about herself was to make other people look bad."

"I never thought of that," Alex said, after a moment. If that were true, it, too, accorded with his findings, a man seeking power to make himself feel important. It also could mean that Cecily was in even more danger than he'd thought. "He'll see the broken engagement as an insult, Cecily."

The sound of him using her name startled her enough, so that she didn't take in what he had said right away. "You were serious, then?" she said, startled. "You think he might try to get back at me?"

"I think it's possible. Which is why you shouldn't ride alone anymore."

"But I've always been perfectly safe!"

"Until now." His eyes, meeting hers, were serious.

"Remember the other night."

Cecily glanced away. "I've been trying not to," she whispered, and a silence fell between them.

"Trust me on this, Cecily," he said, after a few moments. "Riding alone isn't safe under normal circumstances. If you must ride, at least take a groom with you. Or let me know."

Cecily's eyes were as serious as his. "That sounds, sir, as if you are suggesting an assignation."

"I mean no insult, ma'am."

"Oh, no. I've just always wondered what it would be like to have an assignation with a rake."

Alex put back his head and laughed, and Cecily watched him with real pleasure. It struck her then that he had changed since she had first met him—had it only been a month ago? The world-weary air had dropped away, and with it some of the pain she had glimpsed in his eyes. The man he had been then wouldn't have laughed like this. He looked younger, freer, happier, and she wondered, with even more pleasure, if she'd had something to do with the change.

Alex's eyes were brimming with mirth. "I don't know what I'm going to do about you, Cecily, my girl—"

"I'm not your girl." *Am I?*

"—but I'm glad I met you."

"Are you?" Gone was all flirtatiousness; in its place was a soft appeal that Alex found altogether too inviting.

"Yes. Who else do I know who has a dancing horse?"

Cecily made a face. "Oh, so it's the novelty you like."

Partly it was, he admitted. Mostly, though, it was something else. "Don't ever change." All laughter was gone from him. "Don't let them change you into a bored society matron."

"I won't," she said, startled.

"You're very special," he said gruffly, and turned Azrael away. "Come. It's getting late. I'll see you home."

"All right." Cecily fell into step beside him, her mind whirling with the implications and the complications of this encounter. "I hope Papa doesn't find out, though."

"I've a feeling your father won't mind. Come." He gestured toward her, and they rode away together toward home.

Their voices had faded when a man stepped from behind a tree, leading a nervous bay gelding. So, Edgewater thought, mounting and riding away. His plans to take Lady Cecily by surprise during her early morning ride had gone awry. Which was probably just as well. When he had seen Cecily streak by him, head bent low over the head of her mount, he had realized that he could never catch her. He had never liked riding, and consequently he didn't ride well. It was one more thing he could hold against her, one more thing he would have to deal with, that a mere woman could be superior to him in anything. And deal with her, he would. He had to, else she would be too much of a danger to him.

Thoughtful, he rode on, ignoring the bone-jarring gait of his mount, chosen for appearance rather than his ride or his stamina. How he was going to get to her was another matter. Like most other young ladies, she rarely left her house unaccompanied, except for these rides. He'd learned about them some time ago, after bribing a footman. Much good it had done him, though, now that St. Clair had appeared by Cecily's side.

Edgewater's face hardened, and he grasped the reins tighter, so that his mount shied. There was his real nemesis. If not for St. Clair, Cecily would not have left the ball the other evening, and they would still be engaged. Someday, Edgewater vowed, St. Clair would pay for that. There was something else about the man, too, something Edgewater couldn't identify, but which troubled him. He appeared in too many places at opportune times, the Radcliffes' garden the other evening, for example, or the park this morning. It couldn't be because of Lady Cecily's charms, he thought, sneering a bit; those were nonexistent. No, St. Clair was up to something else, and he would have to find out just what. Nothing was going to stop him now.

Chapter Twelve

"The Duchess of Marlow. Lady Cecily Randall, Lady Diana Randall," the footman intoned, and the people gathered in the drawing room looked around. The news that Lady Cecily's engagement to the Marquess of Edgewater had been broken had been announced only that morning, and the room was abuzz with speculation. Cecily was well liked, but nearly everyone agreed on one thing. It had been Edgewater's idea to end the engagement, even if a man could not in honor cry off. Highly placed in society though Cecily was, she was no beauty, while everyone agreed that Edgewater was a catch. What made peoples' tongues wag even more was that Edgewater was present tonight.

"My dears." Smiling broadly, the Countess of Chatleigh crossed the room, her hands outstretched. "Your Grace. How very good of you to come."

"Thank you, Lady Chatleigh," the Duchess said graciously. "Such a crowd as you have here tonight! It is a sad crush."

"Yes, quite sad," the countess said, her face straight. "Chatleigh and I planned to hold only a small do, to announce that we'd returned to town, but I'm afraid that once Aunt Helmsley heard of it things — well, changed." She shrugged, but a smile played about her lips.

"Dear Lady Helmsley. I must have a word with her. Is she here?"

"Yes, Your Grace, on the sofa over there. Cecily, you look lovely! And Lady Diana, your gown is beautiful."

"Thank you, Melissa." Cecily briefly pressed her cheek against Melissa's. Though married, and with an infant daughter, Lady Chatleigh was only a year older than Cecily. The two had become fast friends last year, during Cecily's first season. "It's so good to see you again! I have so much to tell you."

"I can imagine." Melissa took Cecily's arm and strolled with her into the room, alive with conversation and movement and color. "My dear, I must warn you that Edgewater is here."

"Here? Tonight?" Cecily stopped short, unable to hide her dismay, though she was aware of people watching her.

"Here? Where?" Diana demanded.

"I fear so. We had invited him before all this happened, else we wouldn't have. I am sorry."

"Well, I'm not. I don't understand it at all, Lady Chatleigh, do you?" Diana's eyes were very blue and very guileless. "I mean, he's so handsome!"

"I explained it to you, Diana," Cecily murmured. "We decided we didn't suit."

"Well, he didn't look as if he thought so yesterday, after leaving Papa."

Cecily's smile was strained. "People are watching us, Di."

"And it's none of their concern, of course, though I fear you'll be asked a lot of questions tonight," Melissa said. "Lady Helmsley wishes to speak with you."

"Oh, no."

"Don't worry." Melissa smiled. "I believe she wishes to congratulate you."

Cecily glanced at her sidewise. "You never did like Edgewater, did you?"

"Not very much, no."

"Why not?"

Melissa shook her head. "It's past history. But I'd

watch out for him, Cecily. He can be vindictive."

"I'll be careful, I promise." She had no desire for a confrontation with Edgewater, not here, not anywhere.

"Oh, but there is someone here I think you should meet," the countess chattered, leading Cecily into the room. Cecily glanced down at her, radiant in emerald-green satin that brought out the fire in her coppery curls. Lady Chatleigh was not only beautiful, but a kind and generous person. And happily married. Cecily envied her that. "He's a school friend of Chatleigh's and he's been on the Continent the past few years. He stayed at the Hall with us last year and I found him quite charming. And," she added thoughtfully, "more lonely than he cares to admit."

Cecily smiled. "Melissa, please! I've just broken my engagement. Surely you're not matchmaking already."

"Of course not, I wouldn't dream of such a thing. But I do think you'll like each other. Stay right there and I'll find him." She threaded her way through the crowd, leaving Cecily to stare after her, bemused.

"I don't understand it, Cece," Diana hissed in her ear. "Why did you break your engagement?"

"I didn't love him, Di."

"I know you didn't, but you said—"

"I know. I said we'd suit. I was wrong. Isn't it better for us to find out now?"

"But he's so handsome and charming—"

"If you feel that way, why don't you marry him?"

"Really, Cece." Diana pouted. "There's no need for you to snap at me so."

"That woman terrifies me," the Duchess said, returning to them and plying her fan vigorously. "She always asks me questions I can't answer and then smiles! So warm in here, don't you think? She's a dragon, but she has such power, it doesn't do to ignore her. Where is Lady Chatleigh?"

"Gone to find someone she wants me to meet," Cecily said.

153

"Edgewater is here, Mama," Diana put in.

"Yes, so I've been told. I do hope you won't cause a scene, Cecily."

"I—!" Cecily began, and then broke off, her eyes widening a bit at the sight of the man on Lady Chatleigh's arm, coming toward them.

"Oh, gracious, she isn't really going to present him to you, is she?" the duchess exclaimed.

"Mama, remember what Papa said."

"Yes, I know Marlow said we must receive him after the other night, but really, Cecily, this is the outside of enough! St. Clair." The duchess held out two fingers, her smile polite. "How very nice to see you again."

"Your Grace." Alex bowed over her hand, only the look in his eyes telling Cecily what he really thought of this meeting. "A pleasure to see you again, ma'am. May I say how very well you look tonight?" he said, with his most charming smile.

"Why, thank you, sir." Flustered, the duchess put her hand to her hair, as if to check that her feathered headdress was straight, and Cecily, her eyes briefly meeting Alex's, bit back a smile.

"I see you do know each other already," Melissa said brightly. "I'll just leave you then, shall I? I fear I must see to the refreshments."

Her going left an awkward silence. Alex sent an inquiring glance toward Cecily, who simply smiled. She wasn't about to tell him what she suspected the countess of. Matchmaking, indeed! Her eyes were thoughtful, though, as she looked at him, so handsome in black evening coat and pantaloons it made her heart ache. He could have any woman he desired. Why would he be interested in her?

"I see someone I must speak to," the duchess said, her voice, for her, unusually firm. "If you will excuse us, sir—"

"Let me escort you, ma'am. Three such beautiful ladies should not be left alone."

"Gracious!" The duchess stared at him. "Thank you, that is very kind of you." Placing her fingers on his arm, she let him bring her over to some acquaintances, her daughters following. Cecily had to bite back another smile, at the look on her mother's face. Even she, apparently, was not immune to St. Clair's charm.

It was some time before Cecily was able to have a word with Alex, and during that time, her amusement grew as she watched him with others. He had apparently been accepted, scandalous reputation or no, and to see him talking with bejeweled dowagers or painfully shy debutantes was enlightening. He knew quite well how to handle women; he was the epitome of the man about town, and yet every now and then he glanced at her, his expression wry, as if he realized quite well what was happening and was as amused by it as she.

"You have become quite respectable, sir," Cecily said, sipping the punch that he brought her, sometime later. "I heard even Lady Helmsley spoke well of you."

" 'And with every word, a reputation dies,' " he quoted, making her laugh. "You look well tonight, Cecily. I didn't have the chance to tell you before."

"Thank you, sir." Cecily's tone was light, but she was pleased; her gown of rose satin with its blond lace overdress was new, and somewhat more sophisticated than she usually wore. In it she felt adult and very attractive. "The countess is quite beautiful, is she not?"

"Indeed. And very married, as well."

"So she is not one of your flirts?"

"My flirts? But, madam, as you just pointed out, I've become respectable." His eyes twinkled. "Even the Duchess of Marlow speaks to me now."

"Yes, Papa told her to," she murmured, taking a sip of her punch. "I suspect people are talking about us, sir."

"Let them." He scanned the milling crowd. "Edgewater is here. Have you seen him?"

"No, thank heavens. I suppose I shall have to face him someday, but I'd rather it not be here. There's been enough talk."

"Better before a group of people than alone."

Cecily shot him a glance. He really did believe Edgewater might try to hurt her, though the more she thought about it, the less she credited it. Certainly he had scared her the other evening, but he was a gentleman, was he not? And he seemed too languid, too civilized, to attempt anything so savage as revenge. "I'll be glad to put it all behind me."

"Indeed." Alex nodded absently. He wished it were all behind them, too, wished that the plot were known, the conspirators arrested, so that he could be free. Free to do what? At the moment, he wasn't certain he knew.

Other acquaintances came up, speaking to him and drawing him away, so that he lost sight of Cecily. Anxiety clawed at him and he pushed it away. She would be safe enough in this mob. He could relax his vigilance.

"There he is," Diana said suddenly, and Cecily, seated beside her on a satin-striped sofa and talking to Anthony Carstairs, looked up. Across the room, through the crowd, she saw the man she least wished to see. Edgewater.

She froze. His eyes were fastened on her, and the look in them chilled her. They were cold, implacable, inimical. Alex's words of warning came back to her, and she thanked God there were enough people about to protect her.

"Don't you see him?" Diana said impatiently.

"Yes. I see him."

"He is so handsome."

"Something of a peacock, wouldn't you say?" Mr. Carstairs said. Lately he'd taken to emulating Alex as his ideal.

"Oh, no." Diana sighed. "He is a man. Oh, look, he's coming our way!"

"Oh, no." Cecily began to rise, and her sister's hand clamped on her arm.

"You can't go," she hissed. "It will cause a scene, and

156

you know what Mama said!"

Where was her mother? Cecily glanced around frantically as Edgewater continued to bear down on her. And where, oh, where, was St. Clair?

"Good evening, Lady Cecily. Lady Diana, Carstairs." Edgewater's voice was smooth and urbane.

Cecily forced herself to look up. "Good evening, sir." Not by any gesture would she show how much he frightened her.

"You are looking as lovely as usual, Lady Diana. And, Lady Cecily. Your hair is coming down. Also as usual."

Cecily's hand flew to her hair, and she forced it down. "How ungallant of you, sir."

"Is it? But then, you must know I have only your good in mind. Though I wonder now why I bothered to propose to you, when your sister is so much more attractive."

"You are insulting, sir!" she exclaimed, rising, not caring who noticed. He had touched on a sore spot, and though she cared naught for him, it hurt. "I will not stay here and listen—"

"Ah, but you wouldn't wish to cause a scene, would you, my dear?" His voice was silken, but his hand caught her arm in an iron grip. "People are staring at us now."

"Unhand me, sir."

"Why, Cecily, so unkind? We've some things to discuss. Carstairs," he drawled, "you will entertain Lady Diana, will you not, while Lady Cecily and I take a turn about the room."

"I'd be delighted to," Mr. Carstairs said.

"I shouldn't leave my sister alone, sir," Cecily said, making one last attempt to save herself.

"But I'm quite all right, Cece. Do go." Diana's eyes sparkled. "And perhaps you'll have news for us?"

"Perhaps she will," Edgewater said. "Come, ma'am. Let us walk."

157

Cecily cast one more despairing glance around the room, and then gave in. His grip on her arm was too strong for her to break free without a struggle. He wouldn't hurt her, though. How could he, with so many people around?

Leisurely Edgewater pulled her through the crowd, smiling and greeting the people who glanced at them. Later Cecily thought she must have smiled, too, for no one seemed to notice anything amiss. Forevermore, this scene would live in her nightmares: so many people and none coming to her aid.

"Smile, Cecily," he said, ice under his urbanity as they reached a window embrasure, affording them the illusion of privacy. "You look frightened."

"Not at all, sir." Cecily put up her chin, and he chuckled, an ugly sound.

"Ah, that's it, Cecily. Fight me. I like that. Because we'll soon see, won't we, who is the better of us?"

"I don't know what you're talking about."

His urbane mask slipped, revealing a face contorted and ugly with anger. "Don't pretend you don't know! Think you're too good for me, don't you? Well, you'll learn, my pretty — my not-so-pretty." He chuckled again. "You don't like that, do you? But you're no beauty, Cecily —"

"I know that."

"— and you really should be grateful to me. Yes, you should," he went on, at her look of astonishment, "because I took you up when no one else would. You owe me, Cecily."

"Owe you! You must be mad!"

"Oh, must I? Perhaps. I don't take such insults lightly, my dear. Breaking our engagement because you believe you're too good for me —"

"But that's not why —"

"Don't talk nonsense. I know what it is. You're the daughter of the Duke of Marlow, and you think you're too good for me. Everyone thinks they're too good for

158

me! Well, they'll soon find out," he gloated. "Oh, yes. Soon."

Cecily smiled for the benefit of those watching. "I am going to return to my sister, sir and you will let me," she said, as much steel in her voice as in his. She wouldn't allow this man to dictate to her. "And we will not cause a scene."

"Good evening again, Lady Cecily. And Edgewater." Edgewater's head jerked up, and his eyes met Alex's. "Lady Cecily, I believe your mother is looking for you."

Edgewater loosened his grip on Cecily's arm, but he didn't release her. "St. Clair," he drawled. "You are interrupting us, you know."

"Really, Edgewater." Alex sounded equally bored, but his eyes were alert. "This is getting to be quite tiresome. Must you continue to bother Lady Cecily?"

"I fail to see that it's any of your concern."

"I'm making it my concern," Alex said, his voice cutting sharply across the other man's.

"I'll not have your interference in my affairs, damn you!"

"You have no choice. I won't allow you."

Edgewater's eyelid twitched. "You dare threaten me?"

"I dare do more if you accost Lady Cecily again."

"Really, dear boy." Edgewater crossed his arms on his chest and grinned at the people who were covertly watching. "She's not worth it, you know. Fickle, that's what she is. Wants to have both of us."

"That's not true!" Cecily said.

"Of course it's not," Alex agreed, but his eyes flickered. Seeing it, Edgewater chuckled.

"You sound as if you don't quite believe her, dear boy. But then, one never knows whom to trust, haven't you found?"

"I am warning you, sir." Alex's voice was quiet and deadly, and if he'd taken a hit, he didn't show it. "Leave Lady Cecily in peace, or you will have me to deal with."

Edgewater's eyes were hard. "Very well, go. But this

159

isn't the end of it, St. Clair."

"On that we both agree," Alex said. "Come, ma'am. Your mother is this way."

Cecily grasped his arm and took a deep breath. Now that she was safe, she was almost giddy with relief. "Thank you," she said. "I didn't know how I was going to get away from him. It seems you always need to rescue me."

"I wouldn't if you wouldn't persist in going with him."

Cecily stopped short. "Surely you don't think that was my choice!"

Alex turned. "Oh, of course. In a room crowded with people, you let him drag you about. What else am I to think, but that you wished to be with him?"

"Ooh!" Absurd, angry tears filled her eyes, and she dashed them away, not caring who saw. "You are as hateful as he—"

"Cecily." His hand caught her arm, his touch infinitely more gentle than Edgewater's had been. "Forgive me. Of course it wasn't your choice."

"No, it certainly wasn't," she said tartly. "I couldn't break free and Mama said"—her mouth quirked—"not to cause a scene. Which I imagine I've done."

Alex glanced around and several people quickly averted their eyes. "I'm afraid so. But let's not make matters worse. Come." He took her arm. "What did he want?"

"You were right; he was very angry about the engagement being broken. I should have realized." She frowned. "I wouldn't have thought he had such a *tendre* for me."

"He doesn't."

"Excuse me? How do you know?"

"Hm? Oh, sorry." He gave her his thoroughly charming, disarming smile. "I don't think he cares for anyone but himself."

"No. 'Self-love is the greatest of all flatterers.' " Cecily looked down, absurdly aware that her curls were

mussed, as Edgewater had said and that, somehow, she'd gotten a spot near the hem of her gown. Why could she not ever look bandbox perfect, as her sister did? "But, sir" — she frowned — "what does he want with me?"

Alex's smile was abstracted. " 'Ask Cecily Randall,' " he murmured.

"Excuse me? Ask me what?"

Now that was the question, wasn't it? "Why, to have supper with me, of course. Now that I am a reformed rake."

"Thoroughly reformed?"

"Alas, I fear so," he said, giving her that charming smile again, so that she shook her head.

"I doubt that, sir. Very well." She tucked her arm through his. "Let us go." And let the gossips think what they might, she thought, with just a touch of defiance.

"What think you of reformed rakes, Cecily?" Alex asked, and she turned to face him. In contrast to his light tone of a moment before, his face was serious.

"I think he deserves some kind of reward, sir."

"Do you."

"Of course, virtue is said to be its own reward."

"Vice has its rewards, as well."

"Now, sir, you no longer sound quite so reformed."

"No, I don't, do I?" His gaze softened as he looked down at her. "Do I get to choose my reward, then?"

Cecily's heart speeded up. "If you like."

"Indeed. Then, I choose—"

"Why, here you are." Melissa took Cecily's other arm, smiling brightly, and they looked at her, startled. "Absurd to think anyone could be missed in such a crush, but your mother is looking for you, Cecily."

"Oh! Then, I'd best go to her," Cecily said.

"And I shall be taking my leave." Alex bent over Melissa's hand. "A most interesting evening, Countess. You'll make my farewells to Chatleigh for me, of course."

"Of course." Melissa smiled at him as he sketched a

bow, and then turned away. "A charming man," she said lightly, taking Cecily's arm, "and a lonely one, I think."

"Lonely? But he's had his choice of women—"

"I know." Melissa smiled at her guests, who were eyeing them interestedly, scenting something out of the ordinary. "Smile, my dear, they know something's been happening. Yes, lonely. He had rather a difficult time during the wars."

Cecily stopped. "But I thought he wasn't in the war."

"He didn't tell you? Oh, dear." Melissa frowned. "Well, I must leave that to him. You see, he needs someone special. Someone who will care for him, someone he can trust."

"Why tell me?" Cecily asked, and Melissa gave her such a speaking look that she felt herself color.

"Very well, have it your own way," Melissa said, smiling. "But I hope to dance at your wedding someday soon. Do come along now, there's your mother."

"Of course," Cecily murmured, her mind far away, barely listening to Melissa's chatter. What, she wondered, would St. Clair have chosen as his reward?

Edgewater lounged down St. James's, thoughtfully swinging his walking stick from side to side. Last night's events at the Chatleighs' had angered him, but now he had himself under control. His sudden attacks of rage, which lately came more often, bothered him, but not very much. After all, he had every right to be angry with Cecily, even more right to be angry with St. Clair for daring to interfere. He would have to keep watch on that anger, however, until his task was accomplished. Not much time left now, and every second was important. Too important for him to jeopardize with an ill-timed burst of rage, and for reasons that were mostly personal. Cecily, he had decided, was not so much of a threat as he had thought, and though he had wanted the *cachet* of marrying her, there were other ways of achieving it. No,

Cecily he could dismiss from his thoughts. St. Clair, however, was another matter.

Still swinging his walking stick, he walked sedately up the stairs of Brooks's. Handing his stick and hat to the porter, he lounged his way into the reading room, stopping for a moment to glance around through his quizzing glass. Not for him Whites', that bastion of Toryism and conservatism; he preferred more spirited company. And, though many of the members here were in opposition to the current government, he expected to find someone who could tell him what he needed to know. Where, for example, St. Clair had spent the years of the war.

Some hours later, after engaging in a hand or two of piquet, and after taking part in several spirited discussions about the offenses of the government, the marquess strolled out again. With his curly-brimmed beaver on his head, his white thorn stick in hand, he was the very picture of the man of leisure. His brow was serene and untroubled but his brain was working feverishly. St. Clair? several of the people he had spoken to had said. He'd been abroad during the war, everyone knew that. Doing what? Well, that, no one knew and who cared about the activities of such an obvious loose screw? It wasn't until near the end of his visit that Edgewater received a nugget of information. St. Clair? said Lord Hartford, dealing a hand of piquet. Hadn't Wellington mentioned him once? The mention of Wellington's name brought a turn in the conversation; there were still those in this highly Whig establishment who didn't support the hero of Waterloo. It also made Edgewater go very, very still. "Why," he had asked carefully, when the hubbub had died down, "would Wellington have mentioned St. Clair?"

Hartford shrugged. "Heard he said something about him in one of his dispatches," he said, discarding a card. "Something about the war couldn't have been won without the work of men like him. Now, shall we play?"

163

"Of course," Edgewater said after a moment, looking at his cards without seeing them. A spy. St. Clair had been a spy. That was the only explanation for Wellington's message. What was he now if he'd been a spy then?

Edgewater played the hand badly, and lost badly. He was cheerful as he settled up, tossing some notes on the table and rising to take his leave, but his smile faded as he left the room. St. Clair was a spy. That could very well mean that his plot, his very future, was in danger.

Now, walking again down St. James's, he considered what to do. He knew how to deal with spies; had he not dealt with the Cockney who had infiltrated the conspiracy? St. Clair was different, however. He was a peer of the realm. Moreover, he seemed somehow to be connected to Marlow —

Edgewater stopped. Of course. That was it. Cecily had told. The little jade had told what she knew, damn her, and if she didn't realize its significance, St. Clair probably did.

The rage rose within him, and he fought to master it. Now was no time to lose his head. "Damn," he muttered, and walked on again. St. Clair was more of a danger than he'd realized. Once a spy, always a spy, and now his target was Edgewater.

But he wouldn't win, Edgewater thought, with a chilling smile. Oh, no. St. Clair had met his match. He'd deal with him, Edgewater vowed, and soon, and then he would have all the power and position that he craved, that he deserved. And St. Clair, he thought with growing satisfaction, would be dead.

Chapter Thirteen

Parsons stifled another yawn and pulled out the big turnip watch, gazing muzzily at it. Only two hours he'd been here, watching Marlow House, and he wasn't certain this was necessary anymore. For some reason, Lord St. Clair still hadn't absolved Lady Cecily of any role in the conspiracy, and yet Parsons himself would stake his life on her innocence. If, that is, he were still a betting man. Gambling was no longer for him, he thought piously, suppressing a wistful pang. A man set his sights on higher things, found something he could trust. If only Lord St. Clair could learn to trust something, anything, again, he'd be a happier man.

Parsons would be happy when they had all the conspirators rounded up and in gaol. Time was getting short, and they knew neither the target of the assassination nor the location. If Parsons had his way, he'd have arrested that there Edgewater long since, but Lord St. Clair had his own methods. Parsons only hoped they wouldn't come to grief this time.

He yawned again, so widely that he nearly missed the first sign of movement from across the street. Then his gaze sharpened. Jem had slipped out from the mews and was hurrying to the corner, in what Parsons could only consider a havey-cavey manner. Something was up.

In a moment, Jem came back, and reemerged from

the mews with Lady Cecily at his side, dressed in a dark gown. Parsons set off after them at a run, catching up with them just as they reached the hackney stopped around the corner. "Lady Cecily," he called and Cecily, about to climb into the hackney, turned, her face startled.

"Parsons," she said stepping down. "What do you here?"

"You going to the orphanage, my lady?"

Cecily glanced around, but there was no one to see her. "Yes, as it happens, I managed to get away today even though it's not my usual day. I must go, Parsons."

"Lord St. Clair should know, my lady," he said urgently.

"Should he, indeed?" Cecily gazed at him. Was St. Clair, by some chance, having her watched? Ridiculous thought. "I don't really see why, Parsons." Though she wouldn't mind seeing him again, the thought of his ordering her life rankled.

"He'd want to know." Parsons' face softened. "He worries about you, my lady. If he finds out I let you go without telling him, he'll have my head."

"Gracious!" Cecily smiled; the only thing Parsons had said that had any meaning was that St. Clair worried about her. That had to mean he cared, didn't it? "Very well, Parsons. Climb in and we'll go tell him what we're doing."

"Thank you, my lady." Parsons returned her smile, feeling in perfect charity with her. A man needed to trust something. Just might be that Lady Cecily was the one to teach Lord St. Clair that.

A little while later, in front of his lodgings, Alex climbed into the hackney, gazing quizzically at Cecily. "Off on another adventure, Lady Cecily?"

"I hope not. At least, not as adventurous as last time," Cecily answered.

"Let us hope not. I don't think I could take it." He clamped his heart dramatically to his chest, his eyes glinting. "My heart, you know."

"I wasn't aware rakes had hearts."

Alex's eyes gleamed brighter. "It's a well-kept secret. However, there are exceptions."

Beside him, Parsons coughed. Both Alex and Cecily looked at him in some surprise; for a moment they had forgotten they weren't alone. Then, as if by common consent, each turned away to gaze out the window for the remainder of the ride.

"My lady, since you have Lord St. Clair with you, I'll stay with the hackney this time," Jem said, when they stopped in front of the orphanage.

"A very good idea," Alex approved, stepping out and then holding out his hand to Cecily to assist her. "Always make certain you have an escape route."

Cecily glanced at him; though he'd spoken absently, the words weren't merely idle speech. Once again, she wondered just what his life had been like to make him so cynical. "You needn't come in with me, sir. I'm certain I'll be safe enough."

"I'm not letting you out of my sight. Not with characters like that around."

"Characters like—oh!" Cecily glanced at the roughly dressed man who was coming down the stairs toward them. "It's Mr. Driver."

"Lady Cecily." Joe Driver stopped on the stair just above them, effectively blocking their way. Alex's hand involuntarily went to his pocket, where his pistol was. "Glad to see you suffered no harm."

"Thanks, mostly, I understand, to you." Alex eased his hand away from his pistol as Driver's eyes, hard and suspicious, swung toward him. "I believe I owe you an apology," he went on, holding out his hand and Driver's eyes flickered in surprise. "I misunderstood the situation last time. I'm sure you can understand I was concerned for Lady Cecily."

Driver's eyes flickered again, and he glanced uncertainly from Cecily to Alex. "That I can," he said, at last holding out his own hand. "Wouldn't want no harm to come to her."

"Neither would I, Mr. Driver." Alex was aware that he was being measured by as shrewd a pair of eyes as he'd ever encountered. A force to be reckoned with, was Joe Driver. Alex was devoutly grateful he was on their side. "Thank you for watching out for her."

"Yes, Mr. Driver, it was very brave," Cecily said.

Driver looked, if anything, uncomfortable at this un-looked-for praise, and twisted his cap in his hands. "Anything I can do for yer while yer here, m'lady, yer just tell Matron, and she'll see I hear."

"Thank you, Mr. Driver, that's most generous of you."

"And I'm glad to see yer not alone this time," he went on, glancing toward Alex and nodding. "He'll watch out for yer."

"I will." Alex nodded gravely. "An honor, indeed," he murmured to Cecily as they continued into the orphanage. "To have Mr. Driver as our ally."

"Don't tease," Cecily said. The dark dankness of the orphanage reached out to surround them, and Alex resisted the urge to drag Cecily away. "He means well. This time, at least. He really does care about his daughter, you know."

"Peace, little one." He laid his hand briefly on her shoulder, moving it away as her startled glance met his. "I believe you. I don't think the finer feelings are confined only to people with means." His gaze softened. "You see, Cecily, I really do have a heart."

"I never doubted it, sir," she whispered, returning his look. At that moment, Matron bustled into the hall to greet them. Cecily turned away, her polite smile masking her frustration. Every time she and St. Clair had a chance to talk, every time the atmosphere between them turned magical, they were interrupted. It was most annoying.

Alex greeted Matron politely and refused her offer to wait in her parlor while Cecily sat with the children. In-

168

stead, he went around the orphanage with them. His face was, as usual, expressionless, but Cecily was coming to know him well enough to guess that he was as dismayed and horrified as she had been when first she had come here. The rows of cots with threadbare blankets, the dankness from the unhealthy location, the pinched faces of the children, all reached out to her as they always did. Someday, perhaps, she could do more, promising them all a better life, but not now.

"Thank God," Alex said, when they at last walked out, taking a breath of the sooty air that seemed fresh and clean to him after being inside. "Are all the orphanages like that?"

"No, this is one of the better ones," Cecily said.

"Better! God's teeth, the conditions those children live in!"

"But they're clean and Matron doesn't allow her staff any alcohol."

"God's teeth," Alex said again, helping her into the hackney. All he wanted now was to get her out of this unhealthy place; all he desired was to keep her away, to protect her from any harm. At least there wouldn't be a repetition of the trouble they'd faced last time, he thought, raising a hand in salute to Joe Driver, who stood across the street. "I've a mind to tell your father about this."

Cecily stared at him as the hackney started off. "You promised you wouldn't!"

"That was before I knew what that place was like."

"That is why I'd like to see schools built, sir, and new orphanages."

"God's teeth, just breathing the air would make you ill. It's no place for a lady."

"But it is for a gentleman?"

"Excuse me?"

"You've never told me, sir, what you were doing here the last time."

"Indeed." Alex's gaze was expressionless. "And I don't

intend to tell you."

"I see. Tis all very well for you to come here, and Lord Edgewater, but not me—"

"Edgewater?" Alex and Parsons spoke together.

"Yes." Cecily looked from one to the other. "I saw him here one day, too."

"Indeed?" Alex drawled. "And what did he tell you he was doing here? If you were so impertinent as to ask."

Cecily frowned. "He denied it, if you must know. I must say, it did seem strange," she said, her pique dissolving, "but it did look like him. He was dressed in dark clothes and he was coming out of a building across from the orphanage."

Alex craned his head to see. They were passing a low, crooked building, its sign barely legible. The Star and Garter. A tavern. "Was he, indeed," he murmured, disguising his mounting excitement.

"My lord," Parsons said. "While you were inside I did some looking around. Wasn't far from here they found Barnes."

"Indeed." Alex exchanged a long look with Parsons. This was it, then, the link they had been searching for. How, though, did Barnes figure in this? "Did you not think it strange, seeing him there?"

"Of course I did. I said so at the time, didn't I, Jem?"

Jem, who had been sitting quietly, stirred. "Yes, my lady. Glad I was to get you out of there that day, too."

"Oh, for heaven's sake, must we bring that up again?"

"I didn't like it when that man spoke to you, my lady," Jem said stubbornly. "I still don't like it. My lord." He looked at Alex. "Maybe you can make Lady Cecily see how unsuitable this is."

"I'm not sure anyone can, Jem. Except perhaps the Duke."

"It would mean my position, sir, and someone has to make sure she's safe. She'll talk to anyone."

"You needn't discuss me as if I weren't present," Cecily put in.

170

"Indeed," Alex said sounding bored, to cover his intense impatience. There was more to this; he knew there was. "Who was this man you speak of?"

"I don't know," Cecily said. "Does it matter?"

"Perhaps not. Satisfy my curiosity, Cecily."

Cecily looked at him at that, hearing a note of urgency in his voice. What was this? "Oh, very well. I don't know who it was. It was after I'd seen Edgewater, and I was about to leave when a man approached me and asked me if I knew Edgewater. That was why the incident was so strange, you see."

"Indeed. And you didn't know this man?"

"No, I never saw him again."

"What did he look like?"

"Do you know, you are as bad as my father, in your own way? He was short, with gray hair, with the brightest blue eyes I've ever seen—"

"Barnes," Parsons said, and Alex made a quick gesture for silence.

"Barnes?" Cecily looked from Parsons to Alex. "I don't understand any of this," she complained.

"It is of no moment," Alex said. Barnes! She'd seen Alf Barnes that day, and at last he had the answer to the question that had been plaguing him. "Ask Cecily Randall." Ask her whom she'd seen in Whitechapel, and where. That was all. Cecily was innocent. The thought made him lighthearted with joy. "Someone Parsons knew in his misguided past."

"My lord," Parsons said reprovingly, and Cecily looked again from him to Alex. Something was happening here, something she didn't understand. "I see," she said finally, sitting back and pretending to look out the window. Foolish to feel hurt about this. St. Clair was surely entitled to his own secrets, his own life. But of what, she wondered with sudden unease, did that life consist? For the first time, she realized just how little she knew about this man.

The rest of the ride was accomplished in silence. The

171

hackney stopped on South Audley Street, and after extracting a promise from Cecily that she would notify him when next she went to the orphanage, Alex watched her walk away. When she reached the safety of Marlow House, he thumped on the roof of the hackney, which started off.

"Barnes, sir," Parsons said. "It had to be."

"I agree. You realize what this means, Parsons?"

"Yes, sir. Edgewater has to be the leader."

"Of course he is." Alex's voice was impatient. "Though I wish we had more proof of that. To accuse a peer of the realm without it is foolhardy. No, Parsons, I meant about Lady Cecily. She's innocent."

"Of course she is," Parsons returned in the same impatient tone. "Didn't you know that?"

"No. Hoped it, believed it, but knew it? No. Not until now." He stroked his upper lip. "She is exactly what she seems. How unusual."

"She could be in danger, sir."

"From Edgewater? God's teeth!" Alex stared at him. "That's why he wanted to marry her! A wife cannot testify against her husband."

"Damn!" Parsons exclaimed, which earned him a look from Alex. "I'll continue to keep watch on her, sir, shall I?"

"Yes. And I suppose I shall have to continue attending routs and the like. What I do for my country."

"Yes, sir. At least until we capture Edgewater."

"Oh, at least. And perhaps even after." For the first time that afternoon, Alex smiled. They'd done it, by God! They had the leader of the conspiracy. "And we'll get him, Parsons," he said, grimly confident. "We'll get him."

Edgewater stood in a window embrasure at the Duke of Dartmouth's, watching the dancers, at this most select gathering of the *ton*. So select, in fact, that people

172

were able to move about without actually tripping over each other. For all his appearance of being a man about town, Edgewater had found that moments like this, simply watching, were often the most useful. It was when people were unaware they were being observed that one could often learn much about them.

Lord St. Clair, for example. Since learning of St. Clair's prior occupation, Edgewater had set himself to find out more about the man. It wasn't easy; even before his departure for the Continent, St. Clair had apparently kept to himself. However, Edgewater's position in Parliament, as well as his more secret activities in business, led him to sources that otherwise would not be available to him. From them he had gleaned bits and pieces of information and had carefully set them together as one would a mosaic, to gain a picture of the man he was increasingly coming to believe was his most dangerous opponent. Why else would St. Clair always have been on the spot when Edgewater was about to execute some part of his plan? No, he was being watched, he concluded; he'd made a mistake somewhere. That was of no moment, however. He had other resources, other strengths, and he had no doubt that he would win through, St. Clair or no. Especially now that he knew the man's weaknesses.

The whirling dancers parted in a swirl of color. For a moment he could see his opponent waltzing with Lady Cecily and smiling down at her as if she were quite the most beautiful woman in the world. Edgewater's mouth twisted into a sneer. The fool. There, though he probably was not aware of it, was his prime weakness, his ridiculous attachment to that plain, dowdy girl. Edgewater wasn't quite certain how to exploit that weakness yet, but in combination with another flaw he suspected St. Clair might possess, it could be deadly. For Edgewater had thought long and hard on the attributes a spy would need to be successful, and it had occurred to him that the most important one would be a distrust of everyone. A strength in a spy, but a weakness in a man, especially one who appeared to be as enamored as St. Clair. Reformed rakes always did fall the hardest. It would, Edgewater promised himself, prove to be St. Clair's downfall. He knew his opponent now, and that, along with his natural superiority, would carry the day.

As for Lady Cecily—that young miss would get her comeuppance. Because of her jilting him, people had laughed at him—him!—in the guise of commiserating with him. Or they had pitied him, which was far worse. He was Edgewater! Lady Cecily would pay, he vowed, and soon. The knowledge she had of his activities was nothing against this. One day she would regret having jilted him.

In the meantime, her loss had left him with a problem. By himself he could probably carry the day, once his long-planned revolution started. He was, after all, a peer, born and bred to rule, and thus would be far more acceptable to the aristos, once he had taken power. A wife, however, from the highest echelons of society, would have helped cement his position. He hadn't the time to begin courting someone else; Cecily had been carefully chosen and long-courted, before he had proposed. Who could he find now to take her place?

The waltz ended and the dancers began to move off the floor, some to go to other partners, others to seek refreshment or the haven of the card room. In the milling crowd Edgewater lost sight of St. Clair and Cecily, but that was of no moment. Someone else came into his view, a tall, laughing girl with dark hair and sparkling eyes, a girl with quite as much background as Cecily. Edgewater's mouth curved in a slow, triumphant smile. Lady Diana Randall. Why had he not thought of her before?

"Cece? You're surely not going to bed yet!" Diana, the sash of her wrapper tied securely about her, bounded into Cecily's room.

" 'Tis late, Di. I'm tired." Cecily, sitting in front of her dressing table while her maid brushed her hair for the night, smiled ruefully at her sister's reflection. Why was it that even *en dishabille* Diana managed to look attractive and perfectly groomed, while she herself could never attain such perfection, no matter how she tried?

Diana bounced onto Cecily's bed, her eyes alight. "Well, I think it's poor-spirited, when I've so much to tell you!"

"Do you? Thank you, Annie, you may retire." Cecily smiled at her maid as she rose from the dressing table. "Now, Di, what's all this?" she asked, climbing onto the bed and sitting with her arms wrapped around her knees.

"Oh, Cece, the most marvelous thing!" Diana smiled dreamily up at the canopy. *"He* talked with me tonight."

"He? Mr. Carstairs?"

"No, silly, not him! He's the merest boy. No." She smiled. "Lord Edgewater."

"What? What did he want?"

"Merely to talk to me, so you needn't sound so exercised. Or do you still have a *tendre* for him?"

"No!" Cecily spoke more sharply than she'd intended. "Oh, Diana, have you any idea what you're getting into?"

"Of course. He's handsome, wealthy and titled. What more could one want?" Diana said, with one of her rare flashes of practicality.

Some kindness, perhaps, Cecily thought, knowing Diana wouldn't understand. Worse, Cecily knew from experience, any opposition might well make her more stubborn. "Well, I'd want more than that. I will admit that he's charming." *When he wants to be.*

"And so handsome! When he came to ask me to waltz, I nearly swooned, I was so thrilled."

Cecily bit back an exclamation of alarm. It meant nothing. Edgewater was only being polite. And, much as she disliked him, he must find it far more pleasant to be with someone who idolized him, rather than someone who saw him all too clearly, as Cecily had. She suspected he didn't like having his self-image disturbed. "There are many other wealthy, handsome and titled men, Diana. You needn't settle on anyone just yet."

Diana pouted. Cecily made a mental note to practice just such an expression herself, it was so appealing, and then discarded the idea. Such tricks didn't work for her. "You sound like Papa," Diana complained.

"My apologies, Di." She yawned. "Forgive me, but I am prodigious tired, and we have a busy day again tomorrow."

"Oh, yes, I'm to go driving with Danbury!" Diana said, bouncing off the bed and relieving Cecily's mind enormously. If Diana could still be excited by the attentions of other men, her attachment to Edgewater was likely not serious. "Will you be seeing Lord St. Clair tomorrow?"

Cecily paused, and then slipped into bed. "I don't believe so. Why?"

"Why?" Diana's eyes sparkled. "Because I think he has a *tendre* for you, that's why!"

"Oh, nonsense!" Cecily said, but she blushed.

"It isn't! I saw the way he looked at you. And tonight, he always seemed to be wherever you were."

"That's just the way he is." Cecily pulled the quilts up over herself, struck once again by how perceptive Diana could be when she wished. "He looks at every woman like that."

"Oh, no. Just at you."

"Nonsense. Now do go away, Diana and let me sleep."

"Oh, very well, cross-patch." Diana yawned. "But I doubt I'll sleep tonight, I'm so excited!"

Cecily smiled sleepily as the bedroom door closed behind her sister. Had she ever been that young, even when she had first come to London? Her natural reticence had made the season something of an ordeal for her, until she had come to know some people and had relaxed. Now she enjoyed it quite as much as Diana did, though in a different way. Diana was bright, enthusiastic, openly charming, the type of girl who attracted young men in droves. Not St. Clair, however, and that thought made Cecily's smile deepen. It was not Diana who St. Clair had noticed, but her. Imagine that.

Did he have a *tendre* for her? It seemed nonsense that someone like him would be attracted to her, and yet — And yet, there had been the waltz tonight, when the orchestra had seemed to play for them alone, when his hand on her waist had seemed a little warmer, a little firmer, so that she had allowed him to hold her just a bit closer than propriety allowed. There had been the rides in the park, when they had talked in perfect harmony, as if they had known each other forever. There had been that terrible and yet wonderful, moment in Lady Radcliffe's garden, when he had held her and comforted her. And, most importantly, there had been that time in his lodgings, when he had kissed her.

Closing her eyes, Cecily let her fingers drift to her lips, remembering the sensations he had evoked within her. His lips had fit so well with hers; his arms had felt so right about her, strong, but not confining; sure and certain, but not arrogant, demanding. Of course, she reminded herself now as she had then, he knew quite well how to kiss, he'd certainly had experience at it! It was no wonder it had affected her so.

Even as she thought that, though, she knew it wasn't fair. Alex — how she loved saying his name, even if only to herself — hadn't kissed her as if she were just any woman. He had kissed her with an awareness of her that had been missing from Edgewater's embraces. That was what had made the kiss so special. Cecily wondered if, indeed, he did cherish a *tendre* for her. She knew for certain she had one for him.

It wouldn't lead anywhere, of course. Reformed rake though he claimed to be, Cecily doubted he would marry. Certainly he wouldn't choose her, when there were so many more beautiful girls available. But it was nice to dream, and she let herself do so as she at last slipped into sleep. It was very nice to dream.

So nice, in fact, that any concerns she had about her sister's possible *tendre* for Edgewater completely vanished.

Alex was in a good mood as he entered Whites' several evenings later, looking forward to a good dinner, followed by a rout at Lady Sutherland's, where he might very well see Cecily. God's teeth, but he was besotted with the girl, and he wasn't sure why. She was no beauty and yet — and yet there was something about her, about her honey-brown curls, her piquant, heart-shaped face, the clarity and honesty of her eyes. Nor had he forgotten how she had felt in his arms, soft and warm and altogether right. Nonsensical thoughts; he knew quite well there was no such thing as love. However, he could think of worse fates than spending his life with her.

He hailed acquaintances as he crossed the room, Lord Alvanley, the Earl of Rockingham, and then sat at a table, ordering a substantial meal of roast beef, potatoes and vegetables, accompanied by a fine burgundy. Mr. Raggett, the current proprietor, served a good dinner. It was as he was leaning back, savoring his wine, that he became aware of the atmosphere in the room, tense and yet excited. Was it his imagination, or had the muttering increased since he had come in? He looked up, and Rothmere and Ashton, boon companions from his worst days of raking, looked hastily away. Beyond them Lord Beauchamp, the merest acquaintance, glared at him. Alex nodded in greeting. The hairs on the back of his neck rose, and he tensed, though he kept his relaxed slouch. Foolish to think that the tension in the dining room tonight had aught to do with him, or that it presaged danger — but his instincts had rarely failed him before. Something was wrong.

His meal was set before him, and he set to with a will, determined to finish as quickly as possible and leave. He had accounted for half of his dinner when a person appeared before him. Looking up, he saw it was Beauchamp, his face almost purple. "Good evening, Beauchamp," he said calmly, laying down his cutlery, though every nerve was alert. "Would you care to join me in a glass of wine?"

"Join one such as you? Never, sirrah!"

"Never?" Alex leaned back, apparently imperturbable, surveying the other man. He knew Beauchamp very little; the man belonged to his father's generation and beyond that tended to keep to his estate. Aging, balding, increasing in girth, he came to London only to satisfy the whims of his young, and startlingly beautiful, wife. Having met Lady Beauchamp and parried her seductive invitation, Alex in the past had felt nothing but contemptuous pity for the man. Why in the world was Beauchamp approaching him?

"Then, is there aught I can do for you, sir?"

"Yes." Beauchamp picked up Alex's glass and dashed the contents in his face, making Alex recoil, spluttering. "You may meet me at Chalk Farm. My seconds will call upon yours, sirrah." And with that, he turned and, with peculiar dignity, stalked out of the room.

Chapter Fourteen

Alex stood up so fast his chair fell back. Beauchamp had left, denying him the satisfaction of demanding just what this was all about. *God's teeth!* he thought, sitting down again as a waiter scurried across to right his chair, and pulling out his handkerchief to mop his face. Had he really just been challenged to a duel?

The shocked hush that had fallen over the room ended as people began talking. He'd been right. His presence here tonight had caused the tension, though God knew why. He'd done Beauchamp no harm and so what cause had the man to challenge him? Not that Alex intended to meet the challenge, not with everything else that was happening in his life. No matter that he might be branded a coward. Alex had never fought a duel in his life, and he wasn't about to start now.

"Well, old fellow, what have you been up to?" a voice said, and Alex looked up to see Lord Ashton. Ashton was an old acquaintance whose reputation was, if anything, worse than Alex's ever had been. "May I join you?"

Alex waved his hand toward the other chair, trying without any luck to blot the wine that stained his shirt. "Oh, sit. If you wish to be seen with me."

Ashton shrugged, marring the elegant set of his coat for only a moment. "That was in the cards, of course."

"Indeed?" Alex tucked his handkerchief away. He'd have to go home and change before going on to other events this evening. "I wish I knew why."

Ashton grinned, briefly erasing the lines dissipation and hard living had etched upon his face. "Doing it much too brown, old friend. Everyone knows Beauchamp has cause."

Alex looked up, his eyes hooded. "Indeed? And what cause is that?"

"His wife, of course." Ashton's smile grew wider. "Even for you, taking her as your mistress is bold. Considering Beauchamp's temper."

"Who says she is my mistress?"

Something in the quiet tone of voice made Ashton look sharply at him. "It's common knowledge, St. Clair."

"Not to me, sir."

"You deny it, then?"

"I do. I am more, shall we say, particular, than to choose a lady who scatters her favors far and wide."

"Thought so. However, it's on the betting books here, St. Clair—"

"The devil it is!"

"—that Beauchamp would challenge you."

"God's teeth! I swear I've nothing to do with his wife."

"I do believe you're telling the truth, old friend."

"Of course I am. Why should I be interested in her when there's—"

Ashton appeared not to notice the way Alex broke off. "Odd. For the last few days it's all one's heard."

"Is it, indeed. That explains much." It explained the conversations that had been broken off when he entered a room; it explained some comments he'd heard; it explained the atmosphere in the dining room tonight. Had Cecily heard of it? he wondered with sudden urgency. "However, no matter what's been said, it's

181

not true. But it puts me in the devil of a coil."

"I hope you won't ask me to stand as your second. Deuced thing, early rising."

"Why worry about it, old friend?" Alex said laying ironic stress upon the words. "I have no intention of meeting him."

"Never thought you were so poor-spirited, St. Clair."

"Hell, I'm not. This quarrel has been forced upon me. I wonder why?"

"Might you have an enemy?"

Alex looked startled. Edgewater. This would be just like him, working in devious ways to eliminate any opposition. The question was, was the opposition because of Cecily, or the conspiracy? If the latter, then his mission could be in serious danger. He would give much to know who had started the rumors. "That may be it. Or perhaps someone saw me speak with Lady Beauchamp at some rout and drew his own conclusion. Nothing so delightful as a scandal." He looked ruefully down at his ruined shirt. "If you'll excuse me, Ashton, I must go home and change."

"I should hope so." Ashton accompanied him to the vestibule. "Do reconsider, old friend. Matter of honor, you know."

"I know." Alex's voice was grim. "Which doesn't leave me with much choice."

"What are you going to do?" Ashton's eyes were avid to be first to hear Alex's decision. "Beauchamp was a good enough shot in his day. Might even provide a challenge."

"That old man? Hell." Alex took his hat and stick from the attendant. "It looks as if I'm going to fight a duel."

Three mornings later, Alex reached the head of Upper Grosvenor Street to find Cecily waiting for him, astride Dancer. "What are you doing here?" he barked, the tension of the last few days exploding in his voice. "I thought I told you not to ride out alone."

Cecily looked back at him calmly. "What am I doing here? What, sir, did you think you were doing yesterday morning?"

Alex stared at her as she swept by him into the park. "Hell," he muttered, and turned, catching up with her. "Heard about that, did you?"

"Heard about it! The whole town knows about it! Mama is convinced you are beyond redemption."

"I am sorry, Cecily. I would have spared you knowing it."

"Oh, as to that, I don't care," she said, tossing her head. "But it would have been nice yesterday to know what happened and not have to wait, not knowing—"

"Why, Cecily," Alex said, when she didn't go on. "Dare I hope you care?"

"Oh, don't tease!" She turned toward him. "It was terrible, not knowing what had happened. And then to see you last evening at the opera, behaving as if you hadn't a care in the world—if I'd had a pistol, I'd have shot you myself!"

"Cecily." He didn't know whether to laugh or scold as he caught up with her again. "Little one—"

"I am not your little one."

"Cecily, won't you at least let me apologize?"

"Why should I care?" she asked, with that careless toss of her head. "If you go out and fight duels over women who are no better than they should be, what matters that to me?"

Ah. Now he understood. "Cecily." He reached out and laid his hand on her arm. She went very still, her head bent. "It's not true, you know, what they're saying. I've never been with Lady Beauchamp."

"That doesn't matter to me."

"Doesn't it, little one? Look at me, Cecily."

Cecily raised her head, her eyes miserable.

"I don't lie. Lady Beauchamp has never been so much as one of my flirts."

"But—Lord Beauchamp—"

"Got some kind of idea in his head, God knows why. But then, he is known for being jealous."

"But did you have to duel? You might have been killed!"

"If I hadn't fought him, Cecily, it would never have ended. This way, it's over." His lips twitched. "As to my being killed—I put it about that I was a dead shot."

"Aren't you?"

"Fair enough. In any event, Beauchamp apparently had second thoughts and decided to, ahem, drown his fears. By the time he reached the field, he could barely stand."

"And his seconds still let him fight?"

"Beauchamp was beyond listening to anyone at that point. I'll give him this, he was determined to see it through."

"He actually shot?"

"Yes." His lips twitched again. "After he fired, he fell. The shot went wide, I fired into the ground and that was that. And then we went to have a good breakfast."

Cecily stared at him and then rode away, shaking her head. "Men. I will never understand why you do such things."

"For honor, of course."

"Honor." She managed to invest the word with a great deal of scorn. "What was honorable about that? I've a mind, you know, not to ride with you this morning."

"I thought you wanted an assignation with a rake."

Cecily glanced at him, startled, and her sense of humor was her undoing. Before she could prevent herself, she smiled. "You are a complete hand, sir! I am a

184

proper young lady who would never think of such a thing."

"Of course not."

"Now you are funning me, sir," she said, but she smiled. It *did* feel like an assignation, and it was all the more exciting for it.

"Why, Cecily. Would I do that?"

"Yes. Now, will you promise me not to get shot at again?"

"It isn't so very important, little one."

"Getting shot at?" She stared at him as something the Countess of Chatleigh had said came back to her. "Alex, you were in the war, weren't you?"

Alex was quiet for so long she thought he wasn't going to answer. "Not officially, no."

"What does that mean?"

"We have to talk. Come, let's sit." Dismounting, they tethered their horses to the railings that edged the Serpentine and climbed over them, sitting on the grassy bank. In spite of his preoccupation, Alex couldn't help observing the unselfconscious grace with which Cecily sank to the ground, or the beguiling curve of her hips in her breeches. Desire, unexpected and not quite welcome, stirred within him. "You know I was on the Continent during the war."

"Yes. But you weren't in the army."

"No. I was in the war, though."

"I wondered," she said, and he turned to her. "It was the way you looked when we first met, the look in your eyes. I've a cousin who looked like that when he returned from fighting. As if he'd seen too much."

Alex nodded, twisting a piece of grass between his fingers. There was no good way to say what had to be said. "I was a spy, Cecily." Cecily gasped. "My task was to find out what the enemy was up to. And sometimes our own people. A nasty business." He glanced toward Cecily, but she was sitting with her arms wrapped

185

around her legs, her head bent to her knees. "Never knowing whom to trust, never knowing when you might be betrayed. Knowing that if you didn't find the information the army needed, men might die. Knowing that if you did, men on the other side would die. Nasty and dirty."

"Poor rake," Cecily murmured, and he turned to see her watching him with eyes huge with sympathy. "Do you find it so hard to trust, even now?"

Alex didn't answer that; he couldn't. "What happened yesterday may have something to do with it," he said, more to himself than to her.

Cecily's brow furrowed in puzzlement. "The duel? How?"

"Hm?" Alex glanced at her, realizing, too late, what he had said. "Oh, nothing. Thinking out loud."

"No, you meant something, Alex." She knelt up, her hand on his arm. "It's not over, is it? You're still spying."

Alex drew his breath in sharply. It wasn't what he'd wanted to tell her, but Cecily had a way of seeing through him to the truth. Hell, he couldn't tell her, not if she weren't involved. And she wasn't. Was she? "Some weeks ago," he began carefully, "a friend of mine, a man I worked with, was killed. I'm trying to find his killers."

"But it's dangerous. Alex, you could be hurt, you could be killed—"

"I won't be," he said swiftly, catching her hand in his. The sound of his name, used by her for the first time, affected him more than he'd expected. "I promise you that. But this is something I have to do."

"But not anymore after this? Please?"

"Why, Cecily. You do care."

"Oh, don't tease! This is too serious."

"I'm not teasing." His voice unexpectedly grew deep as he reached out to touch her cheek. She was inno-

186

cent, he knew that. Was it so difficult to trust, she'd asked, and now he could answer that question. No. Trusting her was easy.

Cecily drew back, startled, and then relaxed. "Why?"

"Why what?" Back and forth his fingers went, stroking her cheek, her jaw, her throat. Her skin felt like silk under his fingers.

"Why me? I'm not pretty, I'm never neat, I bite my nails and I dress like a boy."

"But you don't look like one," he drawled, looking at her in such a way that she colored. "Because of all those things. Because you're you, Cecily. You're not afraid to be yourself and you're not afraid to be honest."

Cecily swallowed, hard; the continuous, caressing touch was doing strange things to her. She felt restless, alive, and at the same time, languid. "I'm—not so sure of that. I think there's another side of me I'm just beginning to know."

"In all of us, Cecily."

"I—don't think you should be doing that."

"Doing what?"

"Touching me. You're a rake."

He smiled. "Not anymore." No, because of her. And her father had given him permission to pay his addresses to her. Strange thought, but good. He couldn't do anything about it now, though, not until things were settled. Not for one moment did he believe Cecily was involved in any conspiracy. Until everything was over, however, until he was done with his task, he wasn't free to speak. "Don't you know that, Cecily?"

"I don't recall giving you permission to use my name," she said, the prim words at odds with her breathless voice.

"Nor did I give you permission to use my name. But I like it." His fingers drifted over her forehead and down her cheek. "Your skin is like silk, sweeting."

"A most unoriginal compliment. I would have thought a rake could do better."

Mirth sparked in Alex's eyes. "A former rake, sweeting. But I haven't forgotten everything. Shall I show you?"

"I don't think you should," she said, but she didn't move. "Remember what happened the last time."

"Yes, I remember," he said, with such warmth that her lashes feathered down. "And I haven't forgotten that I was a fool to let you go. Cecily." The sudden deep timbre of his voice made her look up as his hand curved around her neck. Gone was the gentle caress. In its place was a purpose that would not be denied. Something within Cecily responded to that purpose, something leaped to life with an answering demand of its own. A moment ago, she might have been able to break away, but not now. Not now.

She studied his face as his hands came up to frame her face, saw his eyes, deep blue with an emotion she didn't recognize, determined, but oddly vulnerable. She saw the faint white line, never noticed before, of a scar on his temple and a mole high on one cheek, a spot she suddenly, irrationally, longed to kiss. She watched, mesmerized, his thin, mobile lips as they came down to hers. And then there was nothing more to see, so she closed her eyes, shutting out the world, shutting out everything save the reality of his warm mouth kissing her, at last, again.

She had remembered that other kiss, oh, how she had remembered it. Time, though, had dulled the memory of its physical impact, of feeling his mouth open over hers, of her own response. Lost in time had been the need that made her press up against him, her arms tight around his neck, so close that she could almost feel his heart beating. And with time had faded the remarkable sensations that were flooding her now, making her limbs go weak, turning her insides to jelly.

188

"Cecily," he murmured, his voice husky, feathering kisses on her eyes, her nose, her cheeks. "Cecily, my love." The arms that had clasped her knees now clasped him and her legs were outstretched, tangled with his as he turned her toward him. It seemed the most natural thing in the world for them to sink down against the bank, their lips still joined, for him to brace himself above her on his elbows, for her arms to cradle him. Her boys' clothes gave him unparalleled access to her body, gave her unparalleled freedom to move. Dimly he realized why women didn't dress this way; they would be safe from no man. He doubted, though, that many would fill out a pair of breeches as enticingly as Cecily did. Or, for that matter, a soft white shirt.

The hand that had been stroking her arm, her shoulder, hesitated, moved to her waist, and then upward, toward more dangerous territory. Cecily made a little sound in her throat, of protest, of acquiescence and his hand stilled. This was new to her. She was responding like this for him. Just for him. Her innocent, untutored kisses told him that, her gasps that held surprise as well as pleasure. For a man who had long had his choice of women, this was new, infinitely sweet, infinitely precious. She had never had a lover before, and he, holding her, felt as if he never had, either.

And because that was so, this wasn't the place for this. He had reformed, indeed. When he finally made her his own, it would be as his wife, on their wedding night. The prospect of being caught in parson's mousetrap no longer appalled him, not if it was Cecily who caught him.

She opened her eyes, and the sweet trust he saw there gave him the strength to stop. "We have to stop, sweeting," he said, kissing the tip of her nose.

She licked her lips, an unintentionally provocative gesture. "Why?" she asked, her voice as husky as his.

"Because this isn't the place." He set himself to

smoothing the curls that had tumbled about her face. "It's getting late," he went on, his voice very gentle. "Someone may come along and see us."

"Oh, heavens!" She sat bolt upright, her hands flying to her hair, her cheeks stained that golden rosy color he liked so much. "I must look a sight."

"You look beautiful."

"Oh, please don't fun me."

"I'm not funning," he said, and his voice was so serious that she at last looked at him, her eyes wide and vulnerable. "Sweeting, I would not see you hurt."

"I won't be."

"No." He rose and held out his hand to her. Not if he could help it. "You'd best be getting home."

"Yes," she said, sounding a little dazed and he caught her shoulders, turning her to face him.

"Cecily. There are things I can't say to you, things I can't tell you yet. But I promise I will, someday. Will you trust me?"

She reached up and briefly touched his lips. "Always."

Always. Trust, so easily given. He felt blessed, and burdened. In his world, trust was a precious commodity. "Thank you, sweeting. Now—"

"Alex." She stopped as he would have helped her mount Dancer, placing her hand on his arm. "You will be careful?"

"I promise, Cecily. And it will all be over soon." He cupped his hands for her to step in and tossed her into the saddle. She moved Dancer away as he mounted Azrael, walking the great horse over to her. "Soon," he said again, and the words were a vow.

"Soon," she agreed, giving him her dazzling smile, promising him a future he had never before dared believe might be his, as they rode together out of the park. She had become very precious to him, and it was a feeling he'd never experienced before. Love? He

190

doubted it. Love existed only in poems, or romances. Whatever it was, though, it was powerful, and it held out the promise of a happiness long denied him. Soon he would claim her as his own, but not yet. He had other things to do first.

That thought made his smile fade, and his lips tucked back in a frown. What lay ahead of him could very well be ugly, and he wanted none of it to touch Cecily. She had to be protected, and the only way he could do that was to catch the man who was a menace both to him and to her. He'd get him. He'd find the man who was behind the conspiracy, of that he was certain. And then he would be free to reach out for happiness.

Diana ran up the stairs late that afternoon, hugging her secret to herself as she flew into her room. At any other time, she might have shared her news with Cecily, but not now. *He* had said not to, had said Cecily might be hurt, implying that he had been the one to break the engagement and not the other way around. It wasn't fair, the way he'd been treated by Cecily and their father! The injustice of it burned in Diana's breast, intensifying her feelings. That, and the fact that he was so very handsome and sophisticated.

Diana sat at her dressing table, carelessly pushing aside the crystal perfume bottles and silver brushes so that she could look at herself. He'd called her beautiful. From him, that meant something. Diana was no fool, for all that she sometimes appeared silly; she knew she'd made a good catch. He'd noticed her, said she was the one he'd cared about all along, and so she was more than willing to meet him whenever she could. The clandestine nature of these meetings only added to their excitement.

That and what he'd implied he had to do. Some secret mission to do with the government, with which she could help. That, too, was something she wanted to share with Cecily, but he'd warned her against it. She was, she thought, really in love, for the first time in her life. For him, she would do anything. No sacrifice was too great if it would help him. She rather fancied herself in the rôle of tragic heroine, though she didn't really think it would come to that. All he asked of her now was that they keep their love a secret, and that, for now, she was willing to do. Soon, he had promised her, they would be able to tell the world.

Diana smiled at her reflection, a silly, fatuous smile. The smile of a woman in love, she thought. Soon. She couldn't wait.

Joe Driver was a troubled man. Born though he had been in low circumstances, he was possessed of a brain both quick and agile, and of a strong sense of self-preservation. He knew his Jenny's Miss Cecily wasn't just anyone, but was Lady Cecily Randall, the daughter of a duke, of all things. And that worried him. Wasn't much went on in Whitechapel he didn't learn about sooner or later, and he knew a man named Randall had been searching for a sharpshooter some time back. As of last night, he also knew what the sharpshooter, one Bob Grundy by name, had been hired to do. The man might be a good shot, but he didn't have the brains of a louse. Imagine blabbing to anyone who would listen what some fine gennulman had paid him to do, instead of keeping his trap shut.

It was what Grundy claimed the job was for, and the coincidence of the name Randall, that worried Joe. Who was this Randall if not someone connected to Lady Cecily? Joe found it hard to believe she was involved, but if she was, she might be in danger. Someone should know, he thought. He'd have to tell someone.

Joe had his ways of learning what he needed, and so now he stood in Piccadilly, outside the house where St. Clair lodged. He'd never paid a visit to a gennulman before, and he twisted his cap in his hands, swallowing hard. In Whitechapel, Joe knew how to deal with people. The quality was different, though. For the first time in many a year, Joe was, quite frankly, scared.

Parsons, his face wooden, opened the door to him and then left him waiting, still twisting his cap. In a few moments he was back and, somewhat to Joe's surprise, gestured him in, leading him to a sitting room that to Joe's eyes, looked opulent and comfortable. Quality sure knew how to live, he thought, but his rising bitterness at the inequities of life was checked by the sight of St. Clair, rising to greet him, his hand outstretched.

"Mr. Driver," Alex said politely, none of his surprise at this unexpected visit showing. "What can I do for you?"

"It's more what I can do for yer, me lord," Joe said as he sat in the chair Alex indicated.

"Indeed. May I offer you some refreshment? Brandy, perhaps?"

"Now that would be fine." He took the glass Alex held out to him and took a long swallow, smacking his lips appreciatively. "Fine stuff, this. Smuggled in through Devon?"

Alex's lips twitched. "I daresay. What is the problem, Mr. Driver?"

"Well, it's like this, sir." Joe set the glass firmly down on the table, his self-assurance returned at Alex's reception of him. "There's been a man name o' Randall going around the stews askin' for a man to do a job."

"Indeed. Parsons! I want Parsons to hear this, too," he explained as Parsons came into the room. "Mr. Driver was just telling me about our friend Mr. Randall."

Parsons drew a straight chair over. "Really, sir?"

"Yeah. Came to me, he could be connected with Miss Cecily."

"We don't believe so," Alex said, after a startled moment. So Cecily's real identity was known in Whitechapel. Dangerous, that, unless Driver stayed on her side.

"Yer know of him, then?"

"We know something of him, yes. But we've been hoping to learn more."

"Might be I can help." Joe drained his glass and Parsons silently rose to refill it. "This Randall found what he was looking for. Weren't hard, after all, plenty of people to do anything for that kind of blunt. Man picked a looby, though."

Alex, sitting with his legs crossed, looked perfectly at ease. "You know who it is, then?"

"Yeah. Fellow name o' Bob Grundy. Good shooter, but a fool. Been blabbin' to everyone about how he's been hired to shoot the Prime Minister."

Chapter Fifteen

Alex went still. "God's teeth. You're sure of this?"

Joe put up his chin. "Yer callin' Joe Driver a liar?"

"No, of course not." Alex stroked his upper lip. "A plot to assassinate Liverpool. Of course. The government would fall, and the way things are now—it would mean revolution. Almost anyone could take power if he tried hard enough."

"With accomplices to stir things up in the rest of the country," Parsons said.

"Yes. When is this supposed to happen, Mr. Driver?"

"Thursday sennight, sir. Heard Liverpool is supposed to attend some sort o' do at Carlton House."

"There's no danger to the regent, is there?" Alex asked, sharply.

"Not so's I've heard. Anyway, anyone gets rid o' that fat flawn would be doing the country a favor."

Alex's lips twitched. "A most seditious statement, Mr. Driver. Tell me. What does this Randall look like?"

"Short, fat, balding on top, crooked nose," Joe replied promptly.

"Our man, sir," Parsons said.

"Indeed. You'd know him if you saw him again?"

"Sure I would, or my name's not Joe Driver."

"Good. You've done well coming to me with this."

"And Jenny's Miss Cecily ain't in no trouble?"

"No." Alex shook his head. "Parsons. It might be worthwhile to see if Mr. Driver could identify Randall any further."

"You mean, bring him to Edge—"

"That's precisely what I mean." Alex gave Parsons a look. "Would you be willing, Mr. Driver?"

"Aye and what's in it for me?" Joe said, unexpectedly truculent. "I didn't bargain for this, me lord."

"So I see." Alex's eyes were chilly, and Joe shifted uneasily under the steady gaze. "I should have realized you'd want some sort of reward."

"Not for what I come here to tell yer, no. But what's goin' to happen to my Jenny if anything happens to me? You tell me that."

"Ah. I see." Alex's gaze softened. "You'll be in no danger, Mr. Driver. We merely need you to identify Randall for us. And you will be rewarded, I promise you that. Perhaps we can find some way for you to keep Jenny with you."

Joe's eyes brightened. "Happens I've always wanted a tavern of my own. Jenny could be with me, then."

"Indeed. Well, we'll see what we can do."

"Now, that's what I call fair, me lord. Yer a right 'un. Not like some o' the quality."

"Indeed." Alex's lips twitched again. "Parsons."

"Yes, sir. I'll take Mr. Driver there directly."

"Good." Alex rose, holding out his hand. "Thank you for coming to me with this, sir. Be assured I won't forget it."

"Weren't nothin', me lord," Joe said, twisting his cap in his hands again. "Anything I can do for Miss Cecily."

"Indeed." Alex at last let himself smile as Joe, escorted by Parsons, at last left the room. Of all unlikely allies! And all because Cecily had chosen to befriend a child living in an orphanage. Life surely took some strange twists sometimes.

His smile faded, however, as he sank back into his

chair, stroking his upper lip again. So. The plan was to assassinate the prime minister at the reception to be held at Carlton House for Princess Charlotte and her new husband, the Prince of Coburg, and then, presumably, seize the government. Now that they knew that, they could prevent that part of the plot from meeting with success. They still, however, had little evidence against Edgewater. How, Alex wondered, were they going to catch him?

Monday evening, and a ball at the Pembrokes'. Alex quietly closed the door of the study behind him, leaving behind Bainbridge, Lord Sidmouth, the Home Minister and Lord Liverpool. It wasn't the first time he'd transacted government business at a social event. Now he was returning to the ball, his duty done for the night.

The clamor below rose to meet him as he set off down the stairs, music vying with conversation and the chaos of guests arriving and departing. Three more days and it would be over. The conspirators would make their move, only to be arrested. And, at last, Alex would be free to pursue his own life.

Three more days. He stopped at the door to the ballroom, instinctively searching for the one person who meant anything to him. Three more days and he could claim her. He could do so now, were it not for his innate caution. His work was finished. Plans had been made, and other men now had taken over. Outside the home of each conspirator waited men in the service of the government to serve arrest warrants. For all, that is, but Edgewater. Incredible though it seemed, there was still little evidence to link him to the plot. They would have to wait until he made his move before they could arrest him. In just three more days.

There she was. Unaware that he was smiling broadly,

Alex went headlong into the maelstrom, going toward the girl in the gown of gold tissue. Cecily. Just now she was dancing a country dance with Lord Danbury, at whom she was smiling in such a way that he might have been jealous, had he not known better. Danbury might have a *tendre* for Cecily, but it wasn't returned; Cecily did not behave in such a way, keeping more than one man dangling after her. She was straightforward and honest, different from the people he had known over the past years. It wasn't easy, this business of giving one's heart over to another person's keeping, but at last he could do it, knowing the gift would not be rejected. She was a girl one could trust. A person he, at last, could trust.

The music ended, and he briefly lost sight of Cecily. If he remembered correctly, the next dance would be a waltz. Having met with Liverpool immediately upon his arrival, he hadn't had a chance to sign Cecily's dance card, but he was certain she'd kept this waltz for him; she had promised as much this afternoon when they had met in the park and chatted about the night's entertainment. He was looking forward to it. It would be the first chance he'd had to speak with her in relative privacy in several days.

A space at last opened before him, and he began to progress across the room, where Cecily sat with her mother and sister. Halfway there, however, he stopped. For there, bowing over Cecily's hand, was Edgewater.

The waltz would be next. When she had met Alex in the park that afternoon, he had mentioned this very dance, and she had decided to keep it open for him. Unfortunately, though, she hadn't been able to. Cecily's dance card always filled quickly. Now she gazed down at it in dismay. Written in for the waltz, in a careless scrawl, was the name of the one man she least wanted to see.

"Good evening, Your Grace. Lady Cecily, Lady Diana." Edgewater bent over the duchess's hand and she and Diana beamed at him. Cecily's own smile felt stiff. "And may I say, Lady Cecily, how charming you look." Edgewater's gaze traveled slowly over her, and Cecily tried not to fidget. She knew he had to have noticed the curls that had come loose, in spite of her best efforts. Alex didn't seem to care about such things.

As if thinking about him had conjured him up, there he was. Alex. She didn't know when she had begun calling him by name in her mind; perhaps it had been since that morning by the Serpentine, the last time they had been alone, when he had kissed her and almost—. Her face flamed.

"Good evening, Your Grace," Alex said, bowing over the duchess's hand, as Edgewater had, and then Cecily's. Her smile broadened. "Good evening, Lady Cecily." The tone of his voice managed to invest the words with the warmth of a caress. "You look lovely tonight."

"Thank you, sir." Cecily's voice was prim, but her eyes sparkled as they met his. For a moment all was forgotten as she gazed at him—her mother, her sister, her former fiancé—all but the truth that suddenly shone, clear and strong, before her. It was as if a veil of gauze had been lifted from her eyes, and she saw Alex differently. Saw herself, too, with such crystal clarity it left her momentarily stunned. *Of course.* No wonder she had been so attracted to him, even when engaged to someone else; no wonder he had made her feel things she had not known she could feel. The thing she had begun to think might never occur had already happened to her. She loved him, had loved him, perhaps since that first meeting in Hyde Park. And, she thought, looking at his eyes, a warm, sunlit sea of blue, she suspected he felt the same.

"My dance, I believe," a voice drawled from behind her, at what seemed like a great distance. Unwillingly Cecily came out of her reverie to see Alex glaring at

199

Edgewater.

"You are mistaken," Alex said coolly, releasing Cecily's hand. "Lady Cecily is promised to me for this dance."

"I am mistaken?" Though the music for the dance was already playing, Edgewater raised his quizzing glass and studied Alex through it, his eye magnified alarmingly. "I fear not, dear boy. Please look at Lady Cecily's dance card."

"He did sign it," Cecily said reluctantly.

Alex's gaze was unreadable, as he looked from her to Edgewater. "I see," he said, and bowed. "My mistake."

"Of course, dear boy." Edgewater held out his arm and, after a moment's hesitation, Cecily placed her hand on it. Edgewater's smug, triumphant smile as they moved away made Alex clench his fists in reflex.

"Hell," he muttered, forgetting for the moment where he was. "He even dances better than I do."

"He is very handsome," Diana said, and Alex's sense of humor came to his rescue, though Diana was clearly unaware of any insult implied by her words. It didn't matter. He was secure in himself, confident of his appearance and abilities, as, he realized suddenly, Edgewater must not be. Why else must he make such a fuss over the way he looked, or assume such an air of superiority over others, unless it was to make himself feel better about himself? He appeared to have everything, and yet he reached for more. It would explain why he was involved in such a dangerous project as revolution. He needed the power, to salve his own inadequacies.

And that, Alex reflected, stroking his upper lip, could make him a most dangerous opponent, indeed. Edgewater wasn't fighting for some abstract cause; he was fighting for his very self. He was not likely to give up easily, nor would he have left himself unprotected. Capturing him might not be as easy as he had thought.

The waltz ended at last. Alex tensed, in case Edgewater again attempted something improper with Cecily, but to his mingled relief and disappointment he saw them returning. Relief, because she was safe; disappointment, because he would dearly love an excuse to tangle with his opponent. "Lady Cecily," he said, again raising her hand to his lips. "You dance well, no matter who your partner is."

Edgewater took a step forward, and Cecily spoke quickly, to defuse the strange tension she could feel emanating from each man. "Lord Edgewater dances well, sir. As do you."

"After all, what else does a rake need to know how to do, but to charm the ladies? And fight duels," Edgewater said in a bored drawl.

Alex's smile was tight. "You would be surprised sir, at what I know."

That smug, superior look Alex so disliked had returned to Edgewater's eyes, as if he were contemplating some secret. "Would I? But then, are any of us precisely what we seem?"

"A most revolutionary idea," Alex said, and had the satisfaction of seeing anger and alarm flare in Edgewater's eyes. Then his polite, urbane mask was back in place, the only sign of his emotion the twitching of his left eye.

"Quite. You will excuse me, I am promised to Lady Wentworth for this dance." Bowing, he left them as the music, a cotillion, began to play.

Alex watched him go, knowing he had just tipped his hand to his opponent, and yet feeling a curious satisfaction. It was not his way to lay low and watch an opponent as he was forced to do now; he would rather confront someone openly. For the moment, however, he'd won; he was now the one with Cecily.

"Mine, I believe," he said abruptly, and Cecily, reacting instantly to that tone of peremptory masculine authority, consulted her dance card.

201

"Let me see," she murmured. "The cotillion after the waltz. I don't believe, sir—"

"It's mine," he repeated, and took her hand, leading her out to the dance floor in spite of the gape-faced suitor who had come to claim his dance. "You'll not get away this time."

"Really, sir, this is most high-handed of you." Cecily's eyes sparkled, belying the reproach in her voice. "Have I no say in the matter?"

"Not this time." He veered suddenly away from the sets that were forming. "Come. We need to talk," he said leading her toward the French windows that opened onto the terrace. In the confusion of the dance and the milling of the crowd, few remarked their going.

"Alex," Cecily protested as he pulled her along, "we shouldn't—"

"No, we shouldn't," he agreed, opening a window for her, "but we are. After you, my dear."

"Everyone is staring at us, sir."

"In a few days, that won't matter."

Cecily cast him a startled glance, and then stepped through the window onto the flagstoned terrace. Flambeaux at the corners of the railings cast golden pools of light and the heavy scents of roses drifted up from the garden below. It reminded her of another night, when she had been so frightened, when she had needed Alex so much and he had been there. "Alex," she began, turning to him.

"You're mine," he said at the same time, and crushed her to him, his lips coming down on hers. No gentle kiss, this, no careful persuasion or wooing, but passion, possession. Something within Cecily, whose presence she had never suspected, rose within her, and she reached up on tiptoes, twining her arms about his neck and returning the kiss fervently. When at last they broke apart, both were gasping for breath.

"God's teeth," Alex said at last, gazing down at her in

the uncertain light. "Who taught you how to kiss like that?"

"You did, sir." Her fingertips traced lightly along his lips, and she felt them turn up into a smile.

"Ah, yes. I remember. And don't you forget it, Cecily." His arms tightened around her. "You're mine."

"Am I, Alex?" Her voice was soft, but her certainty shone in her eyes.

"Always," he said, and bent to kiss her again. It was a gentle kiss this time, but no less potent or persuasive. At last Alex had to pull away. "We'll have to stop. You're bound to be missed soon."

"Perhaps we could meet in the park, tomorrow —"

"No." His voice was firm. No more clandestine meetings for them. When next he saw her, it would be to proclaim her to the world as his future bride. In just three more days. "Just three more days, sweeting," he said without thinking.

"Why?" Cecily's huge golden eyes, gazing at him, were filled with such sweet trust it made his heart ache with joy. "What happens in three days?"

God's teeth, now he'd done it. But there was no reason not to tell her, now that she had been absolved from involvement in the conspiracy. "In three days my work will be done, sweeting and I'll be free." His eyes met hers. "Free to think of my future. And who to share it with."

"Who?" she asked, her voice barely above a whisper.

He smiled, the sudden brilliant smile that so changed his face, erasing all traces of cynicism and sadness from it, making him look young and carefree again. "In three days," he promised, laying his finger on her lips.

Cecily gazed up at him for a moment, and then nodded. Three days. She could wait. At the same time, part of her wished impatiently for the time to fly, so that she could at last be in her beloved's arms. Her beloved. Did he feel about her as she did about him, that their being together was right, natural? Did he, too, feel that aching, overwhelming emotion she had so recently identified as love? He had to. Feelings this strong had to be shared.

"All right." She smiled up at him. "In three days."

"Good." He pulled away from her, slowly, reluctantly. "Come. We must return before we're missed."

"All right," Cecily said again, though she didn't particularly care if her disappearance were remarked. In the space of a remarkable few minutes, her life had changed, and she finally felt free to be herself with the one man who knew and appreciated, who she really was. Though she walked with him into the ballroom, though she chatted with friends and danced the night away, nothing really mattered. Nothing except her future, shining clear and bright before her. Three days! How would she ever survive that long?

Cecily came instantly awake and lay staring at the canopy, with no feeling of confusion or disorientation. Two more days. Forty-eight hours and—how many minutes? A smile curved her lips. She was being foolish beyond permission, but somehow she felt she was allowed it. *Now* she understood the sometimes silly way Diana acted when she had a *tendre* for a man. Funny, Diana was acting that way now, though she seemed partial to no one in particular. But that was of no moment. She dismissed Diana from her thoughts in favor of more delicious dreams of her own future. Dreams of a pair of strong arms holding her close, of a feeling of security and serenity she'd never before known, that she could at last be herself with someone. Dreams of a love so strong nothing could ever destroy it; dreams that he surely loved her in return? That he hadn't said so was the only flaw in her happiness. If she rose, dressed in her boy's clothes and went to meet him, perhaps he would declare himself and—

And more likely, he would scold her. He had sounded quite determined that they meet in the park no longer, and though she would miss those meetings, she wasn't truly disappointed. In just two days, she would be able to see him openly, any time she wished. Well, almost any time, considering the rules and conventions of their society. They could be open about their relationship, however, and plan their future together. That more than compensated for the lost morning rides.

The problem remained, however. How was she ever going to get through the next two days? And just what was going to happen then? she wondered She hoped Alex would give up spying and settle to a normal life. The activities and social events of the season were beginning to pall on her. She wanted to do more than this artificial life allowed. Into her mind, then, came an idea she had considered before, an activity far more worthwhile than attending someone's Venetian breakfast or shopping in the afternoon. It also held out the promise of adventure and risk, and that, in her present mood, was welcome. Yes, she decided, she *would* do it and, swinging her legs out of bed, rang energetically for her maid.

Mr. Josiah Worley was busy at his desk in his City counting house when one of his clerks scurried in, his shoulders bowed and his arms partly raised. "Beggin' your pardon, sir," the clerk said quickly, for Mr. Worley was known to be overquick to use his fists when one of his employees had displeased him. "There's someone here for you."

"Send him away!" Josiah roared. "Can't you see I'm busy, man?"

"Yes, sir." The clerk shrank back a few steps. "Beggin' your pardon again, sir, it's a young lady and—"

"By Jupiter," he exclaimed, for Mr. Worley was a devout chapel-goer, "am I surrounded by dunces? You tell this here lady that this is a place of business and she can go and—"

"Excuse me." A young lady stood in the doorway of the glass-paned office, her smile so sweet that Mr. Worley abruptly swallowed his words. "Please, sir, do not abuse Mr. Perkins. I fear it is my fault he disturbed you. He didn't wish to."

Cecily, clad in her most charming frock, the apricot muslin, batted her eyelashes just as she had seen Diana do. *It worked!* she thought. A dazed Mr. Worley looked from her to his clerk, apparently at a complete loss for words. "I won't take up much of your time," she went on, walking into the office and carefully tugging off her gloves. "I'm sure you must be very busy. Perhaps you don't remember me, sir? I am Lady Cecily Randall. We met once when I was with Lord Edgewater."

That galvanized Mr. Worley into action. "Perkins, back to your desk!" he barked. "And tell those other nosy parkers out there that if they know what's good for them they'll get back to work!"

"Yes, sir!" Perkins ran out of the room with alacrity and went back to his own high desk, mopping at his forehead with a handkerchief. Phew! In a rare taking, Mr. Worley was. Perkins considered himself lucky to have escaped unscathed.

Mr. Worley eyed his aristocratic guest uneasily, all too aware of the panes of glass that usually worked to his advantage, allowing him to keep an eye on his lazy, worthless clerks. Today, though, he wished he had curtains he could draw, or that Lady Cecily, whoever she was, had chosen a more private place for this extraordinary meeting. By Jupiter, but to mention Edgewater, just like that! Mr. Worley had to resist the impulse to pull out a handkerchief and mop at his forehead, just as Perkins had.

"So this is what a counting house looks like." Cecily's eyes were bright with curiosity. "I've often wondered."

"Er, yes. What can I do for you, miss, er, my lady?" He lowered his voice, though no one could overhear this conversation. "Did Edgewater send you?"

"What? Oh, no, of course not! He has no idea I am here. But, please, I must ask you not to tattle on me. My parents wouldn't be pleased." She gave him that charming smile again, and Mr. Worley leaned back, not wholly reassured.

"I'm a plain man, miss — Lady Cecily," he said bluntly. "What is it you want if you're not from Edgewater?"

"Something I hope you will help me with, sir." Cecily leaned forward, dismissing his truculence. Of course her arrival here, unannounced, would be a surprise. "You see, I am very concerned about the poor of the city, particularly the children and — "

"You're one of them there reformers."

"Well, no, not really," Cecily said, a bit confused by the relief she heard in his voice. "But I do care. I do what I can, but it's not enough, and the money the parish gives is barely sufficient for the basic necessities. However, if men of substance like you, sir, would care to contribute — "

"Lord love you, miss, I'll give you anything you want! If you'll just leave."

"Why, thank you, sir. I'm most particularly interested in an orphanage in Whitechapel — "

"Whitechapel!" What little color had returned to his face drained away. "Look. What is it you really want?"

"To help those poor children, of course."

"How do I know I can trust you?"

Cecily looked surprised. "I'd give you my word, sir,

207

but ladies aren't supposed to have a sense of honor. However, I promise the money will go to the right place."

"Oh, it will, will it?" He examined her narrowly. "Tell you what, miss," he said finally, and the fear in his voice had left, to be replaced by the determined tones of the hardheaded businessman he was. "Tell me where this orphanage is and I'll make the donation myself."

"Oh, will you? That would be most generous of you, sir."

Cecily told him the street, and he repeated it. "Fine. Now, if you'll excuse me, miss, some of us has to work for a living."

"Of course." Cecily rose, her hand extended. "I do appreciate your taking this time, Mr. Worley. I'm sure you'll be rewarded for it someday."

"Just tell Lord Edgewater to do his own checking up," he said, truculent again. "I ain't—I'm not going to fail him."

"Of course not," Cecily said mystified. "If I see him, I'll tell him. And thank you again for your generosity." Smiling, she turned and left.

Mr. Worley mumbled something and fell back in his chair before the big rolltop desk. By Jupiter, but that had rattled him. And well it should, her coming in and spouting Edgewater's name like that. Weren't no one was supposed to know of his connection to the marquess, not until the time was right, and that made his temper, never very calm, flare. By Jupiter, Edgewater would hear about this, sending a girl to check up on him!

Cecily, her maid by her side, emerged from the counting house onto the cobblestoned street, climbing into the hackney that had conveyed her here. Across the street, a man who had been leaning against a building, his cap pulled low over his face, straightened up. Crikey, but that *had* been Lady Cecily, Parsons thought in dismay. For some reason, she had gone to meet with one of the conspirators. In spite of his instincts, in spite of Lord St. Clair's beliefs, it appeared they'd been wrong. Lady Cecily was a part of the conspiracy.

Parsons didn't relish the thought of telling Lord St. Clair. Cravenly he considered not saying a word, and then dismissed the thought. St. Clair would have to know and he, Parsons, would have to be the one to tell him. *Damn,* he thought, resorting to the language he had used before he had discovered religion. What was he going to do?

Parsons' instructions had been to keep a close eye on Worley, whom they suspected of being one of the chief members of the conspiracy. Today, his patience was rewarded within a very few minutes after Cecily's departure as Worley's carriage pulled up before the counting house. Parsons signaled to the hackney he had waiting and climbed in just as Worley entered his own carriage. With a sinking feeling, Parsons leaned forward, watching the other carriage and becoming increasingly certain of its destination. Worley was on his way to Edgewater. Banging on the roof of the hackney, Parsons called out new directions and then leaned back, his arms crossed and his face set in grim lines. He was not looking forward to the coming interview.

Alex was sitting at the table in the sitting room, cleaning and oiling his pistols, when Parsons came in. "Ah, Parsons, there you are. Your watch done so soon?"

"No. Sir—"

"I've been thinking about Edgewater," Alex went on in a meditative tone of voice. "I am not certain it's going to be so easy to catch him. I'm also thinking he won't leave anything to chance, and he might very well be there Thursday."

Parsons impatiently brushed back the hair that always insisted on falling down over his forehead. "Sir, you must listen to me."

Alex glanced up from reassembling one of the pistols. "Why? Is something amiss?"

"You might say that, sir," Parsons said, his elbows on the table, leaning forward and staring intently at Alex. "We've got a problem, sir. Seems we were wrong all along."

"About Edgewater? I doubt that."

"No." Parsons swallowed, hard. This was going to be very bad. Worse than that time in France. "Worley had a visitor this morning."

"Yes, so?"

"It was Lady Cecily, sir."

Chapter Sixteen

Alex stared at him for a moment, and then went on with his task. "Ridiculous."

"Yes, sir, but I know what I seen."

"It can't have been her, Parsons. What business would she have visiting a Cit's counting house?"

"What business would you think, sir?"

"No!" Alex exploded into movement, jumping to his feet so fast that the table rocked and the pistol skittered to the floor. "No, damn it, I'll not believe it!"

"Barnes said—"

"We explained what that meant. 'Ask Cecily Randall.' Ask her where she saw her fiancé."

"Ask her anything. Sir, we don't know what Barnes meant."

"Damn it, man, she's innocent! You said so yourself."

"Yes, sir, I did. I don't like this anymore than you do."

"There you are wrong, Parsons."

"But remember there've been people we've each liked who were on the other side."

Alex went very still, and then pounded the table. Parsons waited, hiding his sympathy. It was going to be very bad, indeed, this time.

"Hell," Alex said finally. "Surely I couldn't be so wrong, Parsons, not this time."

"She might be involved without knowing she's involved. If you take my meaning."

"A pawn?" Alex took several strides about the room. "A pawn, yes, Edgewater's using her for some purpose—no, damn it, that doesn't work! If she's really innocent, she's on her guard against Edgewater. I never did find out, though," he added to himself, "what he said to her the other night." No, because he had been so jealous, and so intent on staking a claim on her. What a fool he had been. He could see it now, the plan in all its twisted glory. Seduce Alex, the government spy, with her sweetness, lull him with her innocence, while all the time she was in league with Edgewater. No doubt she and her paramour were laughing at him that very moment. Black rage rose within him, and an anguish deeper than any he'd ever felt. And memory, of another betrayal.

Now, when he least wished to remember, he could still feel the soft warmth of the Frenchwoman's arms about him, smell her earthy scent, feel the blessed relief that he had reached safety, after so nearly being captured. He could feel the wondrous sense that someone cared for him—him—because he was himself, not because he was a wealthy viscount. To be taken in by such a warm, loving woman had been a boon unlooked-for. And even now, he could hear the quick patter of her speech as she told the soldiers that, *oui*, the English gentleman they sought was within. If Parsons hadn't warned him in time, he might not have gotten away that day, away from a betrayal that had seared his soul and taught him forevermore to be wary of everyone.

Now it had happened again, but so much worse. Though he hadn't given his body to Cecily, he'd given her something more precious: his heart. He'd loved her. God help him, but he had allowed himself to fall in love with her. Now, when he at last knew the truth about her, he knew it about himself. He loved a deceitful, perfidious jade. Worse, he had trusted her, and she had betrayed him.

"She'll pay for this," he said, his voice hard.

"Yes, sir." Parsons rose. "Sir, if I may say so, I'm sorry—"

"Damn you, Parsons, I don't want your sympathy!" Alex roared, rounding on him with fist upraised. He wanted to hit something, hurt someone, to assuage the terrible pain within him. "I was a damned fool and I nearly ruined everything. So spare me your mealy-mouthed platitudes."

"Yes, sir."

Alex turned away, and for long moments there was silence. "Where is Worley now?"

"With Edgewater, sir."

"I see. It would appear Lady Cecily brought him some important news."

"Sir, wouldn't she be a strange choice as courier?"

"Hell, Parsons, I don't know what to think anymore. This affair's been strange from the beginning." Wearily, he rubbed his hands over his face. "Is anyone watching Worley?"

"No, sir. I thought you'd need to know of this right away."

"You thought right." Alex bent to pick up the partially assembled pistol, examining it for damage. "Best you return to your post now. Don't forget we're after bigger game than Lady Cecily."

"Yes, sir." Parsons hesitated by the doorway. "Sir, will you be all right—"

"Damn it, Parsons, go and leave me in peace!"

"Yes, sir," Parsons said, and went out, closing the door quietly behind him and catching a glimpse of Alex, standing very still by the table, his head bent. He was right, he thought. It was going to be very bad this time.

* * *

213

One more day. Cecily entered the music room at Lady Rutherford's and glanced around, her eyes bright with anticipation. Already many of the gilt and crimson chairs for this evening's musicale were taken, though it was early; this entertainment was only one of several being held this evening, as on other evenings. She saw a great many people she knew, but not the one she cared most about. One more day. Whatever was to happen tomorrow, she wished it would hurry and be done with. She was eager to begin her future with a certain rake. A reformed rake, of course, she thought, smiling to herself. Then she turned and saw him.

He was standing across the room, in profile to her and her heart speeded up. Then the crowd shifted, and her smile faded. Alex wasn't alone. Standing next to him and gazing up at him with an adoring, saucy smile, was Lady Susan Palmer, who, rumor had it, had once been one of Alex's flirts. Her gloved hand rested on the arm of his evening coat of blue superfine, and though always before this Alex had appeared to dislike such shows of possessiveness, tonight he didn't seem to mind. Instead, he was smiling warmly down at Lady Susan. Cecily's pleasure in the evening faded.

"Cece. Cece. Aren't you even listening to me?" Diana, by her side, demanded.

"Hm? What is that, Di?" Cecily's voice was absent. Across the room, Alex had brought Lady Susan's hand to his lips and was holding it for much longer than seemed necessary. For the life of her, Cecily could not look away, though it hurt. Oh, how it hurt. But he was only flirting. Yes, that was it. He was only flirting.

"I said, Mama wishes us to take our seats. Oh, and did you see Edgewater? He looks so handsome. Honestly, Cece, will you listen to me?"

"I heard you." Mercifully the crowd had shifted again, blocking Alex from her view. Feeling hollow inside, she sat down. In the space of a few moments, everything had changed. He was only flirting, she told herself again, but the feeling of doom remained. Something was terribly wrong.

Her common sense reasserted itself, however, as they listened to the first performer of the evening, Lady Rutherford's sister Catherine, on the harp. What had she expected? A man didn't acquire a reputation such as Alex's for no reason. Of course he flirted with women and probably always would, whether she liked it or not. She had her own ideas on handling that situation. As far as his not having greeted her, that was of little moment. Beyond the fact that he may not even have seen her in all the crush, she had realized in the past few days that he was being remarkably careful of her reputation. Except for those moments on the terrace at the Pembrokes' the other evening, they were rarely alone and never did they dance more than once at an assembly. Of course there had been whispers about them, but very few, considering who Alex was. She should be glad she was attracted to someone so thoughtful.

When the music stopped for the interval, Cecily rose with the others, glad of the chance to look for Alex. Musical evenings were not his favorite form of entertainment; he had once explained to her that though he enjoyed music, he disliked being made to sit through a performance by amateurs with little or no talent. He had probably found a reason to escape to either the card room or the refreshment room long ago. She was rather looking forward to tracking him down.

Diana nudged her as they slowly made their way toward the door. "Oh, look, Cece, Edgewater is over there, watching us," she hissed in Cecily's ear. "I wonder if he'll speak to us."

Cecily turned, forgetting Alex for the moment. "Di, do you have a *tendre* for Edgewater?" she demanded.

"Oh, no." Diana glanced down. "But you must admit

215

he is handsome."

"No, I'm not so certain I agree with you on that." She turned back, vaguely troubled. She knew her sister well and could tell when Diana was being less than honest. What, though, was likely to happen? Diana's infatuations never lasted very long.

"Oh, look," Diana chattered. "Lord St. Clair is with Lady Susan again. I've heard she's making a dead set at him."

Instantly Cecily forgot about Edgewater and her vague suspicions. For a moment, she couldn't move. Not only was Alex still with Lady Susan, but he was smiling warmly down at her, as if no one else in the room existed.

Pain shot through her. It was one thing being polite to another woman, gallant even, if he were trying to protect Cecily's own reputation. It was quite another, however, to look at her in that way, the way he had looked at Cecily herself, especially when Lady Susan, simpering up at him, looked like a cat who had just found a bowl of rich cream. A pampered fat cat, she thought spitefully, all soft, rounded curves, and without a thought in her head. Alex surely couldn't prefer someone like her.

At that moment, as if he felt her gaze on him, Alex looked up, and his eyes met hers. Cecily waited for his smile, the light that came into his eyes when he saw her, but his face remained blank. Then, without so much as a nod of recognition, he returned his attention to Lady Susan, leaving Cecily shaken.

Cecily's new-found confidence in herself began to shrivel, even in her new gown of sea-blue sarcenet, trimmed with azure ribbons and rouleaux about the hem. Why, after all, should he prefer her, slender and plain as she was, when he could have his choice of any woman? No matter that only two nights ago, he had pulled her close and proclaimed her his, in no uncertain terms. He was a rake and he could well be toying with her. She would swear, though, that there was more than that between them. Something else had to be going on here. When she had the chance, she would approach him and find out exactly what it was.

With that decision made, she was able to enjoy the supper interval, spent in company with Diana and Lord Danbury, who had always had a marked preference for Cecily. It was as she was rising to return to the music room that she felt a hand on her arm, and joy shot through her. *Alex!* she thought and turned to face Edgewater.

"Good evening, my dear," he said, his hand tightening in response to her instinctive recoil. "You are looking well this evening."

"Thank you, sir." Cecily's voice was cool, and though she smiled, her eyes were watchful. "I didn't think you enjoyed musical evenings, sir."

"No, I usually deplore amateurs' performances, but I must admit I am enjoying tonight." His teeth gleamed briefly in that cold, smug smile she so disliked. "I see St. Clair has found a new flirt."

Cecily tossed her head. "I hadn't noticed."

"Oh, hadn't you?" He sounded amused. "The word I heard is that he's quite taken with her."

"They are old friends, I believe."

"Yes, quite old. I understand that Lady Susan is growing tired of widowhood and is casting about for a husband."

"St. Clair will never marry her."

"Come, my dear. Did you think I didn't know? It is never wise to underestimate me, Cecily." His smile was chilling. "Lord St. Clair is only toying with you."

"No."

"Though why he should bother even with that when there are so many other beautiful women available. You do lack womanly charms, Cecily."

217

"You are insufferable, sir!" Cecily snapped, and pulled her arm away, aware of curious glances from on-lookers.

"Am I? You may change your mind about that one of these days, my dear. You made a mistake, throwing me over."

"Lady Cecily?" Danbury appeared on her other side, his face alight with enthusiasm and humble admiration. "May I escort you back to the music room?"

"Thank you, sir, I'd like that." Cecily laid her hand on his arm and walked away, without a backward glance. Edgewater was just being spiteful, she thought, so angry with herself for allowing him to upset her that the sight of Alex, still with Lady Susan, only added fuel to the fire. Whatever Alex was doing, she was not going to let him leave her dangling like this. Somehow, she would find out what he was up to, if not tonight, then tomorrow. There was only one more day left.

Today. Alex sat motionless upon Azrael, looking abstractedly at the Serpentine, glassy in the early morning calm, and reviewing once again the plan. Were there any flaws, any points he had left out? No, all seemed to be in place. Men had been dispatched to Leeds, to Plymouth, and to other parts of the country, to watch the members of the far-flung conspiracy. Men constantly, if discreetly, shadowed Edgewater's every move, looking for the evidence that would convict him. Those same men had reported Edgewater's activities last evening, including his attendance at Lady Rutherford's musicale and his conversation with Cecily. Alex's mouth hardened. If he had needed proof of her perfidy, there it was. The two main conspirators discussing their plan, the night before it was to be carried out. God! How could he have been so wrong about her?

Azrael snorted suddenly, tossing his head and Alex,

218

instincts honed by years of living with danger, turned in the saddle. Another rider was approaching, a woman wearing a blue riding habit, mounted upon a large gray. It was the horse that made him recognize her. Cecily.

He watched her approach, his face so expressionless that no one could possibly guess at the tumult of feelings inside him. Not so long ago he had held her in his arms, just a few feet away, kissing her and knowing he had found, at last, the woman with whom he wanted to spend the rest of his life. And she had betrayed him! The anguish of that thought almost made him cry out. Instead, he tightened his lips. He had been betrayed before, and it had hurt. He should have learned from it. He should have known better than to give his heart, and his trust, into any woman's keeping.

Cecily drew Dancer to a stop beside him, her somber face matching his mood. "Good morning, Alex," she said finally.

Alex nodded, not looking at her. "Lady Cecily."

"So formal?" Cecily glanced at him in surprise. She had spent a restless night, tossing in her bed and wondering what had gone amiss. By morning, thoroughly upset and confused, she had decided that she had to confront him. Taking pains with her appearance, she had donned her prettiest riding habit, with its dashing plumed hat. If Alex preferred a more feminine woman, then that was what she would be. For today, at least.

Alex tugged at Azrael's reins, and the big black moved away. After a startled moment, Cecily followed. "Alex," she called, her confusion clear in her voice. "What is wrong?"

Alex stopped. He couldn't do it. He couldn't turn to her and say the harsh, wounding things he had planned to say; he couldn't spit out the accusations that crowded in his mind. Traitor was the least of them, but to say that would tell her that her part in the conspiracy was known. "I made a mistake," he said looking away, his eyes distant, his voice hard.

"About what?"

"About you." Oh, Lord, that was true. He had thought her sweet, innocent, untouched by the world, a symbol of all he had lost, all he had hoped to regain. Even now, he found her perfidy difficult to believe. She had betrayed him, and her country. Yet, to look at her now, with that wounded, worried look in her huge golden eyes, he could still almost believe in her innocence. Almost.

Cecily's brow was furrowed. "What about me?"

"I fear, my dear, that I may have given you the wrong idea. You see, I've been thinking things over the last few days, and I've come to the conclusion this has to end. And if you'll think about it, you'll agree with me."

"What has to end?" she asked, her voice hoarse.

"Our association." His smile was totally charming and totally without warmth. "If you'll think about it, you'll agree with me. You'll only end by being hurt, you know."

Cecily gripped the reins tighter. "Say what you mean. Are you saying we shouldn't see each other again?"

"Yes, my dear, that is exactly what I mean." He smiled again. "I'm grateful for your understanding."

"Understanding!" She wheeled Dancer around and rode a few paces away, the horse's canter showing her agitation. "Understanding! No, my lord, I don't understand any of this! If you'll recall, you were the one who said I was yours. You were the one who spoke of three more days. Today!" She spat out. "What is happening today that is so important?"

"I've come to my senses." He faced her squarely. "Very well, Cecily, if you want plain speaking, I'll give you plain speaking. I wish not to see you anymore."

220

Cecily recoiled. "Come, my dear," he said, his voice gentling. "If you'll think about it, you'll see it's for the best. I may be a rake, but I am not a cad."

"But the things you said to me, the way you kissed me—"

"Ah, but I know very well how to seduce a woman. It was very easy. But boring. You're much too young and innocent. Frankly, my dear, you're not my style."

It hurt. Oh, it hurt. Every word slammed into her like a blow. Every instinct screamed at her to run, to escape and hide, like a hurt, frightened child, but something held her there. Something about the look in his eyes. They were hard and cold, yes, but there was something else. Pain, as if he, too, had been deeply wounded. He looked, she realized suddenly, as he had when she'd first met him. "Fustian."

"What?"

"You're lying. I don't know why, Alex, but I know you better than you think. You're lying to me."

"Why should I bother, my dear? You should know by now I can have any woman I choose."

"So why choose me? I don't know, Alex. You tell me."

"A momentary aberration. You are attractive wearing breeches, you know. But it's true, what I said. You're too young." His smile changed, became a leer. "Perhaps in a few years, my dear, after you're married, we'll meet again."

Cecily recoiled again. "You're insulting, sir," she snapped, and wheeled away. This time she intended to leave, but she couldn't. This wasn't the Alex she knew. Something was very wrong.

She turned Dancer. "I don't know why you're doing this, Alex, but I do know I don't believe a word of it. And I warn you now, I intend to find out why you're acting this way."

There was an odd look on Alex's face. "Do that, my dear. And do come to see me when you're grown up."

"Ooh!" This time Cecily did ride away. The man was insufferable! But she meant what she had said. She had every intention of learning what was going on.

She was gone. Alex sat very still on Azrael, watching her go. Even in a habit, riding sidesaddle, she could manage a horse, he noticed, concentrating on that to block out the other feelings: the pain of knowing that she was not what he had thought her; the loneliness and panic brought on by thinking about a life without her, without someone he could trust; the aching emptiness at being alone. Worst of all was knowing that he could have her back if he said the right word; worst was the temptation to do so, no matter who she was, no matter what she'd done. If he did that, however, it would make everything else he had done in his life a mockery.

Alex turned Azrael away. It might be just as well to leave England, once everything was over. It held nothing for him, though once he had yearned for it. There was always India, or America, or even the Antipodes, places where perhaps he could start afresh, where he could reclaim his life. After tonight, he thought, spurring Azrael forward. Tonight it would all be over, and he could put it behind him. And he would never have to see Cecily again.

Chapter Seventeen

Carlton House was *en fête* this evening, warm and balmy, in contrast to the wet weather that had marked this spring. Each window glowed brilliantly with the light of thousands of candles, and the people gathered to attend tonight's rout were no less brilliant. The cream of the aristocracy was present, of course. Though most professed to disdain the Prince Regent and his policies, few had the courage to refuse one of his invitations. Many memorable evenings had been held here in the past, and tonight would likely be no exception.

Outside, on the other side of the iron railings, the crowds had gathered early, common people waiting to see the nobs and the swells, especially Princess Charlotte, who was popular with the crowd. As each carriage in the long line of vehicles crowding Pall Mall drew up, its passengers would alight and tread the crimson carpet to the stairs, to the loud comments of the mob. Dandies they greeted with derision; ladies, especially well set-up ones, with shouts and whistles of approval, which were largely ignored. It was grand entertainment, and most of the people were enjoying it hugely.

By dint of much pushing and prodding, Alex had managed to secure a place at the front of the crowd. Few would have recognized him; his clothing was old and rough, his lank hair was covered by a dirty cloth cap, and his was face obscured by day-old stubble and a false mustache, expertly applied by Parsons. No one remarked him, but his eyes were everywhere, scanning the crowd, rather than the guests of this evening's rout. Somewhere in the crowd was an assassin. If he could be spotted before the crucial moment, a great deal of trouble would be averted. They'd have Edgewater then. The assassin would lead them back to him.

And, perhaps, to Cecily. *No, don't think about her,* he told himself. Forget her, forget the feelings she had awakened in him, forget that once he had thought he could trust her. Forget, if possible, the pain, though he doubted he ever would. Cecily had brought him back to life. Now any reason he could think of for living, save to finish this job, was gone.

The roar of the crowd increased as another carriage drew up, and he looked up, chagrined that he had allowed his attention to stray. To his relief, it was only an elderly couple, walking past to the accompaniment of jeers and catcalls. Nor was he alone in his vigilance. Foot Guards, also in disguise, were scattered through the crowd, keeping watch and the Household Guards, resplendent in their crimson and gold, were on the stairs. They'd get the assassin. Alex had nearly botched things, but he had the chance to redeem himself. England would not be plunged into revolution, not if he could help it.

Another carriage drew up, this one bearing the Liverpool crest. A footman opened the door of the carriage, and the mutterings of the crowd increased to a roaring crescendo, mostly unfavorable. Silhouetted in the doorway of the carriage were the unmistakable features of the prime minister, the hair receding from his forehead, the long nose, the proud bearing. Alex drew his pistols. The time was now.

Lord Liverpool stepped down onto the carpet, and a shot rang out. Instantly, there was chaos. The Prime Minister dropped to the ground, women began to scream, men to shout and the crowd surged, some to see what was happening, some to escape. Another shot and another, and a man Alex had glanced at only briefly before toppled over, a dark stain overspreading his chest. He fell to the ground, and a pistol dropped from his hand to skitter across the ground. *Hell! The assassin!* Alex thought, turning and saw some feet away a man dressed as roughly as he, lowering a pistol. A man he knew. Edgewater.

For what seemed like eternity they stared at each other. All awareness of the chaos fell away from Alex, to be replaced by red fury and grim purpose. There was the true culprit. Worse than that, overriding all other considerations, was that he had made Cecily part of the plot. For that, he would pay.

Edgewater, an odd little smile on his face, turned, pushing his way through the mob. The sheer gall of it, that he thought he could just walk away, made Alex even angrier. If he accomplished nothing else, he would capture Edgewater. Thus he wasn't thinking quite straight as he turned, struggling for space in the mob of people that surged and pressed forward eager to see what was happening. It was a solid wall of people, and Alex used elbows and feet to push his way through, all the time trying to keep Edgewater in sight. He didn't care who he pushed, whose toes he trod upon, and he ignored the occasional protest or threat that followed him. Until, inadvertently, his elbow struck someone squarely in the midsection.

" 'Ey!" The man, large and beefy, who until this moment had been using his superior height to see what was happening and report on it to his fellows, reared back. "Where you think you're going, mate?"

"Get out of the way," Alex said tersely, and pushed against what felt like a solid mountain of flesh.

" 'Ere, wot do you think you're doin'?" the man said. The look Alex gave him would have been enough to make him quail in normal times, so cold and deadly was it, but this was hardly a usual situation. On top of the excitement generated by the shots, his opponent was imbued with a fighting spirit inspired by gin. "I'll show you, you bastid!" And a dirt-encrusted fist, huge and meaty as a ham, swung straight for Alex's jaw.

Several feet away, Edgewater pushed free of the remnants of the mob and walked on, ignoring both the people who were running to see what was happening, and the melee that had broken out behind him. A close-run thing but, all in all, everything had gone as planned. Liverpool was dead, and his assassin had been eliminated. A good night's work. Now there was nothing to connect him to the plot, except for St. Clair.

Another glance back confirmed that St. Clair was too busy defending himself to care about anything else. Edgewater smiled as he walked casually along, attracting little attention. He'd had a bad moment there when he'd looked up and recognized St. Clair, but other than the fact of his presence there, what did St. Clair have for evidence against him? Nothing. Oh, he'd been very careful, very clever, and he'd soon be rewarded for it. Soon the entire country would know just how clever he'd been, and they'd pay, all those who had mocked him or tried to obstruct his plans. Cecily first, he thought, turning onto Brook Street and then St. Clair—

He never knew what had alerted him. Perhaps it was a sound, or a shadow against his town house. Whatever it was, he suddenly pulled back, pressing against a tree. When there was no immediate sound of pursuit, he cautiously moved forward to look. Tendrils of fog were beginning to creep through the streets, turning an eerie yellow in the gas-lit street lamps, and in the uncertain light he stared hard toward his house. The shadow was still there. A trick of the light? Perhaps. There was no harm, however, in being careful, and watching for just a few moments more.

He had just decided that nothing untoward was about, and was about to come out of hiding, when the shadow moved. Quickly he stepped into hiding again. The fog had grown thicker, but his eyes were good; through the haze he saw the shadow assume the shape of a man standing, and then crouching again. Damn! His house was being watched.

His first, panicky impulse was to flee, but he checked it, standing very still instead, thinking. It could be a burglar, but he didn't think so; on this night of all nights, that would be stretching coincidence. No. There was only one conclusion to be reached. Somehow, he had been found out.

Slowly, ever so slowly, he stepped away from the tree, glad now of the fog that muffled his footsteps on the slate sidewalk and hid him from view. Of all the things he had planned for, this was one contingency he hadn't really expected, and it left him stunned. How had he been found out? He had been careful, clever, more clever than anyone he knew. But, found out, he had been, as St. Clair's presence at Carlton House proved. There was no choice for it but to flee.

At Piccadilly he hailed a hackney and climbed in, giving the driver an address in Chelsea. There he had taken rooms some weeks ago, under the uninspired name of Mr. Smythe-Allen, telling no one, not even Simpkins, about it. It was a drab place, certainly not suited to a man who had nearly brought off the triumph of the century. Damn, where had he gone wrong? No one knew who he really was, except for Worley; he'd been careful of that. And Simpkins, of course. Interesting thought, that. Simpkins had been with him for years, but Edgewater trusted him no more than he would trust a flea. No matter, now. In spite of his situation, he was not without resources. He would wait, biding his time and he would learn who had betrayed him. And then he would get his revenge.

His confidence rebounding, Edgewater jumped from the hackney as it pulled up in front of the narrow, nondescript boardinghouse. " 'Ere, mate, where you think you're goin'?" the driver demanded, and Edgewater whirled on his heel. In the dim light from the streetlamps his eyes glittered eerily, and the driver pulled back in surprise.

"Of course," Edgewater said at last, sounding quite normal. "Pardon me. I forgot."

The driver shifted uneasily in his seat. "That's all right, mate. Happens every day." Surreptitiously he made the sign against the evil eye as Edgewater strolled away. For a moment there, he'd not been sure what was going to happen. Not quite sane, that one, by the look in his eyes. Glad to see the last of him, he was, the driver thought, and drove off.

"Of all things," Alex said, carefully fingering the swelling on his jaw, "I end up in gaol, remanded for brawling."

The duke of Bainbridge crossed his study, a glass of brandy held out to Alex. "I must say, the last thing I expected from this night's work was to be called down to the Old Bailey to go bail for you. But all went well, though you look a little worse for wear." He sat at ease in one of the green leather armchairs, stretching out his legs. "We've the London conspirators in custody, and I imagine the magistrates in the provinces had equal success with the others. I doubt any of them were expecting it."

"No. But, hell." Alex touched his jaw again and then took a careful sip of the brandy. Not only his jaw looked battered; a slight discoloration presaged the makings of a fine black eye, and he was none too certain that one of his teeth hadn't come loose. In the melee that had followed that first punch, he had lost both

228

cap and jacket, and his remaining clothes were soiled and torn. He counted himself lucky to have escaped with his life. "To have seen Edgewater there and not to have got him. That's what galls me."

"He's got the wind up, I fear. It doesn't look as if he'll be returning home tonight."

"So that means he probably has another bolt-hole. Hell. He's damnably clever."

"We'll get him." Bainbridge sipped from his glass. "The important thing is, the Prime Minister is safe."

"True. A good plan, to have someone impersonate him, and the resemblance was uncanny. When he stepped out of the coach, I thought for a moment there'd been a mistake and he was Liverpool. A brave man. Thank God he wasn't badly hurt."

"No, he took the ball in his arm. He was lucky. Had the assassin's aim been more accurate—" Bainbridge downed his drink. "Well. We needn't worry about that. The plot is over, thank God, and the assassin is dead."

"Edgewater shot him," Alex said, setting his empty glass down on the mahogany table that stood between the chairs.

Bainbridge raised an eyebrow. "I would think he's too smart for something like that."

Alex shook his head, an action he immediately regretted. "Smart enough to know that the assassin could lead right back to him. Who else could he trust with such a job? No, he had to do it himself. It must have seemed worth the risk."

"You may well be right," Bainbridge said, after a moment. "In any event, we'll soon catch him."

"Don't be too sure. He's a dangerous man and, a determined one."

"You think he'll try again?"

"I know I won't feel this is finished until he's been arrested. Don't underestimate him, Bainbridge. He's damned clever, and he has all the confidence in the world."

Bainbridge shook his head. "He knows he's a wanted man, and he doesn't dare show his face in public. Even if he does decide to try again, it won't be easy for him."

"Mm." Alex stared morosely ahead, the thought he had been trying to avoid all evening intruding unpleasantly. "What of Lady Cecily?"

Bainbridge shook his head. "Nothing so far. There's a man watching her house, and he's reported only that she went out with her mother and sister. Whatever her involvement is in this, it's not direct."

"But she is involved. Barnes was right, all along."

"Perhaps." Bainbridge leaned back in his chair. "This is a tricky matter, St. Clair. Edgewater was one thing, but Lady Cecily is the daughter of a duke. We'd want to be very certain of our proof before making any move against her, and what, so far, do we have? Nothing but circumstantial evidence."

"Hell, man, she was seen meeting with one of the conspirators — God's teeth," Alex said softly. "The fight must have addled my wits more than I realized."

Bainbridge looked at him. "Why?"

"Because there is one person who can tell us what Lady Cecily's rôle was."

The gate clanged shut behind Alex with such finality that for a moment he feared he might never be allowed to leave. Newgate Prison always had that effect on him, though he'd been here only a few times; its grim stone walls and dank stone floors reminded him inevitably of dungeons, or of Dante's inferno. " 'Abandon hope,' " he murmured and the turnkey, a few paces ahead, turned and looked at him.

"My lord?"

"Nothing." Alex gestured for the man to lead on, down the corridor lit fitfully by torches, his lantern

230

bobbing along.

"In here, my lord." The turnkey opened a heavy door set in the wall and showed Alex into a small, square room, furnished only with a table and some straight chairs. Set high in the far wall was a tiny window, barred against any chance of escape. No daylight was allowed to penetrate into this place of endless night.

"You'll bring the prisoner here?"

"Yes, my lord. If you'll just wait."

"Of course." Alex prowled the room as the turnkey left, wondering what it would be like to be imprisoned here, wondering if this was where Cecily would be incarcerated. The thought hurt so much that he made a motion with his hands, as if pushing it away. No matter what Cecily had done, surely she didn't deserve this. Yet here he was, seeking the proof that would either convict her or set her free. He knew he was foolish to hope for the latter, but he couldn't help it. Everything inside him rose up in revulsion at the thought of Cecily being guilty of treason.

The door opened, and the turnkey came in, holding tightly to the arm of a stout, middle-aged man, his hands held before him in manacles. "The prisoner, my lord."

"Thank you. You may leave us."

"No, my lord. My orders are to stay with the prisoner."

"And mine are to question him alone." From an inner pocket Alex brandished a piece of paper, and though the turnkey could not read well, he could recognize the name of his Prime Minister. Bowing, he left, closing the door behind him.

Alex turned to the prisoner. "Sit down, Mr. Worley. You are Josiah Worley, are you not?"

"And what if I am?" Worley said truculently, but fear gleamed in his eyes. Josiah Worley was, in fact, a very frightened man. When he had been recruited by Edgewater into the conspiracy, he had known things might go wrong. He had not expected, however, that they would go wrong so spectacularly, with him, who had until now been a law-abiding man, gaoled in Newgate, and the marquess still free. Sometimes there just weren't no justice in the world.

"You intend to cooperate, Mr. Worley?" Alex said, his tone light, but his face grim.

"I will if it'll catch that damned marquess," Worley growled. "It true he still hasn't been caught?"

Neither Alex's face nor voice betrayed his surprise. "We think to catch him soon."

"Meaning you haven't. Me dad always told me to stay away from the nobs. Said they'd only cause honest blokes trouble."

Alex permitted himself a small smile. "So it would seem. I rather hesitate to tell you, sir, that I'm a nob. I am St. Clair."

Worley looked in surprise at the hand Alex held out to him. "I can't shake your hand, my lord. Not with these on." The chain on the manacles clanked as he held up his hands.

"We'll take it as given, then." Alex sat down facing the man, his legs crossed, apparently at ease. One would never suspect from his countenance how important the next few moments were to him. "You've been questioned already, have you?"

"Have I," Worley replied bitterly. "They've got a way of making you answer in this place."

"Indeed. Then, you don't deny that your rôle in the plot was to finance it."

"No, sir, I don't deny it. Not if you understand that it was the marquess who asked me to do the financing."

"Which he wouldn't have done if you didn't already have revolutionary leanings. So you knew he was the leader?"

"Course I knew. The others, they were all fooled, but

232

then, they never met the marquess face to face, you might say. Wasn't any way that man would let anyone tell him what to do."

"Indeed. And what part, may I ask, did Cecily Randall play in all this?"

Worley looked blank. "Who?"

"Come, come, man, we haven't all night." Alex leaned forward. "We know she's involved, so if you're trying to protect her, you may as well forget it. What did she do? Was she go-between for you and Edgewater?"

"I don't know who you're talking about, my lord."

"Mr. Worley—"

" 'Struth. I don't know no Cecily Randall."

"Do you mean to tell me," Alex said, his voice deadly quiet, "that you deny having met her at all?"

"'Struth, my lord, I'd tell you if I knew what you was talking about. Weren't no woman involved in this at all."

"Small, golden-brown curls, amber eyes, long eyelashes," Alex shot at him. "She came to your office two days ago with her maid."

Worley continued to look blank and then his face cleared. "Oh, her! The little do-gooder."

"What?"

"That's right, now I recollect. She said she was Lady Cecily something-or-other. Tell you the truth, my lord, I didn't really listen, because she said she'd seen me with the marquess and that had me proper worried."

None of Alex's excitement showed on his face. "When did she see you with him?"

"They was out walking one day, and I made the mistake of greeting him. He gave me a proper dressing down, I'll tell you that. The marquess must have told her who I am."

"So she came to see you—"

"To ask for donations to some charity or other. Some

233

orphanage. A do-gooder, like I said."

"Indeed." Alex sat back, feeling dizzy. She was innocent. Cecily was innocent. Suddenly, none of the night's events mattered, not that he was bruised and battered, not that Edgewater had escaped. Cecily was innocent. "You have been a great help, Mr. Worley," he said rising.

"That's it?" Worley blinked at him. "That's all you want to ask?"

"That's all." Alex crossed to the door, opening it and the turnkey nearly fell in. "You may return him to his cell."

"My lord. What's going to happen to me?"

"I can't say, Mr. Worley. It's not up to me to decide."

"But you'll tell them I helped, won't you? Tell them I'll do anything to help them get the marquess."

"Indeed. Good evening, sir." Alex inclined his head, and only after he was walking out did he allow his distaste for this whole business to show on his face. God's teeth, he would be glad when the whole sorry affair was over. One forgot, in the world of spying, that another world existed, where people went about their daily business and actually trusted other people. It was perhaps no wonder, then, that he had been so quick to suspect Cecily. No more, though. As soon as he could, he would go to her and make some explanation so that they could begin planning their lives together. And never, ever, would he let her suspect what he had once thought of her.

Alex grinned, though it made his jaw ache. No matter that he was still in Newgate, awaiting the return of the turnkey to escort him through the locked gate and doors. For the first time in a very long time, he was free.

Chapter Eighteen

Cecily took two steps into the Gold Drawing Room and stopped. "Oh! I didn't realize you were alone."

Alex rose rather stiffly from the sofa, a bunch of violets in his hands. He was feeling the effects of last night's brawl, but he could not have waited any longer to see Cecily. "Good morning, Lady Cecily," he said without a hint of a smile. "Did your father not tell you I was here?"

"Yes, but he said you would tell me what it was all about." Cecily sank gracefully into a chair, her back straight, her head erect, watching Alex warily. Had it not been just yesterday morning that he had said he was no longer interested in her? "What in the world happened to your face?"

Alex grimaced. "I ran into a spot of bother last night. Looks worse than it is."

"It looks very bad indeed." She studied him. "Is your business over, then?"

"Yes. You may have heard what happened at Carlton House last evening."

Cecily's eyes widened. "Good heavens! The attempt to kill Lord Liverpool?"

"Yes. We had word, some time back, of a plot to overthrow the government. Most of the conspirators have been arrested."

"But not all?"

"No, Edge—no, but we're certain we'll catch them soon." Alex shifted uneasily in his chair. He didn't want to discuss this just now. Already he'd spent an uncomfortable hour with Marlow, explaining how Cecily had been implicated in the plot and what he had been assigned to do. They knew, now, that any mention of her name had been brought in deliberately by Edgewater; he had told his valet, Simpkins, to use the name Randall and had, apparently, considered it something of a joke. To say that the duke was displeased was an understatement. However, he had soon come to a grudging acceptance of the matter, and he was grateful for Alex's efforts to prove Cecily innocent. Alex wanted never to face another such interview.

"Here. These are for you," he said now, with none of his usual charm and crossed the room to hand her the violets.

"Thank you. They are lovely." Cecily buried her face in the bouquet and then raised her face to him. "Alex, why are you here? Yesterday you said you wanted nothing more to do with me. Until after I'm married."

"Hell, Cecily, I'm sorry. That was inexcusable of me. But I had just learned something that upset me, and I'm afraid I took it out on you. Can you forgive me?"

"I don't know," she said softly, gazing down at the violets. "It hurt, Alex, that you lied to me. Oh, don't deny it, I know you did. Do you trust me so little, then?"

"Trust has nothing to do with it." He shifted uneasily again. Trust had everything to do with it.

"Trust has everything to do with it," she said, echoing his thoughts. "Alex, why are you here?"

"Your father has given me permission to pay my addresses to you."

"What!" For a moment she stared, and then a smile crept upon her face. "You've reformed so thoroughly, then?"

"Completely. I swear."

236

"I thought you'd be interested in me only when I'm older."

"Well, yes, of course. And now, too." Suddenly he smiled, the smile she loved so well, the one that transformed his face and made him look young again. No wonder he had been able to charm so many women. In spite of herself, Cecily could feel herself responding. "Cecily, marry me." He leaned forward, his voice urgent. "I'll make you happy, I promise."

Cecily beamed. At last she was hearing the words she had thought never to hear. Everything in her urged her forward, to go into his arms and answer that of course she would marry him, yet something held her back. Something still bothered her. "Alex. What happened yesterday?"

"I can't tell you about that, Cecily. You'll have to trust me."

"How can I, when you won't trust me?"

"It has nothing to do with that, Cecily!" Restlessly he paced the room.

"Then, tell me! I need to know."

"Oh, hell." He stroked his upper lip as he stared out the window, and then turned. "I didn't know what would happen last night. If something happened to me, I wanted you to be able to forget me and go on with your life."

"Fustian," she said crisply. "You're lying."

"Cecily, I swear—"

"Listen to me, Alex! If it has something to do with what happened last night and you can't tell me, I'll understand. But I had the feeling yesterday there was something more personal to it than that. Let's not start with a lie."

Alex looked at her measuringly. He was not used to dealing with women in a straightforward manner; in his experience, most women wished to hear sweet lies, rather than the brutal truth. No matter that she seemed to be able to see into his soul; in the past, his charm had always worked for him.

And so Alex smiled, and made his fatal mistake. "It does have something to do with last night," he said "and that is all I can tell you Cecily." He pulled a footstool over and sat before her, taking her hands in his. "Can't we just put this all behind us? It's over. Once Edgewater is arrested—"

"Edgewater!" Cecily looked startled. "Was he involved in the plot?"

"Hell." He rose again, striding across the room. "I wasn't supposed to tell anyone that."

"Was he?"

"He was its leader."

"Good heavens! Why?"

"How do I know, Cecily? Power, I suppose. I don't know what motivates a man like that, who already seems to have everything, money, position, a beautiful fiancée."

"You thought I was involved," Cecily said, so quickly that Alex had no chance to guard his expression. For a moment, the truth was in his eyes. "You did, didn't you?"

"Hell." Alex sank down onto the footstool, his head in his hands. "Oh, hell. I didn't want you to know, Cecily."

"You really thought that?" she said, stunned. "Simply because I was engaged to Edgewater?"

"No, not just that." He straightened, looking her in the eye. "We had received information that you were involved somehow. We just didn't know how. And you didn't make it easier, Cecily," he accused. "Going into Whitechapel."

"But I explained that!"

"And then being seen with one of the conspirators."

"Who?"

"Josiah Worley."

"What?" She stared at him. "Alex, how do you know all this? No, don't answer. You investigated me, didn't you?"

"Cecily, I had to. Don't you see—"

Cecily rose and went to stand behind her chair. "Then, it was a lie, from the very beginning."

"No, not all of it. I was attracted to you."

"Of course you were, you're a rake. Oh, Alex!" It was a cry of pain. "Oh, how could you do this?"

"Cecily, I never meant to hurt you, I swear—"

"It was a lie, all of it," she said her hands over her face. "Even now, how do I know that you're not using me to catch Edgewater?"

"Because I wouldn't do such a thing! God's teeth, Cecily!" He took a few angry paces about the room and stopped, staring at her. "Do you really think I'd do that to you? Do you trust me so little?"

Cecily lowered her hands and gazed at him, the anger dropping away, leaving behind only an immense sadness. She would not cry. She would not give this man, who had made a career of breaking hearts, the satisfaction of seeing her cry. "How can I possibly trust you, Alex, when you so obviously don't trust me? You don't, do you?"

Alex took a deep breath. "Cecily, I don't trust anyone," he said finally.

"I see." Cecily reached for the bunch of flowers, and then dropped them. "Poor rake," she said, and walked out, leaving behind her the fragrance of crushed violets.

"Cecily!" he called, but she was gone. "Oh, hell!" No woman had ever walked out on him before, never. He had always been the one to do the leaving. Ironic, wasn't it, that the one woman he wanted to marry was the one woman who was unimpressed by his charm. Unfortunately, he was in no humor to enjoy the jest. Hell, he had botched it this time.

Alex sank into the chair Cecily had vacated, his feet propped on the footstool. He was tired, so tired, in his soul more than his body. What did his life hold for him? For a moment he'd thought he had seen his future, shining and bright, had nearly been able to reach out and grasp it. Now it was gone, and the years stretched ahead of him, endless and gray. He had no hope of ever reconciling with Cecily; her parting words had had a terrible ring of finality. And all because, when it had been necessary, he had not been able to put his trust in anyone but himself.

He raised his hand to rub his eyes, remembering, just in time, to avoid his bruises. A necessary habit, that, of trusting no one when he had been a spy. Of course he'd always had a certain reticence, but his life over the past years had only reinforced it. And during that time, he had found himself feeling increasingly lonely, had entered into relationships that were increasingly empty, wondering just what life was about, and never knowing why. Now he did. Now he knew, too late, that the essential connection to life was trust, and love, of another. When he had needed, at last, to let down his barriers and open himself to another, he hadn't been able to do it. Because of that, he had lost Cecily.

The door to the drawing room opened. "Oh, excuse me, my lord, I didn't know you were still here," a footman said.

Alex rose. "I was just leaving. If I may have my hat and my stick?"

The footman bowed. "Of course, my lord. If you'll just follow me."

Alex inclined his head and followed the footman down the stairs. Life wasn't over for him, of course. He'd find something to do, though what did a spy do in peacetime? He'd gone on alone, all these years; he would continue to go on alone and no one would ever suspect the terrible loneliness inside him. Except Cecily. Poor rake, indeed.

At the bottom of the stairs Alex took his hat and walking stick, and then paused, glancing around the hall. In all likelihood this was the last time he would ever come here. "Thank you," he said briskly to the footman, handing him a vail as a tip, and walked out. He couldn't help glancing up at the window he thought might be Cecily's as he passed the house. Several times in the past he had thought that his association with her was finished, only to be proven wrong. There would be no second chance for him this time. Cecily had made that quite clear. He would never see her again.

From her window Cecily watched as Alex walked stiffly away, drawing back when he looked up, though she knew he probably couldn't see her through the sheer muslin of the drape. He was gone. Cecily sank down onto the window seat, at last letting her tears fall. Yesterday, when he had implied he had used her, she hadn't believed him. Today, she did, and it hurt. Oh, it hurt. It hadn't come easily to her, giving her heart; she had done so only when she had realized that she could trust him. What she had learned today destroyed only the trust, not the love. That would take a very long time to die.

Sniffling a little, she went to her dressing table for a handkerchief. No use crying about it, she admonished herself. Crying did nothing for her but give her a headache and red, swollen eyes. It would not bring Alex back, or change the fact that he had used her. Even now, he would have used her if she had allowed it, she thought, anger beginning to replace her grief. The only reason he had ever paid any attention to her was because he had thought her in league with Edgewater. How could he have ever believed such a thing of her?

241

She could understand it, barely, in the beginning of their friendship, but not once he had known her. Not yesterday! He had never really cared about her, never trusted her. How lucky she was to have found out the truth now, or she might actually have married him. She had had a very narrow escape. Why, then, didn't she feel happier about it?

Her handkerchief crumpled into a ball in her hand, she sat on the window seat again, one leg tucked under her and leaned her forehead against the cool glass, unconsciously looking for Alex, though he was long gone. Gone and this time it would be forever. She would have to accustom herself to that fact. She would never see him again.

Few took any notice of the man who stepped down the stairs of the tall, narrow house in Chelsea. On the surface there was nothing out of the ordinary about him. His dress was sober, of decent quality but not the best, in common with that of the other men in this quiet neighborhood, too far from the center of town to be fashionable. He spoke to no one, and no one spoke to him. Were his former acquaintances to see him, they would not have believed the transformation. The marquess of Edgewater intended to do what he had to, to complete what he had come to see as a holy mission.

Several days had passed since he had taken sanctuary here, and the furor over the attempted assassination of the Prime Minister was beginning to fade. When Edgewater first had learned of the failure of his plot, he had been so furious that he had wanted to kill the man who had told him. Fools! He was surrounded by fools and incompetents! Who would ever have thought that the man he had recruited to perform the assassination would have needed to stoke his courage with a large quantity of gin, thus making him miss his shot? And who would ever have suspected that the government would send a substitute for Lord Liverpool, a man who had worn a breastplate of armor under his evening clothes to deflect the assassin's shot? Someone had let the secret of the conspiracy out. Edgewater would give much to know who that had been.

He strode along the King's Road, muttering to himself as he thought of the fiasco, so intent on his thoughts that he walked, full-force, into a man coming the other way. Instead of demanding an apology, however, the man scurried on his way, glancing back over his shoulder as he went and congratulating himself on a narrow escape. The light of fanaticism shone in Edgewater's eyes. Liverpool would have to die. Until he did, the government would remain as it was, reactionary, inept, caring more for the protection of property than for the lives of people. Perhaps then they would appreciate a man like Edgewater; perhaps then they would see him as their savior, a visionary with a clear idea of how the country should be run. By himself, of course. He would come to power yet.

At the corner he paused, and then hailed a hackney. No, of course he would not come to power, he thought, the madness passing. If he stayed in England, he would instead be arrested. Better to go on with his original plans and sail to Jamaica, where he owned a plantation under another name. Before he did so, however, he would finish his mission. That, at least, he could do for his country.

He was ruminating on his plans when the hackney stopped in Westminster. It was chancy, he knew, but he was confident that few would recognize him. It was a risk he had to take. He needed information if he were to succeed. He knew about Liverpool's daily routine. He also knew that the man would be watchful after the attempt on his life. Any moves Edgewater might make would only lead to his arrest, or worse, and that wouldn't do. Failure was not a word he cared to use. Only absolute success would do.

Mulling it over, he walked into a tavern near Parliament and sat with his collar up, slowly sipping at a tankard of ale. Members of the Commons were known to come here before, and after, a session. If he was careful, he might hear something to his advantage. In the meantime, he would content himself with thoughts of revenge against those who had thwarted him. Cecily, now. His eyes grew distant, and an evil smile played about his lips as he contemplated the revenge he would like to take. He knew, however, that he'd never be able to get close enough for that, unless he were to abduct her. That, however, would interfere with his main objective, and so he began to consider his other plan, a more indirect form of revenge. If it worked, the entire Marlow family would feel the scandal. As for St. Clair—

"Can't blame him for wanting to get out of town, after what happened," a voice nearby said and Edgewater's ears perked up. Looking out from under the brim of his hat, he saw two men, one young, one older, take a table across from him. What luck, he thought, congratulating himself on his wisdom in coming here today. The two men, though unknown to him personally, held seats in the Commons and wore the white toppers that had come to denote someone with a radical philosophy. With any luck, he might hear something of interest.

"Bad 'cess to him," the older man replied in a gruff voice, after calling for ale. "The things he's done, makes you wish the shooter succeeded t'other night."

"Keep your voice down!" the young man hissed, glancing quickly toward Edgewater. "You don't know who's listening."

The older man shrugged massive shoulders. "People know how I feel. High time there's a change in things.

You going to tell me you don't feel different?"

The young man leaned forward and said something in a low voice, which Edgewater didn't catch. Then he sat back. "Still, I think it's a good idea he's leaving town."

"Not so sure of that." The older man took a deep draught of his ale. "Heard he'll be meeting with Canning, anyway, and maybe Sidmouth. God knows what they'll think up. More repression, more like."

Edgewater was listening intently. He had already guessed that the two men were talking about Liverpool, who apparently was planning an informal meeting of his cabinet and other trusted advisors at some unspecified location. *Where?* he demanded, silently. *Tell me where!*

"Any event," the older man went on, "be good to see the back of him for a while. Should have a peaceful week while he's at Cranbourne. Another round?"

Edgewater sat back as the two men went on to discuss other matters. Cranbourne Hill, in Hertfordshire. Of course. The estate of Lord Milford, a friend of Liverpool's. Invite the Prime Minister for an informal house party, and allow him to do some business, away from London and possible conspiracies. Or so they thought. Edgewater knew Hertfordshire quite well. He had been born there. All he needed to know was when Liverpool would go, and that should be easy enough to learn.

No one took any notice of him as he rose from the corner table and, after tossing down a few coins, walked out. He wanted nothing more than to laugh aloud with sheer pleasure, but to call attention to himself at this stage of the game would be fatal. Here, at last, was his chance to complete his mission, and the best part of it was that he would be able to get his revenge on Cecily at the same time. He was going to win. There was no doubt in his mind.

This time, he would win.

London's most notorious rake had become even more notorious recently. In whispers, the *on-dits* had spread through the *ton*. St. Clair, it was said, had taken a new mistress, that pretty blond opera dancer at the Haymarket. No, others said, he had already discarded her and had taken up with Lady Wentworth, his past flirt. Or, it was even alleged, both at the same time. He had been seen in a decidedly bosky condition staggering home in the small hours of the morning, and he had punished an opponent at Gentleman Jackson's boxing saloon so thoroughly that Jackson himself had had to step in and end the bout. And his spells of gambling at Crockford's, Brooks's, even Watier's, were legendary. With great abandon he tossed down his markers, not seeming to care whether he won or lost. Most of the time he won, which was just as well. It could be quite expensive, as well as deliciously dangerous, having two mistresses on one string.

Alex sat slumped in one of the green leather chairs in the Duke of Bainbridge's study, contemplating a misspent life. After only a few days of his former activities, he was heartily sick of them. Rumor hadn't exaggerated his recent exploits. He had indeed gambled a great deal; he had also drunk more than his share of wine. His ravaged face had not dimmed the effect of his famous charm, nor had it repelled the females; if anything, it seemed to have stirred up protective instincts in the ample breast of the opera dancer, whom he was considering installing as his mistress. Already, however, her golden charms were palling on him. Her curves were too lush, her hair too brassy for a man accustomed to a slender girl with honey brown curls and huge, laughing amber eyes. Certainly he didn't love her. He wasn't even certain he liked her, which had never mattered before. Dimly he realized the course he was on was self-destructive. What he didn't know was how to change it.

The door to the study opened, and Bainbridge strode in. "Good morning, St. Clair," he said holding out his hand as Alex rose. "Good of you to come this morning."

"Good morning, sir. Has there been word of Edgewater?"

"None, but with everyone in the country looking for him, we'll get him." Bainbridge sat. "Would you care for coffee?"

"No, thank you. No idea where Edgewater is?"

"No. He's harmless now, without his accomplices."

"I'm not so certain of that." Alex's face was sober. He wouldn't rest easy until he knew for certain that Edgewater was behind bars. "Why have you called me here today? Not another assignment, I hope?"

"There is something—but we'll discuss that later. There's someone who wishes to meet you. We thought it more discreet for you to come here."

"Who is that?"

"Lord Liverpool. He's in the drawing room at the moment. If you'd care to come upstairs . . ."

A little while later Alex was ensconced in the same chair in the study, this time accepting the refreshment of brandy the duke offered. He had just spent an uncomfortable few moments with the Prime Minister, receiving his thanks, which made him feel uneasy. What, after all, had he done? Other people had arrested the conspirators; other people had taken greater risks than he had, the man who had impersonated Liverpool most of all. All he had managed was to allow Edgewater to escape, and to wound deeply the one woman he would ever love. It was not, he thought, taking a gulp of the brandy, one of his more successful enterprises.

"On the whole, it went well," Bainbridge said. "The

247

assassin is dead, revolution has been averted, and all without too much fuss. You are to be congratulated, St. Clair."

"Thank you," Alex muttered.

"In fact, we believe you could be valuable to the Home Office."

Alex set his glass down hard. "No."

"No?" Bainbridge raised an eyebrow.

"No. My spying days are done." No more did he want anything to do with that world, where no one could be trusted, no one could be loved. It was too late for him now to have the life he had so briefly envisioned, but damned if he would continue spying.

"Oh, sit down, St. Clair, I agree with you."

Alex paused in the act of rising, feeling foolish. "You do?"

"Yes. Hear me out. Too many people are aware of what you've done for you to be of any value as a spy. However, we could use men like you in the Home Office. You have knowledge of what it actually entails to be a spy."

"So I would direct others, instead of actually spying myself," Alex said slowly.

"If you wish. There's much that needs to be done. I needn't tell you that the country is not in good shape. Any information we can gather to avert revolution is necessary."

"Mm." Alex took a sip from his glass to cover his thoughts. Oddly enough, he had come to agree with Edgewater. Changes needed to be made in England, changes that had nothing to do with the repression the government seemed intent on enforcing, but instead had to do with people's lives. Changes such as Cecily was trying to make, at the orphanage where she taught; changes that would give a man work, and his family enough to eat. Changes that he could possibly help to affect.

Alex shrugged. "I may as well. On one condition."

"Yes?"

"I want to be in charge of catching Edgewater."

Bainbridge opened his mouth, looked at Alex's grim face, and then nodded. "Done," he said, holding out his hand. "We'll be glad of your help."

"Thank you." Alex held up his glass to be refilled as they toasted his future. It wasn't much, but it was something to do. At least it would give meaning to a life that otherwise was empty and purposeless. A life that stretched endlessly ahead of him, without Cecily. He wondered how he would survive it.

"Thank you, Jem," Cecily said, early that afternoon, smiling at the groom as she opened the side door of Marlow House. The groom bowed and she slipped inside, pausing in the hallway to make certain no one was about. Good. Once again she had managed to go to and return from the orphanage without being remarked, and that was a distinct relief. Life had been empty these last few days, purposeless, and the social round had lost all meaning. Teaching at the orphanage had come to mean a great deal to her. It wasn't much, but it gave some purpose to her life.

"Good afternoon, Timms," she said to the butler as she entered the front hall. "Are my mother and sister at home?"

The butler bowed. "The duke and duchess went out sometime ago, my lady, but I believe Lady Diana is abovestairs."

"Thank you." Cecily went upstairs, her serene face hiding her troubled thoughts. The problem was, everything she did now reminded her of Alex. At a ball or an assembly, she always glanced about the room, expecting to see him, only to be disappointed. He was no longer to be found in the park in the early morning when she rode, nor had she seen him today at the orphanage. Of course not. There was no longer any reason for him to keep watch over her. It hurt, still, that he had used her so; it probably always would. Hadn't he cared about her, just a little?

Her room was empty when she entered it, which was a relief; she didn't think she could bear her maid's chatter just now. Pulling off her gloves, she crossed the room to her dressing table. She had just taken off her bonnet and was smoothing her hair when a reflection in the mirror caught her eye: an envelope, propped up on the pillows of her bed.

There was no way she could contain her curiosity. Throwing herself across the bed, she opened the envelope and pulled out the sheet of writing paper within. "Dear Cecily," it began, in Diana's hasty, cramped script. "Edward told me not to tell anyone of this, but I couldn't leave without telling you, dear sister. We are to be married. . . ."

Cecily drew in her breath sharply and scanned the rest of the note. "Oh, the little fool!" she exclaimed, dropping the note from fingers gone suddenly nerveless. Diana had eloped with Edgewater.

Chapter Nineteen

"Thank God you're home, sir," Parsons exclaimed as Alex came into his lodgings, a portfolio tucked under his arm.

"Taking the name of the Lord in vain, Parsons?" he said mildly. He had just spent some hours at the Home Office and already he could feel life returning. He would at least do something useful with his time. "Is something amiss?"

"Lady Cecily is in the sitting room, sir. I told her she couldn't stay—"

"Cecily!"

"—but she insists she needs to talk with you."

"Indeed. I'll see her, Parsons. Thank you." Joy filled him as he strode toward the sitting room. Cecily, here? That could only mean one thing. She had come back to him.

"Oh, Alex, thank God you're here!" Cecily exclaimed, turning as he entered the room. "I thought you'd never come."

"Did you, little one?" He caught her ungloved hands in his and smiled down at her. Her nails were bitten to the quick; evidently she had been no happier than he. "This isn't circumspect of you, but—"

"I had to come." Snatching her hands back, she fumbled in her reticule. "Here, read this."

Alex frowned at the piece of paper Cecily thrust at

251

him. "What's this?"

"Read it! Oh, never mind, it will be quicker if I tell you. My sister Diana has eloped with Edgewater."

The joy faded. So she had not come to mend the breach between them. Even the news that Edgewater had at last come out of hiding could not dispel his keen disappointment. "I see," he said finally, dropping the note onto a table and pacing to a window. "And what am I to do about it?"

"You must help me stop them! Alex—"

"*I* must?" He turned. "Why come to me and not your father?"

"My parents are not at home. Alex, please, we dare not wait. If we don't catch them soon—Alex, you know what Edgewater is capable of!"

"Where is he taking her?" he asked, his interest stirring in spite of himself.

"Gretna Green."

"Gretna—" Scotland, via the Great North Road. Which led through Hertfordshire, which was where—. A hideous thought burst into his mind. Cranbourne Hill, for which the Prime Minister planned to leave today, to spend the next week in discussion with various members of his cabinet, near the Hertfordshire village of Stevenage. God's teeth, Edgewater was still intent on his scheme. "Parsons!" he bellowed, and Parsons came running in through the passageway.

"Yes, sir?"

"Send down to have my curricle set to, and quickly! Edgewater's tipped his hand at last."

"Has he, sir! By God, that's good news!"

"More swearing, Parsons?" Alex said, but he was grinning. He'd catch Edgewater at last. "Thank you for telling me of this." He turned to Cecily, his face expressionless. "With any luck we should catch him before he does any damage. You'd best get home now."

"Oh, no, you don't, my lord."

252

"Cecily, there isn't time—"

"I'm coming with you."

"No. My curricle won't hold you, and there might be danger—"

"Which is why I brought this." Cecily pulled a small, silver-handled pistol from the pocket in her pelisse.

Alex couldn't help it; he smiled. "Cecily, that toy—"

"I assure you, I know how to use it. Damn it, Alex!" She stamped her foot. "He has my sister! Do you think I'll stand tamely by—"

"I'm not taking you anywhere there might be danger. Rest assured I'll bring your sister back safe."

"And what of her reputation? Are you prepared to marry her, then?"

"That pretty widgeon? God's teeth, no!"

"Then, you'll have to have a female along," she said calmly, drawing on her gloves. "I'm ready when you are, sir."

"God's teeth, Cecily—oh, very well. Parsons can drive and I'll ride. But you're to stay out of danger, little one."

"Yes, Alex." Cecily bent her face to hide her smile. She didn't think he was even aware that the endearment had slipped out, and that lifted her spirits immeasurably. Could it be he did care, after all?

A look at his set face dispelled that idea. "Shall we go?" he said holding the door, and Cecily glided through, her face serene. Of course she wanted to find Diana, but she had had other motives when, panicked, she had run to him for help. Foolish, she chided herself. After this, she would put him out of her life, once and for all. She would have to. But she knew, with a pain deeper than any she had ever experienced, that it wouldn't be easy. It was going to be a very bad time.

Diana was enjoying herself as she rarely had. Oh,

certainly she liked attending the assemblies and routs of the season, and she even enjoyed the more rustic life at Marlow, though she'd never admit it to her more *tonnish* friends. This, though, this was adventure and so romantic, too. To be bowling along the Great North Road in a fashionable curricle—well, perhaps it wasn't so very fashionable—with a handsome man, was the height of romance. Whyever Cecily had broken off her engagement with this man, Diana didn't know.

She stole another glance at Edgewater's classic profile, and a little thrill went through her. Since leaving behind London's traffic, Edgewater had sprung his team, a mismatched pair of a bay and a chestnut, who were at least smooth goers. Diana still didn't quite understand why they weren't riding in his wonderful phaeton with its team of blacks, but she didn't really mind, either. The whole escapade had such an element of mystery and secrecy, so much like her favorite novels, that her whole being thrilled to it.

The idea of elopement had startled her at first, but Edgewater had soon managed to persuade her to his way of thinking. Everyone in her family seemed opposed to him, unfairly so. And so, early this afternoon, when it was supposed she was in her room, she had engaged a hackney for the Lombard Street Post Office, where the mail coaches started and met her intended with his hired curricle and job horses. No one would ever expect the dashing marquess of Edgewater to drive such a rig and so their secrecy was protected. That there was apparently some sort of scandal concerning the marquess only made everything more mysterious and romantic.

They had already stopped to change horses several times and were moving at a spanking pace through the Hertfordshire countryside. Of course they wouldn't reach Gretna Green tonight, or even tomorrow night, but Edgewater had promised he knew of some out-of-the-way inns where no pursuers might find them. At that, Diana felt just the slightest bit uneasy. He had made her promise to tell no one of the elopement, but she hadn't been able to resist writing that note to Cecily. They were more than sisters, they were friends, but Diana admitted to herself she'd written the note with pride. After all, it was she Edgewater really wanted, not Cecily, and that made her preen a bit. Cecily awed her sometimes. She was so calm and practical and so rarely made the same silly mistakes that Diana did, that she sometimes despaired of ever living up to her. Now, though, she had the man Cecily had thrown over.

"Oh, everyone will be so surprised!" she chattered, slipping her arm through Edgewater's and hugging herself against it. He started and the team momentarily slued sidewise. "I'm sure no one suspected what we planned, we were so very careful, but once we return, they'll see how suitable this is. Papa will be angry at first," she went on, "but I'm sure he'll come around. And then he and Mama will probably give a wonderful reception for us, and we'll be so happy."

"Of course," Edgewater muttered.

"But, Edward dear, you're so quiet! We've miles to go yet, haven't we? Shouldn't we talk, to pass the time?"

"You do enough of that for both of us, Diana."

Diana paused, unsure at the edge she heard in his voice. He was funning her, of course. "I wish we could have stopped at Marlow, to tell everyone our news. Perhaps on the way home? I do wish, Edward, I could have told more people about this, besides Cecily — oops!"

The curricle stopped, and Edgewater turned slowly to face her. "You told Cecily."

"Well, yes." Diana forced herself to meet his eyes and smiled brightly. "But only in a note, which I am persuaded she won't read for hours yet. I had to tell someone, you see, Edward, and she is my sister —"

"Damn you!" Edgewater's hand raised high. "You fool —"

"Edward!" Diana cried, shrinking back.

"You stupid idiot, now you've spoiled everything!"

"B-but I don't think it will do any harm. You said no one would know you in this carriage —"

"Yes, and haven't we been stopping to change horses? Damn you!"

"Edward! That's no way to talk to me."

"You will not reprimand me." He spoke with chilling finality, and in his eyes was a strange, wild look. "Never speak to me so again."

"No, Edward, I won't," she said frightened into docility.

"I wonder what I shall have to do with you," he went on, in a conversational tone that was somehow even more frightening. "But, damn, I can't worry about that now; I haven't the time." Picking up the ribbons, he set the team into motion again.

From her corner of the curricle, Diana eyed Edgewater warily. He was muttering to himself, and his eyes looked strange. She'd expected him to be annoyed about the note, but not this upset. It was out of all reason; it was not quite — sane. Panic flared within her. She was trapped on a country road with a mad man.

Her first impulse was to jump out, but she was made of sterner stuff than she cared to show. There was nothing she could do about it; at least, not now. If she started to scream, the least that would happen was that he would be angrier, and the worst — well, she didn't want even to consider that. She had to escape him; she just couldn't do so yet. The chance would come, however, at the next posting house. What she must do now was to lull any suspicions he might have about her, as though she hadn't realized the import of his actions. It shouldn't be so very difficult to act feather-brained; she'd been doing so for years.

"I wonder what the fashions are like in Scotland," she said brightly and Edgewater slowly turned to look at her. "Are they like ours, do you think, or does everyone wear plaid? I don't like plaid very much, do you? Though I think perhaps a gown of it might be rather interesting. With a plain bodice, of course." She tilted her head to the side. "What do you think, sir? But you won't be interested in ladies' fashions," she chattered on. "You, sir, are always so elegantly turned-out, you must be more interested in your own clothing! If I had a gown of plaid, it would look well with a green evening coat, don't you think?" Edgewater muttered something under his breath. "What is that you say, sir? Oh, and I've just had the most marvelous thought! When my parents have the ball for us, we can decorate in plaid. Tartan, I believe it's called? Yes, tartan! Why, we'll be the success of the season. Even more than Lady Cuthbert's ball, with the pink taffeta that she had. So *de classe,* don't you think? Did you attend Lady Cuthbert's, sir? She—"

Diana prattled on, about parties she had attended, people she had met, an interesting cloud formation, cows gathered in the fields they passed, different houses, and, of course, ladies' fashions. Edgewater tried to ignore her, but it was difficult; her voice had become high-pitched, and it seemed to penetrate into every corner of his brain. Damn, if he had to listen to this all the way to Scotland, he'd go mad—but he wasn't going to Scotland, and that was the beauty of his plan. Soon he would turn off the Great North Road. They were nearing Lord Milford's estate, and he would, at last, have a chance to complete his mission.

Edgewater chuckled, and Diana's voice faltered for just a moment. Such a beautiful plan as it was, too. No one would suspect him; he had carefully laid clues that indicated he was aiming for Dover, in the opposite direction. By the time any government agents who might be searching for him realized they'd been misled, it would be too late. Liverpool would be dead, and Edgewater would be on a ship, bound for Jamaica. And Lady Diana? She would have her own problems, and he would have his revenge on the Marlows, better than he'd expected when he'd first started paying court to Diana. Even Cecily was certain to be hurt by the scandal.

He chuckled again. Nothing would stop him now. No one knew where he was going, or what he intended. Even if Marlow did send someone after them, Edgewater was certain he wouldn't be found, once he turned off the road. His real source of danger came from St. Clair, but it was unlikely he would hear of the elopement until it was too late. A pity, that. Edgewater would rather have liked to face St. Clair and make him pay for the ruination of his scheme. That he couldn't was the only thing that annoyed him about making the move now. He would have to wait for his revenge. Nothing must detract from his mission. Nothing.

". . . And of course, there was that time at the Duke of Dartmouth's ball," Diana was saying, and Edgewater turned to look at her, his eyes distant and distracted.

"I beg your pardon?" he said, as if he hadn't snarled at her earlier.

"The time you danced with me, silly!" Diana hugged herself against his arm, though it took all her determination to do so. He mustn't suspect. "I knew then, didn't you? Oh, we'll be so happy together. Why are we turning off the road?"

"We need to stop for a while." Edgewater shook off her arm, concentrating on guiding his team down the rutted lane. Cecily had been right, Diana thought. He could hardly drive at all. And he was really a cruel man; the look in his eyes a few moments ago had terrified her. How was it that she hadn't seen it before? No wonder Cecily had broken the engagement. Diana only wished she herself hadn't been so blind.

"There's an inn along here," Edgewater went on. "We'll stop and refresh ourselves."

The look he gave her was so wolfish that Diana nearly shrank back. Oh, how would she escape now, if they were off the main road? She had counted on their stopping at a busy posting inn, bustling with carriages and people to cover her escape. That wouldn't be possible in a sleepy country inn on some narrow lane. She'd never get free. And if Cecily had told their parents, as Diana was certain she had, any pursuers on the road would miss them. Oh, she had handled this terribly! The only thing she could do was to act as featherbrained as she had all along, and await her chance.

And so she began to chatter again, of clothing and parties and gossip and such, until even she was tired of it. What Edgewater thought, she couldn't guess; he responded hardly at all, and that drove her on to more extravagant flights of fancy. "And of course we'll invite the most fashionable people to our home," she prattled.

"That will be too expensive," he snapped.

"Oh, nonsense, Edward, one must keep up appearances! But we won't invite that nasty Caroline Lamb, not after she wrote that book. Mama doesn't know that I read it. Did you read it, sir? Who do you suppose each person is supposed to be? And as for Lord Byron—I don't know what he was supposed to have done to make him leave the country, do you—"

"Do you know of aught else besides gossip and scandal?"

Diana made her eyes grow very large. "Why, no, sir. What else is there?"

"Politics. Government. What is happening in the world. Damn, Diana, don't you have a thought for anything else?"

"You swore at me." Diana's cornflower-blue eyes brimmed with tears. *I should go on the stage,* she thought.

259

In an odd way, she was enjoying this. "Oh, Edward, what have I done that is so very bad?"

"You—oh, never mind." Edgewater sounded thoroughly disgruntled. "You wouldn't understand. At least your sister has more brains than a peahen."

"Cecily? I never did know how you could abide her, sir, she is so odiously practical. And not at all fashionable, as you and I are." Diana steeled herself to snuggle against him. "It will be so wonderful being married, won't it? Just think! Together we can set all the styles. We can have as many parties as we like, and meet with our friends. Could we go to Brighton for the summer? I confess to a longing to see the regent's new pavilion. Oh, we'll just be so *tonnish*, and—why are we stopping?" Edgewater didn't answer, but merely sat, his head bowed. "Edward? There's no inn here."

"Get out."

"Why, Edward—"

"Get out." God help him, it meant the end of his revenge, but he could not abide Diana's chatter one more moment.

"But—"

"This is as far as you're going. Out."

"But, Edward." Protesting, Diana clambered out. "This is so ungentlemanly of you. Was it something I said—"

"You might say so." Giving her his mocking smile, he picked up the ribbons. *"Au revoir,* my dear," he said and drove off, leaving Diana standing in a cloud of dust.

"Good heavens!" Diana stared after the fast-disappearing curricle, brushing the dust from her pelisse. "Well! So much for *his* undying passion." Her face was cheerful, though, as she turned and began tromping back toward the Great North Road, grateful that she'd worn stout shoes. Her strategy had worked, if not exactly as she had planned. She was

260

safe. But where in the world was she?

"Hell." Alex fumed as his curricle got caught behind a slow-moving dray. They had yet to get out of London, and already he chafed at the delay. Here was his chance to capture Edgewater, and to avert a disaster. "At this rate, we'll never catch them."

"According to her maid, Diana was at home this morning, so they haven't much of a start on us." Cecily glanced at Alex, whose hands, seemingly relaxed on the ribbons of the curricle, kept his team in perfect control. She'd never driven with Alex before. She wondered if she ever would again. "I doubt they're very far ahead of us, the way Edgewater drives. He is the veriest whipster, sir. Not like you."

Alex didn't answer this tentative attempt at peacemaking, and so Cecily sat back, nursing the angry injustice that had filled her for the past few days. Once again he was using her, because of her connection with Edgewater. Foolish of her to think he had ever cared, and yet—and yet there had been that look in his eyes when first he had seen her in his lodgings. "I know you think having me along is a dreadful nuisance—"

"Hardly. I always take a girl with me when I chase a dangerous criminal," he said, an edge to his voice. "But then, I am a rake, remember? I use people."

"You needn't be sarcastic."

"And you needn't prattle."

Prattle! The nerve of him! Very well, if that was how he wished it, that was how it would be. Cecily crossed her arms on her chest and settled back in fulminating silence, not even remarking when, by a remarkable display of driving skill, Alex managed to pass the dray, with only inches to spare. She couldn't help stealing little glances at him, though, at the hair that riffled across his forehead, at his lips, set in their habitual straight, thin line, at the hands that held the ribbons, strong and hard and yet, as she well knew, capable of gentleness, too. But not for her. Never again for her.

Parsons galloped back to them as they at last emerged from London's traffic onto the Holloway Road and began to pick up the pace. "Found 'em, my lord," he called, turning to ride with them. "They changed horses at the posting house in Finchley, not more than two hours ago."

"Good! Then we have a chance. Fine work, Parsons."

"Thank you, sir," Parsons said and galloped off.

"We'll catch them, then," Alex said, more to himself.

"I hope so. I hate to think what Edgewater is doing to my sister," Cecily said.

"Your sister, ma'am, apparently went quite willingly."

Cecily bristled for just a moment. "Yes, I know. She doesn't have the best judgment, but she isn't really stupid. Of course, Edgewater can be very charming, when he wishes."

"You should know, ma'am."

"Oh! Must you be so odious?"

"Yes, it appears I must."

"I don't like this anymore than you do," Cecily said in a tight voice. "But I would like to find my sister and get her home before dark."

Alex glanced up at the sky. The fast-moving clouds made the day appear later than it was. "Not much chance of that, ma'am. At this rate, you'll both be compromised." His smile held little humor. "And if you think I'll marry you—"

"I wouldn't marry you, no matter how compromised I am!" Cecily snapped, and turned away, fighting back tears. Where had it all gone wrong? She had been attracted to two men, and both had wanted her for the wrong reasons. Would she never find someone who wanted her for herself? Someone who loved her?

"They're not making much effort at secrecy," Cecily said, determined not to give in to melancholy.

"Edgewater doesn't expect to be followed," Alex answered, absently. "It's what's finally going to bring him down."

"What?"

"His overconfidence. He thinks he's superior to everyone. This time, he's wrong."

Cecily glanced at him curiously. "You sound as if you have a personal grudge against him."

"Whyever would I feel that way?" he said, with that edge to his voice, making Cecily look at him again. What was there in that for him to be sarcastic about?

Alex could feel Cecily's gaze on him, but he had no desire to explain. She had made it clear she didn't want him; why should he tell her that his chief grudge against Edgewater was that he had been engaged to her? It seemed as if in all Alex's encounters with the man, Edgewater had come off the winner. Not this time, though. He was acutely aware that they were approaching Stevenage. If they didn't catch up with Edgewater soon, he would have to put Cecily off and go after him.

He had just decided that he would stop at the next inn when, looking down the road, he saw a woman trudging toward them, a bundle in her hand. She looked so bedraggled that he didn't recognize her until Cecily spoke. "It's Diana!"

"God's teeth! It is," he said and brought his team to a halt just as Diana ran toward them.

"Thank God you've come," Diana said, gasping for breath as she reached them. "I didn't know what I was going to do."

"Where is he?" Alex said tersely.

"He took a turning up ahead and left me off." She smiled, suddenly. "I think I bored him."

"Oh, Diana," Cecily said. "What in the world did you

think you were about?"

"Oh, give over, Cece! I've had a terrible day." Her smile faded. "He really scared me. I think he's gone mad."

Alex handed the ribbons to Cecily and jumped down. "Climb in," he said to Diana. "Cecily, do you know how to drive?"

"Yes, but—"

"There's an inn up ahead. Go there and wait for me."

"You're going after him. Oh, Alex—"

"The inn won't allow us in," Diana said unexpectedly. "Not two females, unescorted."

"Hell, there's no time!" Alex looked up at them. "And no room in the curricle for three."

"Cecily can sit in my lap."

"Yes. Alex, please—"

"Oh, hell," he said, but he knew there was no hope for it. Without an escort, the George Inn, which he knew catered to the nobility, would not allow the two girls in, let alone give them a private parlor. If they wished to get out of this with their reputations intact, he would have to go along. "Hell. All right." He clambered back in and by squeezing together, the girls managed to make room for him. There was so little time. He couldn't afford to let Edgewater escape.

They drove in silence, except when Diana pointed out the turning she had taken with Edgewater, until they saw a figure riding toward them. "Parsons. Thank God," Alex said.

"You've got Lady Diana?" Parsons called. "Where's Edgewater?"

"Gone down the last turning. There's not a moment to lose! As I recall, it leads to Cranbourne."

"I'm on my way, sir."

"I'll join you when I can." Grimly Alex leaned forward, setting his team, nearly exhausted now, to as fast a pace as he could manage.

264

Cecily stared at him. "Cranbourne. Isn't that where Lord Liverpool is staying this week?"

"Yes."

"Good heavens. Alex, you don't think he's going to try again!"

"I know he is." Alex's face was as grim as his voice. "And I have to stop him."

"Then, go after him. Don't worry about us—"

"Not until I know you're safe," he said, pulling into the inn yard with a flourish.

"I don't understand," Diana protested.

"You'll stay here until I can come for you. Though God knows we'll be lucky to reach London by nightfall."

"I don't care. You can't face him alone, Alex."

"I'll have Parsons. We'd like your best private parlor." This last was addressed to the innkeeper, who bowed and scraped at what he knew was the Quality. "You'll be safe enough here."

Cecily barely glanced around the snug little parlor, with its sturdy table and comfortable chairs. "But what of you? 'Tis dangerous—"

"He has to be stopped. And I suppose you're thinking I used you again to get to him."

"No, Alex, I—"

"It doesn't matter. Stay here until I return," he said, and stalked out the door.

Cecily stared after him. "He'll get himself killed!"

"Cece, what in the world is going on?" Diana asked.

"There's no time to explain now. I have to go after him."

"But he said not to leave—"

"He might be killed! I couldn't bear it."

"Cece! Are you in love with him?"

"Yes." Oh, Lord, yes. "Be a good girl, Di, and stay here? I can't let him go alone."

"But, Cecily—"

265

Cecily kissed her quickly on the cheek. "I'm glad you're safe," she said, and whirled out the door, leaving Diana to stare after her. This had been the most confusing day.

Cecily ran down the Great North Road, heedless of passing traffic and the stares she was receiving. In other circumstances she would have been concerned about her reputation, but today that was the least of her worries. Now, when it was too late, she at last knew that it was Alex she loved, Alex she needed. She belonged by his side, no matter where he was, and if he were in danger, she wanted to share it. The cool, practical Cecily, who would have realized there was little she could actually do, was gone. In her place was a woman in love, ready to risk all for her man.

The turning seemed farther down the road than she had expected, but at last she reached it. Instantly she was plunged into a shadowy, silent world, as the road narrowed to little more than a lane. She had once been to Cranbourne Hill; but this road was new to her, and she had little idea of where she was. All she knew was that Alex was ahead someplace, and that he was in danger.

A distance down the road she passed a shabby curricle, its team of job horses stamping and blowing, tied to a tree. Of Alex and Parsons there was no sign. Except for the curricle, she might have been alone, and she began to feel profoundly uneasy. It was too quiet. No birds sang; no animals rustled in the underbrush. To Cecily, a girl raised in the country, that meant only one thing: The animals scented a threat. The humans were about somewhere.

That meant she might very well be watched, right at this moment. The skin between her shoulder blades prickling, she spun around, but she saw no one, nothing, only the thickening gloom as the daylight began to fade. It was time she took some precautions herself. Spotting a break in the trees, she turned into the forest. Here the undergrowth was thick, impeding her progress. Try though she might to be quiet, she couldn't help stepping on twigs or brushing against the branches that seemed to reach out to snag her clothing. This was no good. Without knowing exactly where Alex was, what could she do?

She had decided to return to the road when a branch snapped up ahead. Cecily froze. Someone was there! Her hand crept into the pocket of her pelisse to find her pistol, and she withdrew it with shaking fingers. At that moment, a shot rang out, and she dropped to the ground.

Chapter Twenty

"Come out," a voice called, and Cecily raised her head.

"Alex?"

"What—God's teeth! Cecily!" Alex appeared through the trees ahead of her. "What the hell are you doing here?"

"You shot at me," Cecily said, rising shakily and dusting herself off. In the tree near to where she had been standing was a fresh scar in the bark. "Not too well."

"Would you have preferred my aim to be accurate?" he snapped. "God's teeth, what are you doing here?"

"Looking for you." She plucked a dead leaf from her pelisse. "I see I needn't have bothered."

"Looking for—oh, for God's sake." Disgusted, Alex turned away. "Go back."

"No." Now that the shock of being fired upon had worn off, Cecily stood her ground. "I may be foolish beyond permission, but I can't let you face him alone."

"What are you going to do? Protect me?"

"You needn't be sarcastic! I do know how to use a pistol."

"And have you ever fired at a man? No, I thought not. Leave, Cecily. You'll be worse than useless. You're a liability. I don't want you here."

Cecily flinched at each word. "I'm not going."

"Hell, Cecily, don't you see? I can't protect you and fight Edgewater at the same time."

"Oh." Now she understood, and for a moment her heart warmed. Only for a moment, though. He was a gentleman, after all, and a gentleman would feel obliged to protect a lady. She put up her chin. "I can protect myself, sir. And," she went on as he began to protest, "if I go now, Edgewater may find me. I think I'd best stay with you."

"Hell." She was right. She was in danger if she stayed with him; she might be in more danger if she left. "Oh, all right," he said ungraciously. "Follow me and —"

Another shot rang out, this one coming from the direction of the road. Without stopping to think, Alex threw himself at Cecily, knocking her to the ground and falling atop her. Frantically he fumbled for his pistol, managing at last to pull it free. "Stay down," he commanded, and rose to a crouch, his eyes alert, his muscles tensed. In the wake of the shot, the silence rang eerily, and in spite of Alex's command, Cecily lifted her head to watch him. Gone was the elegant man about town she was used to seeing; the veneer of civilization had been stripped away, revealing the essence of the man, a hunter, deadly and savage, and yet somehow magnificent. Something stirred deep within her at the sight, some primal force. Edgewater, no matter how dangerous, paled next to this man.

Far off in the underbrush, branches crackled, and Alex was up and running, as lithe as a cat. Left alone, Cecily slowly rose, aware of bruises from her fall, and crept to the shelter of a tree trunk, pulling her pistol out. She felt defenseless, uneasy, though she doubted Edgewater would actually come back. If it came down to it, could she defend herself? She had never shot a man. The thought of doing so made her ill.

The branches crackled again, and Cecily stiffened. Swallowing hard, she raised her pistol, just as Alex came into view. "Lost him," he said briefly, extending a hand to help her stand.

"Was it Edgewater?" she asked, holding his hand for a moment longer than necessary. Now that the danger was past, at least for the moment, her legs were decidedly shaky.

"Had to be. I didn't see him, though. Are you all right?"

"Yes. I'm glad I didn't have to use this, though," she said, gesturing with the pistol.

"Keep it close by," Alex said, so grimly that for the first time the danger of this situation came home to her. This was no game. This was life and death, and it was something Alex had engaged in before. In such a situation, whom did a man trust?

She was standing stock still, absorbing the shock of that revelation, when Alex, who had already walked a few paces away, turned. "Come. There's a path a few feet away. I suspect it leads to the estate. Try to be quiet."

"Yes, Alex," Cecily said, so meekly that he gave her a look. It was as well that Alex, tense, alert, was watching for danger as they walked along the path; Cecily was following her thoughts. In the past years, Alex had lived in a dangerous world, a world where betrayal might be only a few words away. In such a world, he would learn quickly to keep his own counsel, and to rely on few. It would be very hard to unlearn such lessons, just because the war was over. It was obvious to her now that Alex was very much, in his own way, a warrior, though he'd never actually fought a battle. His war had been a different one, and it was still going on. If he had evidence, no matter how sketchy, that a certain Lady Cecily was involved in a conspiracy, why should he believe otherwise? And yet, in the face of danger, he had acted to protect her, not himself.

Alex suddenly stopped, his hand held up, and Cecily, not attending, walked directly into him. He turned quickly, but the remonstration on his lips died when he saw her eyes, huge, questioning, framed by those long lashes, gazing up at him. How could he ever have thought her guilty for so much as a moment? But he hadn't, not really. In spite of the evidence against her, he had known from the beginning, deep within himself, that she was innocent. He had done her a grave disservice. He wondered if he could ever make it up to her.

"Is something wrong?" Cecily whispered, and he abruptly became aware that he was staring at her.

"Ahem." He cleared his throat. "No. The house is just over there."

Looking past him, Cecily could just see through the trees the long, curving drive and the west wing of the great house. There was no one about; in the fading light of early evening, the manicured lawns and formal gardens were empty. "How will Edgewater know where to find Lord Liverpool?"

"I suspect he's going to watch for the carriage coming up the drive. How he'll do it, though, I don't know, though he must have some plan. He values his own skin too highly to endanger it unduly."

"Do you think he'll try for us first?" she asked with creditable calmness, sinking down onto the ground next to him.

"No, and for the same reason. Any shots would alert the house that something is wrong." He peered forward, his eyes intent. "He's come this far; he's not going to give up now."

She looked over at him, crouched beside her in the shrubbery that lined the parkland. "Alex, I owe you an apology."

"Why? All you've done is possibly ruin my chance of catching an assassin."

"I hate it when you're sarcastic!" she flared. "Oh,

why should I bother? I thought I misjudged you, but maybe I haven't. You can't trust anyone, can you? Not even to—"

"Why should I? Most people have proven quite untrustworthy."

"Not even to show your feelings, so you hide behind sarcasm."

"I don't need your pity," he said, biting off the words.

"Pity? That was contempt! Is that how you're going to live your life, Alex, forming brief attachments, never letting anyone get too close—"

"Be quiet."

"—never really getting involved with someone, holding people at arm's' length—"

"Cecily, I am warning you."

"—never feeling love?"

"God's teeth, who says I don't feel love?" he demanded, and fastened his mouth on hers. After a startled second, Cecily responded, moving her mouth eagerly against his, and when at last the kiss ended, both were breathing unevenly.

"You're experienced at this," she said at last, her voice as shaky as her breathing. "You know what to do to affect a woman."

Alex reached out to tuck an errant curl behind her ear, his hand unsteady. "No, Cecily. Only you. I've never kissed anyone else like that."

"Only me?" Joy flared within her. "But how can I believe you, when you don't believe in me?"

"Cecily." He leaned his forehead against hers. "Trust is hard for me, with the life I've led."

"I know. I finally realized that."

"But I do trust you." He pulled back to gaze at her. To her surprise, his eyes were anxious. "I do. If I didn't, I wouldn't have let you stay."

"And here I thought you were concerned about my safety."

272

"That, too. And I wanted you with me." He leaned against her again. "I *am* a poor rake, Cecily. I'm all that you said, and more. But I don't want to be that way and I'm trying. It will take me time, sweeting."

"Oh, Alex." She reached up to touch his cheek. "We have that."

"Maybe." He straightened, looking regretful. "Of all times for this . . ."

"I don't know, it seems appropriate, somehow. Considering how we first met."

He flashed her a brief smile, and then turned serious. "It'll have to wait for London, sweeting."

"I can wait." Her eyes met his. "I trust you, Alex."

Alex caught her hand and kissed it. "Thank you, sweeting."

"Now." Cecily's voice became brusque. "What are we going to do about Edgewater?"

"Catch him." Alex's face had gone grim again. The hunter was back. "I'll not let him escape this time."

"I think we should go after him."

Alex turned toward her, grinning. "Do you know, Cecily, I think in your own way you're something of an adventuress."

Cecily's eyes sparkled. "Such a compliment, sir! But really, Alex, don't you think we should hunt him down, instead of waiting for him to show himself?"

"Yes, I do." He rose, reaching out his hand to her. "I'd like to leave you here. You'd be safe enough, I think. I doubt Edgewater will wish to run into us."

"No. 'Whither thou goest.' "

"I don't think that quote is particularly apt," he said, but he was smiling. "Very well, then. Let us go catch an assassin."

Some distance away, the marquess of Edgewater crouched near some bushes, looking out at the house

273

and considering his alternatives. The drive, where soon Lord Liverpool would be arriving, was too far for his shooting, superb though it was, to be effective. He had to get closer to the house, but not so close that he couldn't elude capture. What he needed was a diversion, or a hostage. A hostage, yes, that was an idea and he knew where one could be found.

The idea was so perfect, he nearly laughed aloud. When he had heard the shot, sometime earlier, he'd known he was being pursued. Somehow, he hadn't been surprised to see St. Clair, but the sight of Cecily had been startling. Now he could see it for what it was, the intervention of some kind fate, allowing him to take his revenge on both Cecily and St. Clair, as well as to complete his mission. It confirmed what he had always known. He was one of the special ones, one of the chosen, and he would win out. Anything less was unimaginable.

Wearing the mocking smile that never reached his eyes, Edgewater rose. He had work to do, and he would succeed. His destiny was within reach.

"Stay close," Alex cautioned as he and Cecily began their slow progress through the belt of woods between the house and the lane, "and keep as quiet as possible."

"I wish I'd worn my breeches," she whispered, and he flashed her a quick smile. "Did you see him go this way?"

"No, but it stands to reason he's here somewhere. He has to get close to that drive." He held a branch back so that she could pass by, and though he smiled at her, it was clear to her from the tense set of his shoulders and the way his eyes searched the trees behind her that she wasn't uppermost in his mind. She didn't mind. In an odd sort of way, she was enjoying this. She felt for the first time that someone was seeing her as she really

274

was, and that she, in turn, was seeing the real Alex, a sight she knew few had been privileged to have. Why he had suspected her, she neither knew nor cared. That was behind them. This afternoon had forever changed her, and she would never be quite the same again.

The gloom among the trees deepened as they continued to struggle through the underbrush, keeping the house and the drive always in view to their left. It was so peaceful that Cecily found it hard to believe that danger lurked nearby, except for the continuing silence of the birds. Whether it was their own presence that had alarmed the birds, or Edgewater's, she didn't know, but she hoped Alex was wrong. She hoped Edgewater was far away by now.

They both heard it at the same time, the sound of a vehicle of some sort, and the pounding of hoofbeats, carried to them by a trick of the wind. Alex turned back, his eyes startled. "The lane," he said, forgetting to keep his voice down and changed direction. Cecily followed. If this were Lord Liverpool's carriage, perhaps they were in time, after all. Following Alex, she stepped from the grassy bank onto the lane and at that moment someone grabbed her from behind.

Cecily shrieked, and then went very still as she felt the unmistakable pressure of a gun barrel against her jaw. For a moment terror overwhelmed her so strongly that she thought she would faint, and only willpower kept her from sagging against her captor. It was Edgewater; the scent of sandalwood, now mixed with other, less pleasant odors, told her that. The arm that held her against him was so hard and strong that she wondered why she had ever considered him weak.

In the distance, the sound of the carriage grew louder. Alex, having taken an involuntary step forward, lowered his pistol. "A wise move," Edgewater said, his voice so close to Cecily's ear she had to force herself not to flinch. "As you see, I seem to hold all the aces."

Alex gazed at him for a moment, his face unreadable. "I congratulate you, Edgewater," he said at last, with that edge to his voice that told Cecily he meant exactly the opposite. He seemed relaxed, one hand in a pocket, but the muscles in his neck stood out corded and hard. "You've sunk to hiding behind a woman."

"Ah, but not just any woman," Edgewater gloated. "Your woman. It will give me great pleasure to take her away from you. The famous rake. Who would have thought it?"

"You're not going to win this time."

"Oh? Who will stop me?"

"I will."

"I think not." Edgewater pressed the gun harder against Cecily's throat. "Not while I have her."

"Coward."

"Shut your trap!"

"Piker. Cad. Coward."

"I said shut your trap, or she gets it!"

"You're sounding commoner by the moment." Alex examined his fingernails, for all the world like an idle fop pretending boredom at a ball. "The great marquess of Edgewater."

"You'll learn how great. I've waited for this day for a long, long time."

"Pity you're going to lose. Do you hear that carriage?"

"I hear it." Indeed, they could hear individual hoofbeats now, the jingling of harnesses, the shouts of the coachmen. It was coming closer, closer.

"I'll lay a wager it's Liverpool. And then what do you do? Go after him, or us?"

"I'll have you both!" Edgewater yelled. "Both, do you hear? You'll pay; I'll make you both pay, and then I'll get him, I'll complete my mission—"

"Over my dead body."

276

"It may come to that, dear boy."

"Best decide, Edgewater. You can't have both. Liverpool, or us?"

For the first time, Edgewater looked uncertain as again the wind brought the sound of the carriage closer than it really was. "I'll have both! I'll—"

"Fail. You've failed, Edgewater," Alex taunted. "Failed. Lost. Been beaten—"

"Be quiet!"

"—and where are all your fine plans now? Oh, you've really shown everyone how superior you are, haven't you, shielding yourself behind a woman—"

"I am superior! I'm better than everyone and I can beat you—"

"Oh, really, Ted? Ted the toad—"

"Shut up!" It was a shriek. "Shut up or I swear she gets it right now—"

"Make up your mind, Toad—excuse me, Ted. You haven't much time—"

"Damn you!" Edgewater shrieked again, just as the carriage swept around a curve in the lane.

Several things happened at once then. Cecily, who had been too frightened to move, suddenly found courage as Edgewater's hand wavered. She jammed her elbow hard into his midsection. His breath went out with a *whoosh!* and his hold slackened, enough for her to pull away, dropping instinctively to the ground. Alex was already in place; his pistol barked, just once, but Edgewater, with the reflexes of a cat, moved just in time, taking the ball in his arm. And then his own pistol spoke and Alex fell to the ground.

"No! Alex!" Cecily screamed, scrambling to her feet. Behind her she was aware of the carriage speeding by, and that Edgewater was chasing after it, shouting. She didn't care; he could have Liverpool if he wanted. All she was concerned about was Alex.

"Oh, God," she sobbed, over and over, dropping to

277

her knees beside him. "Oh, God, oh, God, don't be dead, Alex, don't be dead, not now, not when we've found each other." But he lay ominously still, a stain of red quickly spreading across his shirt. "Oh, God. Alex, please!"

"Damn you!" Edgewater cried behind her, but not near. "Damn you, I'll get you yet, now that I've had my revenge."

Revenge. The word penetrated the panic in Cecily's mind. Cold comfort, but it was all she had. Her fingers slipped into the pocket of her pelisse and curled around the grip of her pistol. She had never before shot a man, but that wouldn't stop her. Alex was dead. Somebody had to pay for that.

With calm deliberation, she turned and crouched, raising the pistol and taking aim. Her hand was remarkably steady, she noted in a detached way. Strange. Just now she didn't feel anything, except an overriding purpose. Revenge.

The carriage was long gone. Edgewater, muttering to himself, walked back toward her, his head down. "Edward," Cecily said, gripping the pistol with both hands.

Edgewater raised his head, and stopped. For a moment he simply stared at her, and then began to laugh. "You wouldn't," he said. "You don't have the nerve."

"Try me."

"Oh, I don't think I'll have to, my dear," he said walking toward her again, that mocking smile on his face. "Give me the gun."

"You killed Alex."

"Oh, did I? How remiss of me. But he deserved it, you know. No one calls me 'toad.'"

"Stay back!"

"I tire of this game, Cecily. Give me the gun."

"No," she said but her arm was no longer steady. Now that the moment was here, she couldn't do it. Perhaps someone else could fire at a man in cold blood, but she couldn't. Not for herself. For the prime minister, though, who was still in danger and for Alex, she could.

Alex. Cecily squeezed her eyes closed and fired.

Chapter Twenty-one

The sound of the shot was very loud in Cecily's ears. Slowly she opened her eyes, and the pistol fell from her nerveless fingers. Edgewater was still standing, but a stain of red bloomed on his chest. "You," he began. "You," and then, with a look of almost comical surprise on his face, he crumpled to the ground.

"Oh, God!" Cecily exclaimed, and with instinctive revulsion kicked the pistol away from her. What had she done, what had she done? "Oh, Alex, what have I done?"

There was a crackling sound, but Cecily had her head in her hands and didn't look up, until she heard a voice, to see Parsons bending over Edgewater's body. "Good shooting, my lord," he said.

"Thank you," another voice answered weakly from behind her, and Cecily whirled.

"Alex! You're not dead!"

"No, not yet, little one." He held out his hand to her as she crawled over to him, and on his face was a look of deep tenderness, and pride.

"Oh, thank God. Thank God." She bent over him, unaware that her tears were falling onto his face, and he raised his hand to touch her cheek.

"That was very brave of you, little one."

"Not brave. Oh, Alex, I killed him."

"No, my lady," Parsons said. "I was watching. Your

shot went wide."

"It did?" Cecily stared at Alex. "Then who—"

"I make it a practice to carry two guns." He had done it. Thank God. When he had needed to, he had mastered his anger at Edgewater and done what was necessary. The Prime Minister, and Cecily, were safe.

His gaze shifted to Parsons. "And where the hell were you?"

"Sorry, sir, Watching the house. I got here just as you both fired."

"Edgewater?"

"Gone."

"Good. Was it Liverpool's carriage?"

"Yes, sir and he's safe. Where are you hurt?"

Alex grimaced. "Shoulder. Same place as last time."

"Last time!" Cecily exclaimed. "That's it. You're retiring."

"Yes, sweeting. Hurts damnably, but I'll live."

Parsons had stripped back Alex's shirt and was expertly inspecting the wound. "Ball's still in there. I'll put something on it, and then we'll have to bring you back to the inn."

"Where they've probably never seen anything like this. Cecily?"

"Yes, Alex, I'm here." Cecily fell to her knees next to him, handing Parsons a pile of wadded cloths. "Here, Parsons, use this."

Alex's eyes glinted. "Your petticoat? Such a sacrifice, my dear."

"Oh, hush!" Cecily's cheeks were very pink. "Could you not be a gentleman, just this once?"

Alex grimaced as Parsons shifted him to knot the bandage securely. "Not with my reputation, my dear."

"There, that ought to hold it for now," Parsons said. "I'll get Edgewater's curricle. Can you drive, my lady?"

"Yes."

"Good. I'll ride along with you to the inn."

Alex grimaced again as Parsons left. "I didn't want any of this to touch you. But there goes your reputation."

"I don't care, not after today. There are other things that matter more."

"So you don't mind that I've compromised you beyond all hope?"

Cecily reached out to smooth his hair back from his face. "I can't think of anyone else I'd rather be compromised by."

"Cecily." His eyes were serious suddenly, and his hand clasped hers. "You do realize what this means, don't you?"

Cecily opened her mouth to answer, but at that moment Parsons drove up in the curricle. She smiled down at Alex and then set about the difficult task of helping Parsons get him into the carriage. Once he was settled, she climbed in, taking up the ribbons with expert hands and turning the carriage on the narrow lane. She had often driven at Marlow, or in the park, but never under such circumstances. She wondered what society would say, were they to see her now.

Their arrival at the inn was greeted with consternation and sidelong looks, making Cecily acutely aware of her bedraggled state and the strangeness of the situation. It was Diana, oddly enough, who rescued her. "Cece! I was getting worried," she said coming out of the parlor and taking Cecily's arm. "Come inside and tell me all."

Cecily looked helplessly toward the stairs, where Alex was being carried. "But—"

"Come inside." Diana tugged at her arm and Cecily, suddenly exhausted, gave in. Only when the door had been closed behind them did Diana allow her to speak.

"My word, Cece!" she said when Cecily had finished her tale. "Such things as you do get into!"

Cecily raised a shaky hand to push back her hair. "I

didn't expect this. I thought we'd find you and bring you back to London, and that would be that. And now—I'm sorry, Diana. Now your reputation is ruined, too."

"Well, I've been thinking about that, Cece. Do you know who lives near here? Lady Throckmorton."

"Aunt Caroline?" Hope flared within Cecily. Lady Caroline Throckmorton was a distant connection, somewhat of an eccentric, who enjoyed living near enough to town to hear all the gossip, but who rarely left her estate. She was also possessed of an impeccable reputation. If they claimed they had paid a call on her and had lost track of time, forcing them to stay overnight, they would be saved. "Oh, Di, do you think she'll take us in?"

"Of course she will, silly! She'd die to hear a story like yours."

"But I must know whether Alex is all right before we go."

"Yes, I agree." Diana studied her. "Cecily, are you going to marry him?"

Cecily colored, remembering certain moments in the woods and what Alex had hinted at. "I don't know."

"Oh, I do hope you do! He's so romantic."

"Diana, haven't you learned anything after today?"

"Yes. Never trust a man who cares more for his clothes than he does you."

Cecily laughed, but in a few moments the laughter turned to tears. In her sister's arms she sobbed away all the fears and the upsets of the day, leaving her feeling weak and curiously at peace. The future would take care of itself. She could wait, now that she knew that Alex would be all right. And if he thought he was going to get away from her, he'd soon learn differently!

The sun was shining almost horizontally through the

trees when Cecily rode into the park through the Grosvenor Gate. Summer was here, and Parliament had nearly finished its session. People were already leaving town, some for such fashionable watering places as Brighton, others to their estates. Cecily's family soon would be returning to Marlow, something she usually looked forward to. Not this year, however. Not when she, and her future, were both still unsettled.

Nearly a week had passed since the adventure near Lord Milford's estate. She and Diana had both escaped with their reputations intact, though there was a rumor going about that Alex and Edgewater had fought a duel over Cecily. As if nothing had happened, they had taken up their lives again, though Cecily was, for the first time, finding the social round stifling and dull. She was not the same girl she had been at the beginning of the season. Perhaps she was, as Alex had said, something of an adventuress.

Alex. At the thought of him, Cecily glanced around, but of course he was nowhere to be seen. He had returned to town a few days ago and had sent her a note saying he was doing well, but other than that, she hadn't heard from him. Society, and prudence, dictated that she not go to him, though she wanted to. She would have to wait for him to make the next move, if he ever did. The closeness they had shared in the woods seemed very far away.

She was so deep in thought that she didn't hear the clop of hoofbeats until they were nearly upon her. When she did, she started and turned to see who it was. "Alex!" she exclaimed, staring at him, momentarily speechless. He simply stared back, grinning. Mounted on Azrael, he looked much as usual, except that his left arm was in a sling and his face was thinner.

"I thought I might find you here." His grin widened as his eyes leisurely perused her. "In breeches, too."

Ridiculously, Cecily blushed. "But what are you doing here? You shouldn't be riding, not with your shoulder."

"Azrael is a well-mannered old nag," he said easily. "But I don't think I'll try a gallop yet." He fell into step beside her. "I got damn tired—excuse me—of waiting to get better."

"Well, I think you're being remarkably foolish," she said, but her eyes sparkled.

"Do you, little one?" he answered, with such warmth that she looked away, her cheeks going pink again. "I do like it when you blush."

"You are the most difficult man."

"I try." They rode in silence for a little while. "Have you heard anything from the government?"

"Yes. Lord Liverpool spoke with Papa. Oh, was he angry!"

"Liverpool?"

"No, Papa. He was so angry at what I did that he wanted to send me to Marlow early. Diana, too. Fortunately Mama convinced him that would only cause a scandal." She smiled. "He's been giving me the oddest looks. I'm not sure he really believes it."

"Sometimes I don't believe it, either. The worst moment of my life was when Edgewater grabbed you."

"The worst of mine was when I thought you were dead." She stopped, turning and touching his arm. "You will retire, won't you?"

"Why, Cecily. Dare I hope you care?"

"Don't be more foolish than you can help! What will all the ladies do without their favorite rake?"

Alex looked at her for a moment. "Find someone else, I imagine. I've been offered a position at the Home Office, by the by. No, not spying, little one. Those days are behind me at last. Thanks to you."

"Oh." Her voice sounded breathless. "Won't you miss it?"

"Perhaps, but now that the Continent is open again,

we can always travel. After all, a rake and an adventuress need some excitement in their lives."

Cecily stopped. "We?"

"Yes. We. You and I."

"Alex—"

"I love you, Cecily," he said, so simply that she stared at him, whatever it was she had been about to say flown from her head. "And that's not something I say easily. No matter what else I've done, I've never said that to any woman. Never. Do you believe me?"

"Oh, Alex." She reached up to touch his cheek, her eyes brimming. "Of course I do. I trust you. You see," she swallowed, hard, "I love you, too. I think I always have."

"Do you?" He caught her hand in his good one and brought it to his mouth. "God's teeth, but I am a lucky man. I don't deserve you, Cecily."

"Who says you have me?"

"What—"

"Isn't there a certain question you'd like to ask?"

"Minx." He grinned at her. "Last time I asked it I nearly had my head snapped off. But, oh, very well. Shall I go down on my knees?"

"No, silly, you might wrinkle the knees of your pantaloons."

Alex looked startled, and then laughed. "Very well, then, on horseback, it will be. Cecily." His face grew serious, his voice deep. "Will you marry me?"

Cecily tilted her head to the side. "Well, I don't know, sir. Are you thoroughly reformed?"

"Yes. Thoroughly."

"Well, in that case—Alex, you can't kiss me here; someone might see!"

"To hell with them," he growled, gripping her about the waist with his good arm and pulling her close for a long and most satisfactory, kiss. When at last it ended, Cecily rested her head against his shoulder.

"Mm." She raised her head to look at him, and her eyes sparkled with mischief. "I see what I must do."

"What is that, little one?"

"To make sure you stay reformed. I shall just have to keep you happy at home."

"Indeed?"

"Indeed."

A stylishly dressed couple, up unfashionably early, were riding at a sedate pace when they were brought up short by the sight of Viscount St. Clair kissing Lady Cecily Randall, clothed, most surprisingly, in breeches. "Well!" the lady exclaimed, in mingled outrage and fascination. "How scandalous!"

"Quite," agreed her companion, but he was wondering how to start a fashion of women wearing breeches in such an enchanting way. Neither averted their eyes as they rode by; this was too delicious a titbit to ignore.

Neither Cecily nor Alex noticed the presence of anyone else, nor would they have particularly cared. They were far too interested in other things. For, in Alex's arms, Cecily had found her future, the one man who accepted her as she was, loved her as she was. And, in Cecily's arms, Alex had found something much more, love, trust, a world he hadn't been sure existed. The former rake had, at last, gained his reward.